THE FURY BOILING WITHIN BLOODSONG ERUPTED IN A RAGGED SCREAM OF RAGE.

She started forward to do battle, shook off a companion's attempt to pull her back, her emotions overflowing out of control, sweeping away all rational thought.

Decaying bodies lay everywhere. Howls and shouts of Odin's name mixed with the moaning of the Hel-wind as the Berserkers kept fighting and the Death Riders continued to reap their harvest of death, corpse-faces glaring down in triumph at those they were killing from atop their blood-splattered white steeds, black swords rising and falling like executioners, tirelessly, relentlessly, eyes of purple fire flaring brighter with each kill, skeletal mouths grinning the smile of Hel, the grimace of Death.

Then suddenly a howl ripped the air which gave even the Death Riders pause. Fiery purple eyes looked up from their grim harvest. Hel-horses shied nervously. Black swords stopped in mid-stroke.

With another howl, a berserking, raven-black beast leaped amongst them, began tearing at dead throats with stiletto fangs, slashing through sunken, mail-clad chests with razor claws, howling and slavering with boundless bloodlust and fury…

Also by Asa Drake

Warrior Witch of Hel
Death Riders of Hel

Published by
POPULAR LIBRARY

Death Riders of Hel

ASA DRAKE

POPULAR LIBRARY

An Imprint of Warner Books, Inc.

A Warner Communications Company

POPULAR LIBRARY EDITION

Copyright © 1986 by C. Dean Andersson
All rights reserved

Cover art by Boris Vallejo

Popular Library books are published by
Warner Books, Inc.
666 Fifth Avenue
New York, N.Y. 10103

 A Warner Communications Company

Printed in the United States of America

First Printing: March, 1986

10 9 8 7 6 5 4 3 2 1

For the three Bs:
Brian, Boris and Bloodsong

Prologue

At the summit of a jagged mountain, wreathed in wisps of overhanging clouds, edged in ice and snow, loomed the castle of the Hel-Witch, Thokk.

The massive walls and steeply roofed towers of her castle were of black stone shot through with crimson veins, and although those walls and towers reared far above the summit of the mountain, the fortress existed as much below ground as above. Into those black depths the pale mistress of the house was now descending.

Tall was Thokk, hair hanging in long, glistening black coils like restless serpents. Beautiful of face and figure, her appearance had not changed in more than one hundred years. But her lips and nails were the grayish-blue of a corpse beneath their scarlet rouge and paint, and the spicy-sweet herbs with which she perfumed her flesh and breath could not entirely conceal the underlying stench of the grave, for she worshiped and served the Goddess Hel, Queen of Death, Sovereign of Darkness and Decay.

Thokk came to the top of yet another stairway, this one

narrower with stone steps more crumbling than any she had yet descended. Her lips parted slightly in anticipation as she began to descend the narrow stairs, brushing spiderwebs aside as she went, ignoring the crawling things that swarmed over and around her bare feet.

Her breathing came faster as her excitement mounted. Her anticipation increased, pulse throbbing, naked feet padding through chilled dust, the ice-sheathed stone walls reflecting the flickering orange light of her torch as she went down and down.

Thokk came to the bottom of the stairway and unlocked a heavy, nail-studded wooden door. She walked through into a small chamber, then closed and locked the door behind her.

In the center of the chamber sat a dais of intricately rune-carven stone, and upon the flat upper surface of the stone slab lay the naked body of a tall, blond-haired young man in his mid-teens.

The Hel-Witch placed the torch in the wall bracket and slowly approached the dais, her large, wide-set green eyes sweeping hungrily, anxiously, over the young man's flesh. Save for the slight vestiges of decay still remaining on his face, no signs of death could be seen upon his body. Soon even his face would be that of a living man, for the time Thokk had long planned and awaited was fast approaching.

"Soon now, Lokith," she murmured soothingly as she stroked the youth's hair, "soon your flesh will be whole. Soon I will bring your sister to you. Soon her first woman's blood will flow. Soon Hel's plan will be complete and our conquests will begin. . . . " Her voice trailed away beneath a smile.

Thokk's pale, slim-fingered hands reached up and opened the clasp that held her black cloak around her shoulders. The cloak rustled to the floor, leaving her naked. She concentrated her will, intoning words of power. The flame of the torch died away, leaving the chamber in total darkness.

The Hel-Witch stretched out on the slab next to the young man's corpse, gently covering his cold flesh with her warmth.

For several moments the only sounds in the chamber were

Thokk's quickening breathing. Then she focused her concentration, began to whisper, to hiss incantations. Her voice gradually rose in volume to echo from the walls until suddenly her voice was not the only sound in the blackened chamber. The youth's chilled flesh began to stir, and faint moans of pain crept from his stiff-muscled throat while Thokk's incantations ceased and other sounds flooded from her, sounds half pain, half pleasure, as she worshiped Death once more, giving herself over to the frenzied passions of the grave and drawing upon the sexual energies thus released to further heal the youth's dead flesh.

In time, only sounds of pleasure remained.

1
First Kill

In a small, one-room cottage three women lay sleeping.

Nearest the hearth slept a crone, Norda Greycloak, her silvered hair glittering crimson in the firelight. Though the night was warm, she wore a thick gray robe and had wrapped a blanket tightly around herself, for with age had come a persistent chill that she could never seem to dispel. Norda was not sleeping well, her lips moving soundlessly, eyebrows drawn into a frown as she fought a bad dream.

Against one wall of the cottage, naked beneath a yellow cloak, slept Huld, a young woman with elfin features and long blond hair. She was also frowning in her sleep, fighting a bad dream, sweat glistening on her skin.

To one side of the door, clothed in a thin, white sleeping shift slept Guthrun, a girl on the brink of womanhood, her face strong-featured even in its youth, her hair long and raven-black.

Norda and Huld were Freya-Witches. Guthrun intended to become one too.

Guthrun was also frowning in her sleep, her head flinching from side to side, her breathing heavy and labored as she fought to awaken. Then suddenly she succeeded. Her eyes snapped open. She lay panting softly, still tensed, trying to remember the nightmare. Then she heard something that swept away all thoughts of the dream: *Outside the cottage, muffled whispers . . .*

Guthrun reached for the sword she always kept near her bed and drew the blade from its leather scabbard. Her heart racing, she slipped quickly but quietly to Huld's side and gripped the young Witch's bare shoulder. "Huld!" she whispered urgently. "Wake up!"

Huld moaned but could not awaken, sleeping on as if drugged or ensorcelled.

The door crashed open. Men rushed into the cottage, swords gleaming in the firelight.

Guthrun screamed a war cry and rushed forward. Her blade sliced air and jerked to a stop as it cut halfway through a surprised warrior's neck. A fountain of warm blood sprayed her face. She had killed her first man.

Reacting as her warrior-mother had taught her, she wrenched the blade free, parried a cut, feinted, lunged, and killed a second man. But the warriors were all around her now, the surprise of her attack fading as they cursed and pressed closer, overwhelming her by sheer numbers.

Her arms were gripped from behind, and her sword arm twisted. She gritted her teeth against the pain but refused to drop her sword. Her arm was twisted farther. She cried out in agony as her blade fell to the ground. A sword point touched her throat, slowly pressed inward, the scar-faced man who held it savoring her last moments.

"No!" shouted a blond-bearded man as he hurled the warrior away.

"She killed Thorir and Jon!"

"Sheath your sword, Ragnar. Carelessness and overconfidence killed Thorir and Jon."

"But she's just a girl!"

"You were told that she was Bloodsong's daughter and would know swordcraft. And Thokk told you she might not be affected by the sleep spell."

Hearing Thokk's name, Guthrun struggled wildly in the grip of her captors.

"Thokk's orders stand," the tall leader continued. "She must be taken to Thokk alive."

Guthrun saw other men lashing Huld's and Norda's hands behind their backs with leather thongs, the two Witches still sleeping under Thokk's spell. A moment later Guthrun felt thongs tighten around her own wrists.

The warrior who wanted to kill her stood staring angrily at the tall man a moment more, blade held in a white-knuckled grip. Then slowly he straightened out of his tensed crouch and slammed his sword back into its scabbard. "They were my friends, Tyrulf."

Tyrulf nodded and slapped the man's shoulder. "What Thokk has planned for her and the other two will no doubt be quite unpleasant, Ragnar."

"Pray Odin it is," Ragnar growled, glancing angrily at Guthrun.

"Allfather Odin will have nothing to do with Thokk," Guthrun spat, "or with men who work for that Hel-Witch!" The look of doubt that flitted over Ragnar's face told her that she had hit the mark. "No Valhalla for you when you die," she continued, grinning coldly, "but only an eternity of horror in Hel's cold embrace. The Death Goddess Hel will never let your soul fly to Odin, not after you've helped her servant, Thokk."

Ragnar growled low in his throat. "Make her bonds tight," he urged the men tying Guthrun's wrists. "Neither General Kovna nor Thokk said she had to be comfortable on the journey."

A warrior slipped to Tyrulf's side and whispered something Guthrun could not hear.

Tyrulf followed the man back to where Norda lay, squatted down beside her, and placed his fingers on the crone's neck.

"Norda?" Guthrun said, realization dawning. "Norda!" she cried, twisting desperately, wrenching at her bonds.

Tyrulf rose to his feet with a curse.

"But how?" the warrior asked. "Why? We didn't touch her, save to bind her hands."

Tyrulf cursed again. "Perhaps the sleep spell . . . maybe she fought against it. Maybe her heart gave out. She was an old woman."

"Thokk will be angry," the warrior whispered, eyes glinting with fear.

Tyrulf cursed a third time, then began giving orders. "Take the girl and the other one to the horses. Leave the crone's corpse. Fire the cottage."

"No!" Guthrun shouted, struggling as she was pushed toward the door. "I will avenge you, Norda!" she vowed as she was pushed past the crone's body.

"Wait!" Tyrulf commanded. The men holding Guthrun stopped. Tyrulf walked to face her. "How much have these Witches already taught you, girl?"

Guthrun said nothing.

"We know you can use a sword," Tyrulf said. "Perhaps you can also wield some Witchcraft. I don't take chances."

He drew his dagger, reversed it, and brought the pommel down to crack against Guthrun's skull. She slumped unconscious in the grip of her captors.

Guthrun and Huld were lifted onto horses. The cottage was set afire. Then, through bright moonlight, Tyrulf led his men at a gallop down the forest trail, leaving the Witches' cottage blazing, the corpse of the beloved Freya-Witch Norda Greycloak charring in the flames.

They were too far from the cottage to hear when that charred corpse screamed and then slowly, determinedly, began struggling to stand.

2
Eirik's Vale

Atop a hill overlooking the sleeping village of Eirik's Vale, a warrior stood alone in the moonlight. Despite the warmth of the night the warrior was dressed for battle in a steel helmet, mail shirt, and brown leather breeches, boots, and gloves. A broadsword and shield were strapped to the black-haired warrior's back, and a dagger hung in a sheath from a broad leather belt around the warrior's trim-muscled waist. The warrior's name was Bloodsong, her stern-featured, battle-scarred face pale in the moonlight, deep-set dark eyes brooding beneath a frown.

Bloodsong had lived in the village once before, after leading a slave revolt and escaping from Nastrond, the fortress of the sorcerer-king Nidhug. But in time King Nidhug had found her, massacred the villagers who had befriended her, tortured her husband and son to death, burned the village, and left her to die. Bloodsong had eventually returned the favor, destroying Nidhug and Nastrond. Then she and those who had fought by her side returned to the village and rebuilt it with the help of freed slaves.

Now, seven years later, the village she had named Eirik's Vale, in honor of her dead husband, bore little resemblance to the village Nidhug had destroyed. It had grown larger than the original village, and there was now a fortified encampment at its center, protection against the bands of raiders that had begun terrorizing the countryside after Nidhug's fall. Warriors' barracks were encircled by the fortification's towering earthen ramparts, around which were clustered the village's cottages and longhouses. Beyond the village stretched rich farmlands and pastures in which cattle and sheep grazed. Farther still rose thick pine forests. To the north loomed the jagged peaks of mountains.

But Bloodsong was not thinking about her village. She was thinking about her daughter, Guthrun, and about Guthrun's decision to study Witchcraft with Norda Greycloak and Huld, the young Freya-Witch who had helped Bloodsong destroy Nidhug.

Though Bloodsong herself had found it necessary to use Witchcraft in defeating Nidhug, she had a warrior's distaste for magic-working. Guthrun, however, though now well trained in the skills of a warrior, felt otherwise and had been drawn more and more to the lure of the Unseen, the whispering mysteries of moonlight, the secret shadows and powers within the human mind and soul.

Bloodsong glanced up at the bright moon. Considering her daughter's background, the circumstances of Guthrun's birth and early childhood, perhaps she should not have been surprised nor upset that Guthrun wanted to become a magic-wielder. But it *had* surprised and upset her, and beyond that, she missed Guthrun deeply, felt a lonely ache for the daughter who, for the last seven years, had never been away from her mother for more than a few days' time.

Movement caught Bloodsong's eye. She watched as a figure emerged from one of the four gateways cut into the fortified earthen rampart encircling the warriors' barracks. Moonlight flashed from a steel helmet and glinted from the pommel of a sword strapped across the figure's back.

The warrior began running through the streets of the sleeping village.

Bloodsong waited, watched, determined to stop brooding over Guthrun and to trust her daughter to carve a good future for herself, even if the weapon Guthrun preferred to wield turned out to be Witchcraft instead of a sharp steel blade.

Dressed for battle in leather armor, sword and shield strapped to her back, the young warrior ran on through the streets of Eirik's Vale, seeking escape from the memories that haunted her, from the nightmares that had again awakened her before dawn.

The warrior's name was Jalna. She had once been one of Nidhug's slaves. Her nightmares were of that time, of the torture and terror she had survived, memories that could be most quickly driven away by a physical assertion of her freedom and strength.

After Nidhug's destruction, Jalna had asked Bloodsong to teach her swordcraft so that she might never again be made a slave. Because she had helped Bloodsong defeat the sorcerer-king, the warrior-woman had agreed, and Jalna was now one of Bloodsong's deadliest and most relentless warriors. But still the nightmares came, and still she awoke, imagining that she felt manacles clamped around her wrists, the decaying hands of Nidhug's death slaves pawing her naked flesh, Nidhug's venom wand searing her bare skin.

On and on Jalna ran, pushing herself harder and harder, beyond the outskirts of the village, down a narrow trail that cut through the fields and pastures, until finally she reached the distant edge of the forest.

Jalna slowed her pace along the trail, feeling strong and free and confident again, cooling down as her eyes adjusted to the moonlight-dappled shadows beneath the pines. She wiped the sweat from her eyes and removed her steel helmet, running a hand through her short, black, sweat-soaked hair. She replaced the helmet, beginning to catch her breath from the long run while still jogging leisurely on through the trees.

The attack came without warning. Suddenly she was surrounded by men with drawn blades. She reached for her sword, but before she could grasp the hilt, a man reached her from behind and grabbed both her arms. She kicked back, hammering her boot down hard on his instep. He cursed with the pain. His grip on her arms weakened.

Jalna wrenched her right arm free, drove her elbow back into his solar plexus, whirled as he released her other arm and chopped into his throat with the flat of her hand, crushing his windpipe.

As he fell she crouched low and whipped her blade from its sheath on her back, catching an approaching attacker by surprise. He felt the sharp steel edge of her sword slice through his flesh to crunch against the bones in his sword arm.

She parried a cut on her left, saw movement out of the corner of her eye to the right, and evaded a thrust from in front. She heard a sound from behind and to her right.

The young warrior dove to her left and behind. She hit the ground, rolled, came smoothly to her feet outside the ring of attackers, sliced sideways to her left, and ignored the man's death cries as her return stroke made another attacker scream.

She backed away from the remaining three, quickly unstrapping the round shield from her back during the moment's respite. Then they rushed her.

Steel met steel, sparks flying, the clangor of battle once more rending the night.

Bloodsong watched until the warrior disappeared into the forest.

Jalna, she thought, *still pursued by Nidhug's evil*.

She did not know all that had happened to Jalna before Nidhug's defeat. Jalna had never talked about it to anyone. But Bloodsong had spent nights camped under the stars with the young warrior and had been awakened by Jalna's moans and cries as she tossed in the throes of a nightmare. She listened as Jalna talked in her sleep, alternately cursing Nidhug and then begging him for mercy, pleading, praying for the pain and horror to end.

Bloodsong cursed Nidhug's memory and hoped that the Goddess Hel, whom he had once betrayed, was still enjoying making him scream.

But suddenly Bloodsong's thoughts were shattered as the sounds of battle—men's screams and steel striking steel—drifted faintly to her through the night from the direction in which Jalna had gone.

Bloodsong began running toward the forest, stopped herself with a curse, and began running toward the village instead. Jalna would have to fend for herself. An alarm had to be sounded, warriors awakened, the village alerted.

Freya give you victory, *Jalna*, Bloodsong thought, and ran on toward Eirik's Vale.

3

Hel-Warriors

Not all of the warriors of Eirik's Vale slept in longhouses within the fortified earthen walls.

Bloodsong halted at a cottage near the walls and hammered on the door. "Valgerth! Thorfinn!" she called. She hammered on the door again and called out once more. She heard a muffled voice from inside and then the sound of a bar being pushed to one side. The latch clicked; the door opened.

"There's fighting in the woods," Bloodsong explained to the black-bearded man who opened the door. "Alert the village. Get the people inside the walls."

Not waiting for Thorfinn's response, she turned and ran toward a gateway, shouting orders for it to be opened. Inside the walls she sounded the alarm and began bullying sleepy warriors to move faster, to dress and arm themselves for battle.

The sky was graying with the coming dawn when the villagers were finally safely within the walls. Those who could not wield a blade were ordered to stay safely out of the way within one of the four longhouses that served as barracks.

"It was Jalna," Bloodsong said to Valgerth when the tall

warrior-woman, her reddish-blond hair glinting coppery in the morning sunlight, mounted the ramparts to look out over the village with her. Thorfinn followed behind, talking with a warrior whose training he had undertaken but who had not yet been tested in actual battle.

"Jalna." Valgerth nodded, understanding. The young warrior's nighttime runs were not a secret.

"Your children?" Bloodsong asked.

"Safe in a barracks, though Thora wanted to come with me to fight," Valgerth chuckled, "to fight with her wooden training sword. Imagine!"

Bloodsong nodded. "I've been brooding over Guthrun's absence. Perhaps it's best that she's with Huld and Norda, though she would not shirk a battle, I'm certain, if a battle comes."

"You think there may not be a battle?" asked the young warrior with whom Thorfinn had been talking.

Thorfinn and the two women looked at him. He rubbed his beardless chin and shrugged.

"Whoever is out there," he continued, "probably hoped to take us by surprise. Now that they have not, maybe they will go away. Or there might not be any but a few, mightn't there? Of course, I hope there *is* a battle," he added, trying to sound brave.

Thorfinn gripped the youth's shoulder. "Perhaps, Ole," he said, "there won't be, and perhaps there will, but if there is, just remember all I've taught you. And don't worry about getting hurt or killed. If you do, you stand more of a chance of having that happen. Think about taking the lives of the enemy. Don't think about saving your own."

The young man named Ole walked away with Thorfinn along the rampart, still talking. Bloodsong and Valgerth stood looking out over the brightening landscape, saying nothing for a long while.

"When we defeated Nidhug," Valgerth finally said, "we thought there would be nothing but peace. It hasn't gone quite that way, has it, Freyadis?"

Bloodsong frowned at the name Valgerth had called her, the

name by which Valgerth had known her when they were both slaves in Nastrond, before they had been trained as arena warriors and she had taken the battle name of Bloodsong. No one but Valgerth ever called her Freyadis now.

"No, it hasn't gone quite the way we'd hoped," Bloodsong agreed, "but compared to Nidhug's reign of terror . . ."

"Aye. Anything's better than that. I wasn't complaining. I have two fine children now. And—"

Bloodsong suddenly cursed, interrupting Valgerth. "If she hasn't returned by now, she's probably dead," she said, thinking of Jalna.

"Or captured," Valgerth suggested.

"For Jalna, better death, I think, than to again know captivity."

When the last attacker had fallen, Jalna had begun to run back toward Eirik's Vale. The men she had killed might have been a scouting patrol for a larger force. The village had to be warned. But just as she'd reached the edge of the forest, she'd heard the alarm being sounded in the distance. She'd stopped, decided that someone must have heard the sounds of her battle, turned, and headed back into the forest, leaving the trail, determined to do some scouting of her own before returning to Eirik's Vale.

Making scarcely a sound, stopping every few steps to listen and stare into the shadows, sword and shield held ready, Jalna had moved through the trees, all her survival instincts alert. It was nearly dawn when she heard voices in the distance ahead— many voices—and the occasional nickering of horses.

She moved even more cautiously now, keeping to the shadows in the rapidly brightening forest, moving slowly and silently as Bloodsong had taught her to do.

Jalna circled to her right, placing a thicket between herself and the voices. Finally she reached the thicket and moved carefully within it, far enough to peer through to the other side.

Hundreds of warriors were there. She was chilled. It was more like an army than a raiding party. And then she saw a

strongly built man with gray hair and beard sitting atop a
massive black charger, giving orders.

Kovna! Jalna thought, recognizing the man who had once
been the commanding general of King Nidhug's army. She
looked closer at Kovna's men and saw that many wore remnants
of soldiers' uniforms. So intent was she on Kovna and his army
that she did not at first see the others. But then she did see
them, and her chill deepened.

Sitting astride gaunt white mares, protected from the brightening sky by the shadows of tall trees, shunned by Kovna's
men, nine warriors clad in black steel and leather faced a
hooded figure in a black cloak who sat atop a black stallion.
The nine were of the Dead, most little more than skeletons,
silently watching and listening to the hooded one with the
infinite patience of the grave.

Hel-warriors, Jalna realized, and shuddered, gripping her
sword even tighter.

The hooded figure gestured to the brightening sky, made a
negative gesture, as if to reassure the Hel-warriors, then turned
the stallion to face the east and pushed back the hood, revealing
the pale face of a beautiful woman, long black hair hanging
in glistening coils.

The woman lifted her pale, thin-boned hands and closed her
eyes, tracing runes in the air with her fingers, moving her full
red lips soundlessly.

The light began to darken. Above the trees black clouds
appeared, thickening rapidly, shutting out more and more light.

Jalna backed silently out of the thicket, forced herself to
move slowly until beyond the sound of the voices, then began
to run, desperate to tell Bloodsong what she had seen.

Behind her, the incantation to darken the sky complete, the
Hel-Witch Thokk frowned and turned her head in the direction
of the thicket where Jalna had hidden. "Kovna!" she shouted,
"we have been seen! A spy was hiding in that thicket but a
few moments past!"

Kovna's head snapped around toward Thokk. "Then send
some of your vile magic to slay the spy."

"Fool! I must conserve my magical energies for the battle to come. Send some men. I sense that the spy was on foot and should be easily overtaken by mounted warriors."

Kovna cursed beneath his breath, then nodded and shouted, "Tyrulf! Take some men. You heard what Thokk said."

Tyrulf had been expecting it, had already mounted his horse and decided whom he would take. "Ragnar! Ketil! Harolf!" he called, then, ignoring their grumbling curses as they mounted their horses, the blond-bearded warrior kicked his steed into a gallop in the direction in which Jalna had gone, the three he had chosen soon following behind.

"And the rest of you!" Kovna shouted. "Mount up! Pass the word! It is time to begin the attack!"

4
Traitor

As Jalna ran on through the forest the light around her faded more and more, darkening until she was running through a twilight gloom. Then, behind her, she heard the sound of horses, turned with a curse, and prepared to fight, moving to stand near two closely set trees, thinking to use them to reduce the effectiveness of the mounted warriors' charge.

A warrior in mail and a steel battle-helm bore down upon her, followed in the distance by three more. The riders' drawn blades glinted dully in the gloom.

The first warrior saw where she stood near the two trees, guessed her intent, reined up, slammed his sword into its scabbard, and jerked a short, mounted archer's bow from its saddle thongs.

Jalna rushed forward before the warrior could nock an arrow, cut his horse's legs from under him, sliced downward as he hit the ground and rolled, cursing, fumbling for his sword.

Her blade drew a thin line of blood along his cheek, but his quickness evaded the killing cut she had aimed at his neck. Then he was on his feet, sword drawn.

The other three were nearly to her now. She had to make quick work of the first one before they arrived.

"You!" the blond-bearded warrior suddenly cried. "I . . . I thought you dead! How . . ."

Jalna ignored what she assumed to be a clumsy trick and attacked.

"No!" the warrior said, backing away. "Wait! Look at me, woman! I am Tyrulf!"

Guessing that he was trying to buy time for the others to arrive, Jalna continued to attack, silently and fiercely, while the warrior continued to back away, parrying but refusing to return her strokes.

"Damn you, Jalna! It's me! Tyrulf!" he panted, hard-pressed to fend off her killing thrusts and cuts. "From Nidhug's dungeons! The guard who wanted to help you!"

Jalna whirled to face the other three, keeping the warrior who wouldn't fight in view from the corner of her eye in case his cowardice changed to bravery with the arrival of the others.

"Wait!" Tyrulf ordered, throwing himself in front of the three mounted men.

Jalna grunted in surprise as the three reined up. She started to cut at the first man's neck while his back was turned, decided against it, memories returning, and finally recognized him as the dungeon guard who had wanted to help her during her torture.

"We heard Kovna's orders," Ragnar growled. "What foolishness is this? Stand aside, Tyrulf. There will be plenty of wenches who do not wield swords for the taking after we have taken Eirik's Vale."

"I know this woman," Tyrulf replied. "We will not harm her."

"If he knows the spy, perhaps he is a traitor," Ketil suggested.

Ragnar grunted. "Stand aside, Tyrulf. I've no desire to slay you, but I will if you—"

The hilt of Jalna's dagger suddenly appeared in Ragnar's neck, its blade deep within his flesh. Jalna rushed passed Tyrulf and cut at one of the horse's legs. Harolf cursed as his horse went down. He leapt clear. But he was not as fast as Tyrulf had been, and Jalna's downward stroke ended his cursing in a gasp of blood-bubbled agony.

Ketil jerked his horse around, not willing to face both Tyrulf and the spy, galloped to a safe distance, turned, and jerked his bow from its saddle thongs. But Tyrulf had already retrieved his bow and nocked an arrow. Tyrulf's bowstring twanged first. Ketil screamed and fell dead to the ground. His horse galloped away into the forest.

"Only one horse left," Jalna said as she sheathed her sword and began to mount Ragnar's steed. "I need it."

Tyrulf's hand clamped around her arm, pulled her back, spun her around. She jerked free and reached for her sword. He grabbed her wrists and held tight.

"No!" he said. "Listen!"

Toward them came the thunder of hundreds of horses, Kovna's army galloping to attack Eirik's Vale. And mixed with the thunder was a moaning sound.

"That moaning . . . " Jalna shuddered.

"The Hel-wind upon which the Hel-warrior's white mares tread," Tyrulf explained. "The moaning of shadow-wind demons, so I have been told."

"The fortifications . . ."

"Earthen walls will be no hindrance to the wind-treading Hel-horses. We must save ourselves, Jalna. There is nothing we can do to stop what is about to happen. Eirik's Vale is doomed."

Jalna again jerked free of Tyrulf's grasp. "My place is by Bloodsong's side," she growled, and began to mount the horse once more.

Tyrulf jerked Jalna's steel battle-helm from her head and brought it down against her skull.

Jalna sagged, stunned, fighting unconsciousness.

Tyrulf caught her with one arm and struck the horse. As the beast galloped away he lifted Jalna into his arms and began running toward a closely packed stand of trees.

Jalna moaned and began struggling in his arms as he reached his goal. She cursed weakly and fumbled for her sword. Tyrulf pushed her to the ground.

The thunder of the galloping army was nearly upon them. Tyrulf gripped her wrists behind her back with one hand and put his other hand over her mouth. She tried to bite him but was still too weak to break the skin.

"Curse it, woman! I'm trying to save you!"

Jalna only struggled harder, and again tried to bite his hand.

Skirting the closely packed trees where Tyrulf and Jalna lay in hiding, Kovna's army began to gallop past. Jalna stopped struggling, finally conscious enough to understand what was happening.

From where he lay Tyrulf watched as his comrades of a short time before swept by. The enormity of what he had done suddenly struck him. *Traitor*, Harolf had called him, and traitor he was, except . . .

Lying next to him was the woman he had thought dead these seven years past, the woman whose memory had given him no peace, the beautiful, dark-haired, dark-eyed slave woman he had helped chain to the War Skull of Hel . . . she whose naked and bleeding body he had later been ordered to carry into the dark chamber of Nidhug's death slaves to die. Her final screams as that portal had closed had echoed in his mind and nightmares ever since, weighing him down, reminding him of his cowardice in not finding some way to help her, no matter the cost to himself. But what could he have done against the combined strength of his fellow warriors and Nidhug's sorcery? Even if he had killed Jalna to give her a quick and clean death, Nidhug could have brought her back from the grave to torment her anew.

The last of Kovna's army thundered past. The rumbling of pounding hooves and the moaning of the Hel-wind faded into the distance. He released his hold on her wrists and mouth.

Jalna jumped to her feet. She reached for the hilt of her sword, swayed, and nearly fell, pain throbbing within her skull, making her vision swim.

Tyrulf steadied her. "You intended to slay me just now," he said, easing her back to the ground. "I didn't save you in the dungeon, but I *have* saved you from Kovna and Thokk. And your thanks is to try to draw your sword."

"Thokk?" Jalna asked as she fought to clear her vision. "The Hel-Witch? So *that's* who she was."

She climbed back to her feet, her vision nearly clear, the pounding in her skull less severe. "Where's my battle-helm?" she asked, looking around.

"I dropped it after using it to crack your skull."

"And my shield?"

"With your helm. There wasn't time to—"

With a curse Jalna began running toward Eirik's Vale.

"Bloodsong's daughter is Thokk's captive," Tyrulf said as he caught up and paced along beside her.

Jalna glanced at him and kept running.

"Bloodsong's daughter and a blond-haired Witch were taken to Thokk's castle before we came here," Tyrulf continued. "I helped capture them a few days ago."

"Guthrun and Huld," Jalna said, cursing. "Both Thokk's captives. Another reason you should die."

"We two can't stop Kovna and Thokk alone," Tyrulf assured her. "The village is truly doomed."

"Try again to stop me from reaching Bloodsong and I *will* kill you," Jalna promised, and kept on running.

5
Death Touch

"Those clouds . . ." Bloodsong said, staring at the dark shapes that had suddenly boiled into existence above the forest and were rapidly spreading outward, dimming the light of the rising sun. "Sorcery!"

She turned, shouted to the warriors on the ground below, "Bring Witch Gerda to me! Hurry!"

"Gerda's Witchcraft has weakened in the past year," Valgerth observed, "along with her health."

"Do you know of another Witch in Eirik's Vale? And how else can we fight sorcery but with magic?"

"I know, Freyadis," Valgerth said, watching the growing black clouds. "If Huld and Norda were here—"

"They *should* be here," Bloodsong growled. "I think Huld would have agreed to come here and teach Guthrun, but Norda's cursed stubbornness . . ."

Two warriors helped a small, white-haired woman to mount the ramparts, carrying her most of the way up the stairs to speed her arrival.

"Most undignified," Gerda Snowmeadow complained, pat-

ting her hair and green robe back into place when she'd been
deposited before Bloodsong.

"Those clouds"—Bloodsong pointed—"they suddenly appeared over the forest and will soon cover the sky. It must be
sorcery, Gerda. Can you do anything to help?"

The crone peered upward at the spreading cloud and thrust
out her tongue as if tasting the air. Suddenly she swayed on
her feet, eyes tightly closed. Bloodsong and Valgerth caught
her before she could fall, both surprised at how thin and frail
she had become.

Gerda pushed them away, determined to stand on her own.
"I'm all right now," she said, panting, then frowned up at the
boiling black clouds. "I was caught by surprise." The last of
the sky had now been covered, shrouding the land in a preternatural twilight.

"Hel-magic," Gerda told them distastefully. "Strong. Sick-
ening. Death-tainted."

"Who is casting this spell, Gerda?" Bloodsong asked. "Can
you help us? Can you send away the clouds?"

"Since Nidhug's passing," Gerda answered, "I know of only
one person who could wield such powerful Hel-magic. Thokk.
I'm certain you've heard many Freya-Witches warning that
something like this might occur, now that Hel has the War
Skull back, which has increased her power."

"Yes," Bloodsong said. "We've all heard those warnings,
but I have never apologized for having returned the War Skull
to Hel, and I never shall. I would do it again for Guthrun's
sake."

Gerda shook her head disapprovingly. "Hel-worshipers have
been reappearing," she said, staring accusingly at Bloodsong.
"Some say they are flocking to the castle of Thokk."

Bloodsong glanced skyward. "Can you do anything to help
us, Gerda? If you can't, you may return to the barracks to wait
in safety."

"I will try," Gerda promised, eyeing the boiling black clouds,
"but undoing the evil caused by returning the War Skull to Hel
is more than a matter of dispersing clouds."

The Witch closed her eyes, mumbled lilting syllables under her breath. Bloodsong recognized the musical language she'd heard Huld and Norda use when invoking the aid of the Goddess Freya.

Gerda's weather spell began to work, the clouds thinning above the fortress. Blue sky appeared overhead. Then suddenly Gerda screamed and staggered backward. Valgerth and Bloodsong caught her, cried out with pain, and released their hold, the old woman's body suddenly glowing with a purple light. Gerda writhed on the ground and screamed in agony. Her face became a skull. She screamed again and burst into purple flames, within moments becoming no more than a pile of greasy, smoldering ashes. Overhead the clouds thickened once more, covering the patch of blue sky.

Bloodsong cursed, trying to conceal her fear as she looked at the warriors on the ramparts who had seen. "Witchcraft, be damned!" she cried to them. "Ready your weapons! If there is a battle, remember that I destroyed Nidhug, and if *he* could be destroyed, *any* magic-worker can be destroyed, especially one who merely makes black clouds and kills those who are already weak and near death!"

"Are you all right?" Thorfinn asked, running up to them, the young warrior named Ole close behind.

"We're fine," Valgerth assured him, "but Gerda..."

"Look there!" Bloodsong shouted, pointing to the edge of the forest.

Emerging from the trees galloped an army of warriors, the sound of pounding hooves thundering rapidly closer. In front of them all came nine black-clad warriors atop gaunt white steeds.

Bloodsong cursed. "That explains the dark clouds," she said. "Hel-warriors. The steeds they ride tread the wind and cannot stand the rays of the sun. They will sweep over the walls on those steeds and try to open the gates for the others." She quickly shouted orders as she drew her sword and readied her shield. Warriors hastened to obey, many leaving the ramparts to stand ready in defense of the gates from within.

The riders swept on toward the fortress. Just out of bowshot, the main mass of the army reined to a halt. The Hel-horses rose higher into the air, were soon level with the ramparts, and hurtled on toward the defenders of Eirik's Vale, hooves treading the moaning black shadows swirling beneath them.

As the Hel-warriors sped nearer their corpselike nature was revealed to the watchers on the ramparts. When Bloodsong had fought Nidhug in Hel's name, she had herself been a Hel-warrior, but a living one, not like the death-horrors nearly upon them, black-bladed swords drawn, purple fires flickering within the empty eye sockets of their skullish faces.

"They're like the ones Nidhug had with him when he led the Hunt of the Damned against us!" Valgerth cried, "and only the Hel-ring you wore was able to defeat them!"

"Perhaps they're not *quite* the same," Bloodsong said hopefully. "I never regretted Hel taking back that cursed ring and the Witch-powers it gave me, until now..."

Valgerth shouted orders to her archers. A volley was fired at the approaching death-horrors, then another. Shafts struck their targets and embedded themselves deeply into riders and mounts alike. The Hel-warriors and their steeds took no notice. Valgerth cursed.

The black-clad corpse-warriors shot over the ramparts. Black blades flashed downward nearly too fast to see. Men screamed. Beside Thorfinn, Ole fell without a sound, blood and brains pouring from a cloven skull.

The Hel-warriors came to the ground within the walls, slicing left and right as they divided up, two heading for each of the four gates. The ninth rider jumped from his steed and ran toward the entrance to one of the barracks.

"My children are in there!" Valgerth cried.

Several warriors left the gates to block the ninth Hel-warrior's way to the barracks.

"Go help them," Bloodsong ordered.

Valgerth and Thorfinn hesitated, torn between their duty on the ramparts and their desire to do as Bloodsong had said.

"Go!" she shouted. "The battle is down there, anyway, not up here!"

Valgerth and Thorfinn headed down to join the battle.

Bloodsong glanced back to the army outside the fortress. Flames had begun to rise from some of the dwellings. An image of the massacre she had witnessed thirteen years before rose in her mind. *It won't happen again*, she vowed. *I won't let it*.

The army outside the gates was spreading out, encircling the fortress, ready to enter once the Hel-warriors had opened the gates.

Bloodsong looked to see how many Hel-warriors yet remained. A chill shot through her. The eight who had attacked the gates still sat on their skeletal steeds, slaying to left and right. Only a few warriors were left to oppose them at the gates. The ninth rider was pressing ever nearer the barracks, advancing with frightening ease through those who fought him. And then she saw that even when a Hel-warrior's blade did not slice flesh, defenders still died, crumpling to the ground and screaming in agony even if their weapons so much as contacted the swords or bodies of the Hel-warriors. *Merely touching them causes death*! Bloodsong realized, sickened, suddenly knowing that against such warriors her own had no chance, that the battle could end in only one way...

No! she vowed, and began running along the ramparts, shouting empty encouragements to her warriors, ordering the archers to stand ready near the gates should the main army charge. And then she saw Valgerth and Thorfinn racing to help fight the Hel-warrior near the barracks. She glanced outside the fortress one last time and saw that there was nothing more she could do there. She threw herself down the stairs toward the hopeless battle raging within the fortress. *Thank Freya that Guthrun is safe with Huld*, she thought as she reached the ground. She raced for the gate that had the fewest warriors left to defend it and saw, as she ran, that only Valgerth and Thorfinn remained to stop the ninth Hel-warrior from entering the barracks. The Hel-warrior suddenly drew back, refusing to fight them, refusing even to let their weapons touch him, and moving with a preternatural speed to evade their cuts.

Bloodsong stopped running toward the gate and ran toward the barracks instead, wondering why the Hel-warrior was drawing back and if there still might be a way to stop those at the gates.

"He has a death-touch!" Valgerth shouted as Bloodsong came to a stop beside her.

"What did you do to make him draw back?" Bloodsong demanded, watching as the Hel-warrior evaded yet another cut from Thorfinn's sword.

"Nothing!" Thorfinn called.

"Except attack him, like all the others were doing. But he must not want us dead," Valgerth concluded.

"Then you two can help at the gates if the others act the same way."

"And you?" Valgerth asked.

Bloodsong understood and stepped toward the Hel-warrior. He drew back from her too.

Suddenly a small form slipped by Bloodsong and ran at the death-horror, a young, blond-haired girl brandishing a wooden training sword.

"Thora!" Valgerth screamed, and made a grab for her daughter.

The Hel-warrior avoided the child too.

Valgerth reached Thora, held the child tightly, and dragged her back toward Thorfinn and Bloodsong.

All defenders at the north gate had fallen. The two Hel-warriors there were opening the gates, ignoring the arrows being embedded in their flesh from archers on the ramparts. The army outside was already thundering through, shields held over their heads to fend off arrows.

As the mortal warriors poured into the fortification shouting war cries, the Hel-warriors at the gates sped away. The one who had attacked the barracks mounted his Hel-horse and followed close behind, his steed galloping skyward upon the moaning shadow-winds and over the ramparts. With his departure the sky began to clear, morning sunlight again bathing the fortress as Bloodsong and her warriors battled within.

Nearly half the warriors of Eirik's Vale lay dead and decaying from the Hel-warrior's death touch, and though those who remained fought with all the skill and ferocity Bloodsong had taught them, the attackers were too many. In the midst of the battle, warriors surrounded Bloodsong and threw a heavy net over her, as if she were a beast to be captured. As she struggled to cut her way free she saw nets being thrown over Valgerth and Thorfinn too.

It was soon over, the battle lost. Bloodsong, Thorfinn, and Valgerth stood sweating near the barracks, their hands bound tightly behind them, warriors with drawn swords watching them closely as the few defenders who yet lived were herded out the northern gateway.

Other warriors forced those within the barracks outside and out the northern gateway, too, all except Thora and Yngvar, Valgerth and Thorfinn's daughter and son, who were pushed to where their mother and father stood, bound.

Beyond the northern gateway screams began to rise.

Bloodsong started forward, memories of the massacre years before tearing at her. A sword touched her throat and prodded her back against the barrack's wall.

"What are you doing to them?" she cried.

Those guarding her said nothing, merely exchanged knowing grins.

Through the northern gateway rode a man and a woman, he with tanned skin and gray hair, the woman with pale flesh and long black hair hanging in glistening coils.

"Kovna!" Bloodsong cursed, recognizing the man.

"And the woman?" Thorfinn asked.

The woman was too far away to have been able to hear, but her eyes turned upon Thorfinn and held his gaze as she rode nearer. "I am Thokk," she announced as she and Kovna reined to a halt nearby. Her gaze shifted to Valgerth and the children, then settled upon Bloodsong. Her red lips smiled coldly.

The screams beyond the walls were growing louder, more numerous, more agonized.

"You're wondering what's happening to them," Kovna said, eyes boring into Bloodsong's. "You will see," he said with a laugh, "before you die."

6
The Hill

Jalna paced in frustration at the edge of the forest, gripping her sword and shield in a white-knuckled grip. She cursed under her breath, watching as the massacre of the survivors of Eirik's Vale began. Kovna's men were amusing themselves with the captives, killing them in a great variety of ways, none quick or painless. Having suffered torture herself, Jalna's fury grew with each ragged scream she heard.

"We have to *do* something!" she finally cried, glancing accusingly at Tyrulf.

Tyrulf shook his head. "Perhaps later..."

"When they're all dead?"

He said nothing.

"Curse you," she said, and returned her gaze to the distant scenes of horror, watching as her friends and comrades in arms screamed again and again.

Tyrulf watched her, feeling angry that there was nothing he could do to help. It was much as it had been in Nidhug's dungeons when he'd wanted to help Jalna, except that this time she was safe. If not for him, she would either be already dead, or screaming in the distance with the other people of Eirik's Vale.

"At least you need not worry about Bloodsong's life," he told her.

Jalna stopped pacing and came nearer, angry eyes upon him. "Tell me what you know."

"We all had orders to spare her, along with another woman named Valgerth, a man named Thorfinn, and their children. Thokk did something, worked a spell, I suppose, and their identities and appearances came into all our minds."

"Why?"

"We only knew that they were to be taken alive, nothing more. We even trained to use nets in order to capture them."

Jalna began pacing again, thinking of desperate plans.

A heavy rope tied around Bloodsong's neck ran to Kovna's saddle. He and Thokk rode ahead, leading her like a beast out of the village toward a hill, upon which grew one ancient tree. Near the base of the tree were two oval graves outlined in stones, one grave smaller than the other, the graves of Bloodsong's husband and son.

Their destination clear, Bloodsong struggled even harder to free her hands, her eyes locked on the approaching hill, but the tight cords held her wrists unyieldingly behind her. Kovna turned in his saddle, noticed the expression on her face, and laughed.

All around Bloodsong were scenes and sounds of death and horror. Most of the surviving warriors were now mercifully dead, but their screams had been replaced by those of the other villagers. *Even the children*! Bloodsong thought, sickened and enraged. Fire was spreading rapidly throughout the village, and soon it would all be in blackened ruins again.

Just like before, Bloodsong thought, shuddering. It was all happening again as it had thirteen years ago, and there was nothing she could do except follow helplessly along behind her captors like a beast on a leash, just as she had all those years in the past. And she had no doubts that Kovna planned the same for her on the hill she had suffered once before.

Could I have foreseen this? Prevented it? she wondered bitterly. *Did I miss warnings? Ignore advice I should have heeded? I have failed those who trusted me to protect them. Thank Freya that Guthrun is safe with Huld.*

Huld remembered nothing of the past few days. The last thing she remembered was going to sleep with Norda and Guthrun in the cottage, planning the next day's lessons for Guthrun, reminding herself that it would soon be Norda's birthday and she must complete the surprise she had been creating for her beloved teacher. Then, with sleep had come nightmares from which she could not awaken, until now. . . .

The young Witch gritted her teeth against the pains of returning awareness. Even with her eyes open there was only darkness. Her shoulders and wrists ached sickeningly. She tried to move and managed slightly to flex the muscles in her arms and legs. Chains rattled coldly with her scant movements.

She was standing upright, chained naked. She struggled harder, panic sweeping through her. *No matter*, she told herself, trying to grow calm. *I can easily free myself with the spell to open locks.*

Huld concentrated her will, softly intoned the lilting phrases of the spell, and waited for the yellow-gold light of Freya's power to glow around the manacles that held her wrists and ankles. The darkness remained. She tried again and then again. She remained bound.

Spell-chains? she wondered, panic returning. *Like the ones Nidhug used on me?* But Nidhug had been destroyed, transformed into a monstrous, maggotlike dragon by the Goddess Hel and condemned to scream forever in a dark corner of Helheim. Huld had seen his transformation and disappearance from the Earth with her own eyes. Who, then, had placed her in spell-chains? She thought of Norda's old enemy: the Hel-Witch, Thokk. Yes, it might well be Thokk's doing, but if so, why? Revenge? And if she were in Thokk's dungeon, was she there alone? Or had Norda and Guthrun also been captured?

"Norda?" she called into the darkness. "Guthrun?" She tried several more times, but received no response.

The air was cold and moist. A faint scent of decayed flesh underlied its musty odor.

Huld strained onto tiptoes to relieve her aching shoulders and wrists. She considered the way she was chained, her legs and arms splayed out so that her nude body formed an X. *A living Gipt Rune*, she thought. Might there be a purpose in that? She knew that the X rune was often used in operations of sex magic, representing as it did the interaction of two forces. . . .

She tried to discount the notion and control her fears. Something touched her naked foot, something covered with stiff hairs. She took a deep breath and yelled as loud as she could, heard what she assumed to be a rat squeal in fright and scuttle away. *A small victory*, she thought.

The muscles in her calves began to tremble and cramp from maintaining her tiptoed position. She sagged in her chains once more, pain returning to her wrists and shoulders, and hung helpless in the darkness, cold, frightened, confused, angry, waiting for she knew not what.

"Bloodsong!" Jalna exclaimed. "I see her now. There"— she pointed—"walking behind Kovna and Thokk, headed toward . . . ." Her voice trailed away.

"Gods," she whispered. "Sweet Skadi, no. They're taking her to that hill where . . ."

"Where?" Tyrulf prompted.

"Nidhug tied her to the tree on that hill after recapturing her thirteen years ago. Then he tortured her husband and son to death as she watched and left her there to die. I don't want to believe that they'd do that to her again, but . . ."

"It would be like Kovna," Tyrulf commented. "He was undoubtedly with Nidhug that other time. But maybe she'll escape death again, Jalna. She did before."

"No," Jalna quietly said, "she did not. Not the way you mean. I'm going to circle around through the forest so that I'm nearer. You need not come with me."

Try to stop me, Tyrulf thought as he set off beside her through the trees.

While Kovna and Thokk watched, warriors with drawn swords prodded Bloodsong to the lone tree on the hill, then turned her to face her captors. Kovna stepped closer.

"Do you remember me from thirteen years ago?" he demanded.

Bloodsong met his gaze but said nothing.

"She remembers you," Thokk said with a laugh. "She remembers *all* of it. She also guesses what's coming and is struggling to keep her fear and panic from showing."

Kovna nodded, concealing his distaste for the magic that allowed Thokk to so easily penetrate the minds of others. He remembered that King Nidhug had been able to do that, too, but not in the same way, not so effortlessly. Thokk had obviously discovered certain secrets that Nidhug, for all his power, had not. He returned his attention to Bloodsong.

He walked nearer to the bound warrior-woman and smiled unpleasantly, anticipation building steadily within him. "Then you also remember," he continued with a soft laugh, "that Nidhug stripped you naked before tying you to the tree, as befitted an escaped slave about to be executed."

Several of Kovna's warriors chuckled.

Bloodsong ignored them and kept her eyes locked with Kovna's.

Kovna leaned closer to her face. "I'm going to have your hands untied. You will strip yourself naked and place yourself against the tree to be tied there to die."

"She's thinking that as soon as her hands are free—" Thokk began.

"I can *guess* what she's thinking, Witch," Kovna growled, "but she's not going to try any arena warrior's tricks, for several reasons." He lightly touched Bloodsong's long black hair. She jerked her head away. He laughed harshly.

"We don't have your husband and son to torture this time," he said, "but if you don't cooperate, we can substitute your friends, Valgerth and Thorfinn, and their children. And if you don't care about them . . . " He gestured to Thokk. "Show her."

Thokk had been holding a long, thin object wrapped in leather that she had taken from her saddle. Watching Bloodsong's eyes, she unwrapped the object with a flourish. Guthrun's sword fell at Bloodsong's feet.

"No!" Bloodsong cried, started forward. Swords instantly pressed her back.

"If you don't cooperate," Thokk told her, "I can give your daughter great pain. She is a prisoner in my castle, but even at this distance I can make her scream, even kill her. I can even arrange for you to hear her cries in your mind. Shall I give you a demonstration?"

"I'll do as you ask," Bloodsong quickly said, "if you'll set Guthrun free."

"You'll do as Kovna asks"—Thokk laughed—"or I will make your daughter scream. She will not be freed."

"How do I know she's even still alive?"

"You don't." Thokk smiled.

Bloodsong's gaze probed Thokk's.

"She will cooperate," Thokk said, turning to Kovna. "She won't risk harming her daughter."

"A fatal weakness," Kovna said with a chuckle, "though there's nothing she could do anyway, except seek a quick death on one of my soldiers' swords. Free her hands."

Bloodsong rubbed circulation back into her wrists, stalling for time, thinking furiously, seething inside.

"Perhaps, while we're waiting," Thokk said, "I might amuse myself by making one of Guthrun's eyes—"

"All right!" Bloodsong cried. "Curse you all!"

Everyone laughed at her outburst.

Bloodsong looked down at Guthrun's sword, kept her eyes on the blade, and began to strip, trying to ignore the gazes and remarks of Kovna's men as more and more of her flesh was revealed, struggling to find a way to yet turn defeat into victory, finding no hope.

Bloodsong threw the last of her clothing onto the ground

and stood naked in the sunlight, fists clenched at her sides. She looked up from Guthrun's sword, raising her chin defiantly. The warriors no longer laughed. Seeing the numerous scars her body bore reminded them that she was a seasoned warrior, a swordswoman who had survived many battles, a warrior deserving their respect. But Kovna and Thokk still smiled, relishing Bloodsong's defeat.

"Against the tree," Kovna said, ordering Bloodsong. He kicked her clothing toward a warrior. "Burn her clothes," he commanded. "She won't be needing them again."

They won't win, Guthrun! Bloodsong mentally vowed. *We'll beat them somehow. . . .*

Detecting her thoughts, Thokk laughed. "She's stalling again. Perhaps while we're waiting I'll—"

Bloodsong cursed, strode the few steps to the tree, turned to face her captors, leaned back, and let the rough bark dig into her flesh.

7
Friends

"Guthrun," someone whispered. "Guthrun..."

Guthrun stopped pacing the small windowless room. It was the first voice, other than her own, that she had heard since awakening a prisoner in the locked room.

Because she had heard Thokk's name mentioned during her capture, she assumed that she was in the Hel-Witch's castle. Judging by the number of meals that had been slipped through a small opening in the door, and because of the distance from Norda's cottage to the castle of Thokk, she estimated that several days had passed since her capture.

In the chamber was a comfortable bed covered in shiny red fabric, a richly carved table of dark polished wood upon which burned an oil lamp that mysteriously never went dry, and a single cushioned chair with gilt arms and legs. She still wore her thin white sleeping shift, but it was torn, smudged with dirt, stained with the blood of the two men she had killed. The marks on her wrists from being bound on the journey had nearly disappeared.

"Guthrun..." came the whisper again.

She slipped to the iron-banded wooden door, found it still locked, got down on her knees, and peered through the tiny food slot. Beyond the opening she could still see nothing but darkness.

"Release me!" she demanded.

"Guthrun . . ."

The voice was not coming from beyond the door, she now realized, but from within the small chamber.

"I am here," Guthrun finally said, frowning, reviewing in her mind the things Norda and Huld had taught her about spirits and how to deal with them. "Who are you and what do you want?"

"To play, Guthrun," the voice whispered. "I want to play. Don't you remember me? We used to play. . . ."

Guthrun's breath caught. She *did* recognize the whispered voice, but she had not heard that voice for seven years, not since leaving her childhood home in Helheim where she had been born.

"Inga?" she asked, chilled, remembering the childhood friend she had left in Hel's subterranean Land of Death.

When she spoke Inga's name, a ghostly image wreathed in pulsing purple light materialized only a few paces from her.

Inga looked as she had seven years before, a young child with long blond hair framing a corpse's face, sunken eyes staring. "Guthrun!" Inga cried. "How I've missed you! I can't stay long. Mother Hel misses you too. Why did you leave? Won't you come back to us? Come home? All of your friends miss you so. . . ."

Guthrun started to speak, shook her head, and did not.

"Guthrun?" Inga said, her ghostly form reaching out as if to be embraced. "You look different, Guthrun. You've grown older. Don't you want to play with me anymore?" the child asked, her voice catching. "Don't you like me anymore?"

Tears welled up in Guthrun's eyes. Again she had to stop herself from speaking, knowing that to do so might give the specter more power over her.

"Come *home* to us," Inga begged, starting to weep. "Please?

I have to go now since you won't talk with me. But please do as Thokk asks. Mother Hel wants you to do that. So do I and all your friends. I will come back, if I can. . . ." The voice faded along with the ghostly image.

Guthrun choked back tears, raised her fists. "It won't work, Thokk! You won't trick me! You won't win, whatever your game!"

There was no response.

A long time later another meal was delivered. Guthrun at first vowed not to eat it, still upset by the vision of her childhood friend, but then, reminding herself that she needed to keep up her strength in case there was a chance to escape, she began eating the cold, tasteless food, food similar to what she and her mother had eaten while together in Helheim.

Helheim, Guthrun thought with a shudder, remembering the countless gray-skinned corpses with whom she had shared the first six years of her life. After her mother had destroyed the Hel-traitor Nidhug and returned the War Skull of Hel to the Death Goddess, Hel had released Guthrun to walk the Earth with her mother. But Guthrun still woke some nights, thinking that she was back in Hel's icy world, momentarily forgetting that the night's darkness would pass at dawn, that the chill air would warm with the rising of the golden sun.

What if I'm back there now? Guthrun suddenly thought. *What if I wasn't taken to Thokk's castle but back to Helheim? What if Inga's visit was real, was not a trick? What if Inga's mentioning Thokk was a trick to make me think I am still upon the Earth's surface? Could Inga even have visited me if I were not within Hel's realm?*

Guthrun began pacing the small chamber again, fighting to control a rising panic.

Far below the chamber where Guthrun was held prisoner, Huld still hung naked in her chains, each breath becoming more and more of a struggle because of her strained position. She had lost all feeling in her hands. Her shoulders burned with pain, and her cramping legs refused to raise her to give her shoulders relief. She was growing steadily weaker from pain, exhaustion, and the lack of food and water.

I could die here, she suddenly thought. *Freya's teeth! No! I'm not going to die! I refuse to give in!*

The stiff hairs of a rat brushed against her naked foot again. Huld gathered her strength, screamed raggedly with rage and fear and pain.

A faint purple glow began to pulse before her. Slowly it grew brighter. Within the glow a form materialized, gigantic, half again Huld's height, its face that of a grinning skull, tattered flesh clinging to its skeleton's body. It glided forward toward her.

I am your death, spoke a toneless voice in her head, *and your life. I am your lover. Through me you shall know the ecstasies of the grave, the passions of the Dead.*

Huld fought her chains as the horror came nearer. "In Freya's name," she cried, "begone, thing of Hel!"

The towering vision of Death did not respond, kept coming, reached her. Skeletal hands gently stroked her long blond hair, caressed her face. Then the bone-cold touch slowly moved lower. . . .

Huld strained against her chains, throwing herself wildly from side to side the scant distance the chains allowed, watching, feeling, shaking her head violently back and forth in denial of the way the monster was touching her body, the fleshless fingers stroking and kneading and teasing her nakedness in the manner of a lover.

"No!" she screamed, outraged. "In Freya's name I command you to stop! I . . . please! Don't!" She sobbed helplessly, unable to stop what was being done to her chained flesh.

Suddenly the skeletal hands withdrew. The death's-head of the monster turned to one side. Another glow was growing there, yellow-gold light, pulsing softly.

The skeletal thing hissed like a serpent.

"Freya!" Huld cried. "Aid me! Destroy—" She choked off her words. A corpse stood within the yellow glow, blackened, charred, unrecognizable except for the eyes, the eyes of Norda Greycloak, filled with hatred and pain.

Streams of fire shot forth from Norda's hands, striking the skeletal monster. The death-horror was hurled backward away from Huld, struck a crumbling stone wall, and burst into golden flames. It writhed silently on the floor a moment, became ashes, and was gone.

"Norda?" Huld whispered as the charred corpse within the yellow glow came nearer. "Norda? I . . . what has happened? How . . ."

Charred hands touched the manacles on Huld's spread ankles. The locks sprang open. Huld pulled her legs together beneath her, moaning at the pain of moving the long-immobilized muscles. Norda's blackened hands touched the manacles around Huld's wrists, freed them too.

Huld tried to stay on her feet, could not, went to her knees on the floor, sobbing with pain.

You must save Guthrun, Norda's voice spoke within her mind. The young Witch looked up into the eyes of her teacher.

"What has happened, Norda? Who did this to you? Tell me what—"

Thokk has imprisioned Guthrun in the castle above. She intends to awaken the dark powers we sensed in the child. You must not let that happen. I . . . there's no more . . . time. I have done all I can do . . . transporting myself here . . . finding and freeing you. The rest is up to you. I have . . . loved you like a daughter, Huld. I—

The charred corpse suddenly screamed, fell to the floor, burst into flames, writhed spasmodically, and became ashes. The yellow glow faded. Total darkness returned.

"Norda!" Huld cried, struggled to stand, but found the pain still too great. She slumped sideways, then onto her back, lay panting with pain, tried to move again, could not, and began to weep.

"Freya give you peace, Norda," Huld prayed, "and me strength. Thokk will know my revenge!" she vowed as she fought to retain consciousness, again tried to stand, was overcome by exhaustion, horror, and pain, sprawled unconscious upon the cold stone floor, darkness seeping deep within her.

8
Hel-Praying

"When you destroyed Nidhug," Kovna said, standing before Bloodsong, "you destroyed the throne I intended to usurp. Instead of being a king, I have been reduced to leading a band of roaming warriors. I've wanted revenge upon you these seven years, and now I have it!"

Bloodsong forced a laugh. "You should thank me, Kovna. You're still alive, which you wouldn't have been if you'd tried to destroy Nidhug."

"If a mere woman could do it, I—"

"I didn't do it alone! I had the aid of the Goddess Hel, and the help of a Freya-Witch, as well as—"

"The Freya-Witch, Huld," Thokk said, interrupting, "who is also a prisoner in my castle, no doubt wishing that she were dead by now."

Bloodsong hung against the tree, tied tightly by the splintery ropes that circled her waist, held her arms stretched high above her head, and kept her ankles pulled painfully back and up above the ground on each side of the gnarled trunk. The pain was constant and growing steadily worse. Sweat bathed her

42

body, making her bare skin glisten in the sunlight. She turned her attention from Kovna to Thokk.

"And you, Thokk?" Bloodsong asked, her voice tight with pain. "Do you want revenge for some imagined wrong too? Is that why you have taken my daughter and helped to destroy my village?"

"Nothing so petty," Thokk answered, then smiled at Kovna's reaction. "I serve Hel, as you once did. I have motives someone like Kovna could never understand. I want power, yes. But not just for myself. You returned the War Skull to Hel so that she again wields substantial power, power that now extends somewhat beyond the borders of Helheim. But with my help she and I will soon extend the reach of her power farther. *Much* farther.

"Many who worship and serve her have flocked to my castle, and soon now, with Guthrun and . . . " Her voice trailed away. She walked to stand next to the smaller of the two graves near the tree.

"Isn't there a detail you've forgotten, Kovna?" Thokk asked. "Didn't Nidhug tie the corpse of Bloodsong's son to her body as if nursing, to mock her? Shouldn't you dig up what remains of the child and—"

"Let my son's bones rest!" Bloodsong commanded.

Thokk's laughter rang out.

"Perhaps you are right," Kovna said, relishing the notion. "I will have some men—"

"No," said Thokk, stopping him. "They would find nothing within the child's grave. I removed the body myself—"

"No!" Bloodsong cried.

". . . thirteen years ago," Thokk continued to Kovna, ignoring Bloodsong, "after she died."

"You're lying!" Bloodsong shouted, straining against the ropes.

"She . . . died?" Kovna asked. "We all thought she had somehow escaped."

"You didn't know?" Thokk purred, walking to stand within reach of the bound warrior-woman. "She was a Hel-warrior when she destroyed Nidhug."

"Yes. But she was not, *is* not, like those dead things who aided us during the battle."

"There are varieties of Hel-warriors, Kovna. Some, like Bloodsong, are granted a return to living flesh when they die Hel-praying, as she did. Others, like those who aided us, are animations of dead flesh. They are Death Riders. To touch even their weapons in battle is to die."

"Admit that you are lying, Hel-Witch," Bloodsong demanded, "lying about my son."

"Ah, a mother's anguish." Thokk laughed, gently stroking Bloodsong's long black hair. Bloodsong tried to jerk her head away, but her bondage prevented it. "I can tell from your thoughts that you know Nidhug returned to this place and made a death slave of your husband's corpse. I can also tell that you have wondered why he didn't do the same with the corpse of your son. Now you know the answer. The corpse of your son was no longer buried here. I had already taken it away." Thokk smiled sweetly at Bloodsong, kept stroking her hair. "Your thoughts tell me that you are beginning to believe. Yes. It is true."

"What..."

"Have I done with him?" Thokk finished. "He's quite well, in my castle."

"He's ... w-well?" Bloodsong stammered.

New laughter exploded from Thokk. For an instant the beauty of her face became the obscene mask of a demoness. Then she calmed herself, reached out, and began stroking Bloodsong's hair again.

"How I've longed to tell you about him," Thokk told her. "He's a handsome, well-grown young man. I have healed him, you see. Helped him to grow."

"Thorbjorn is ... *alive*? You *must* be lying. I asked for his resurrection to be part of the bargain before I died Hel-praying, but Hel herself said that it wasn't possible, that he'd been dead too long."

"Lokith is his name now. And no, he's not actually alive. Not yet. But soon, when I introduce his sister to him, and when her first woman's blood flows, he will taste of that sweet crimson draft and arise to—"

"No!" Bloodsong screamed, throwing herself against her ropes. "You will *not* make a Hel-monster out of my son!"

"Monster?" Thokk asked, pretending shock.

"Don't let her do it, Kovna! Surely even you cannot condone such a thing! Do something to stop her! Torture and kill me, but I beg you not to let her—"

Kovna's laughter stopped her. "I never thought you would ask for *my* help! Truly my revenge is complete. I thank you, Thokk. You have caused Bloodsong to *beg* of me!"

Bloodsong spit in his face. His fist came around and cracked into her jaw. She sagged, unconscious.

"Curse you!" Thokk cried. "Leave me alone with her. Or do you wish to risk Hel's wrath and my own?" Embers of purple fire flickered deep within the Hel-Witch's eyes.

Kovna stood his ground a moment longer, then cursed, ordered his men to follow him, and strode away down the hill. At the bottom he stationed warriors to keep watch.

Thokk controlled her anger, concentrated her will, traced runes in the air, spoke a word of power.

Bloodsong's eyes slowly opened.

"Warrior," Thokk said with a smile, "you may yet see your son and daughter again. The choice is yours."

Bloodsong's vision cleared. She looked for Kovna.

"This is just between the two of us and the Goddess Hel," Thokk assured her. "I have sent Kovna away."

Bloodsong stared into the Hel-Witch's eyes. "Say what you will. I can't stop you."

"Nor should you want to stop me. I have agreed to let Kovna have his revenge upon you, and I will keep my word. Your fate means little to me but much to my reluctant ally. I suppose, however, that you have many unpleasant days ahead of you, slowly dying here, of starvation and exposure. But then, you already know how it will be, having experienced it before. And at the end, when you know that death is near, there will again be whispers within your mind, the voice of Hel, though louder this time, now that she again has the power of the War Skull at her command. Die Hel-praying when Hel bids it, Bloodsong. Become a Hel-warrior again, and in time you shall see Guthrun and Lokith once more."

Bloodsong shook her head negatively.

"Don't be so certain," Thokk replied. "Every warrior who died here today, every person, even the children, heard the whispers of Hel within their minds at the point of death, offering resurrection in return for service. Many there were who accepted, I assure you. Thus has it been since you returned the War Skull to Hel. Join those who pledged service to my Goddess, Bloodsong, and see your children again. Refuse and . . . " Thokk shrugged.

"I will *never* serve Hel again," Bloodsong vowed.

"Even though your children will be doing so? I do not think you a fool, warrior. You will not accept absolute death if there is an alternative. Your children will one day make you proud. Of course, your thoughts tell me that you are already proud of Guthrun, but you shall be prouder still. They are very precious to Hel, Bloodsong. Guthrun is a Deadborn, born in Helheim of a mother who had herself died."

Thokk brushed strands of Bloodsong's hair back from her face, wiped away a trickle of blood Kovna's blow had caused to flow from the corner of her mouth. "You did not know that Guthrun would be so special to Hel when you agreed to Hel's bargain and died Hel-praying to save yourself and your unborn daughter. But Hel sees far into the future. That is why, as the saying goes, she always laughs last."

"Curse you, Witch. And curse Hel."

"Your thoughts tell me that you've wondered about Guthrun's interest in Witchcraft. Perhaps now your mind will be at peace, seeing that for a Deadborn it is only natural. Power slumbers within Guthrun like a serpent, Bloodsong, the Coils of Old Night waiting to strike in Hel's name. And Lokith—"

"Thorbjorn, Eirik's son, was and *is* his name, no matter what you have done with his corpse."

"Lokith," Thokk continued, "will rise to lead the Death

Riders of Hel, a Hel-warrior himself whose sorcerous powers will surpass your imagining. Oh, yes, Bloodsong, they are children of which you can be justly proud.

"I have waited and planned long for this, as has Hel. If you had not defeated Nidhug, Guthrun and Lokith would now be preparing to do battle with that Hel-traitor and retrieve the War Skull. But you *did* defeat him, and they are now free to embark on the next phase of Hel's plan.

"She was once a Goddess of both Life and Death. All the Earth was her domain. But then Odin and his allies drove her into the darkness beneath the Earth, stole the War Skull from her, made her a Goddess solely of the Dead. She had hoped that when the War Skull was restored to her, so might all her powers be. But she has been a Goddess of only the Dead for too long. Now, because of what was done to her, when she returns one day to her rightful place upon the Earth's surface, the Earth will become a dead world, shrouded in darkness, covered in ice and snow."

"If you want that to happen, Thokk, you are truly insane," Bloodsong said with disgust, "to turn all the world into a vast grave, to let the darkness and ice of Helheim spread over the Earth. How can you even think of such a thing? How has your mind become so warped that—"

"Hel has been terribly wronged, Bloodsong," Thokk said, interrupting angrily. "Those of us who worship her, the first and true ruler of the Earth, are pledged to right that wrong."

"But to work for the death of the Earth? Nothing can justify that, Thokk. Nothing!"

"I tire of your stubbornness and stupidity, warrior. Perhaps I was wrong to waste my time explaining matters to you. You have two choices—and only two. Either die Hel-praying and rise to ride with your children as we spread Hel's power over the Earth, or die and rot in some unmarked grave. I do not really care which you choose. Neither does Hel. It is up to you."

Thokk held Bloodsong's gaze a moment more, then turned and walked away, leaving Bloodsong alone.

9

Bloodsong and Freedom

Hands still bound behind them, surrounded by Kovna's warriors, Valgerth and Thorfinn walked up the hill and stood before Bloodsong.

Valgerth stepped closer, eyes burning with rage at what was being done to her friend. Bloodsong's eyes were closed, the lines of her battle-scared face drawn tight in pain, her breathing labored.

"Freyadis?" Valgerth softly called.

Sunset was near. Bloodsong had hung on the tree most of the morning and all of the afternoon. Pain and exhaustion had finally driven away consciousness. But now, hearing the voice of her friend, she slowly opened her swollen eyes.

Valgerth bent forward and kissed her lightly on the cheek.

"I feared that they had slain you," Bloodsong said, her voice dry and cracked. "Are your children unharmed?"

"Yes." Valgerth nodded. "We are being taken to Thokk's castle. She has promised not to hurt our children if we cooperate."

"Cooperate? How?"

"She hasn't told us yet," Thorfinn answered.

Bloodsong nodded and forced a smile. "It's not the first time things seemed hopeless for us, eh, Valgerth?"

"Aye, Freyadis. If we could escape Nidhug's slave pens and return to destroy him, anything is possible."

The two women looked deep into each other's eyes for several long moments, then Bloodsong's clouded with pain, and a spasm of suffering shuddered through her.

"Guthrun and Huld are in Thokk's castle too," Bloodsong said after a moment, "and . . . my son."

"Your son? But . . ."

"Thokk claims to have stolen his body and used her magic to make him grow older. She intends to awaken his dead flesh so that he may become the leader of Hel-warriors like those who attacked the village. Death Riders, she calls them. And she wants to turn Guthrun into a Hel-Witch. She intends to use my children to spread Hel's power, to turn the Earth into a dead world shrouded in darkness and ice. We have to find some way to stop her. If I die here, it will be up to you."

"If only we could get our children to safety," Thorfinn said.

"Be warned that Thokk can read thoughts," Bloodsong warned. "There's one other thing you should know. Thokk says that I will be offered the chance to die Hel-praying, to return as a Hel-warrior once again."

"And . . . will you?" Valgerth asked.

"I have told her that I will not."

Valgerth nodded. "But if it's the only way to survive?"

"I don't know, Valgerth. I just don't know. . . . " Her voice became a groan as another spasm of agony shuddered through her.

The sun passed beneath the horizon. A faint moaning sound arose from within the forest north of the village and grew steadily louder.

Through the twilight came the nine Death Riders upon their wind-treading steeds. Five riderless Hel-horses followed the mounted ones, embers of purple fire glowing in their eyes.

Thokk came up the hill and smiled at Bloodsong and her

two friends. "Time to ride the wind," she said, gesturing down the hill to the Death Riders who had just reined up nearby. Kovna's warriors were binding Thora and Yngvar each to an empty Hel-horse saddle. Yngvar had begun to cry.

"If you harm my son . . ." Valgerth warned.

"He'll enjoy wind-riding once we get started," Thokk assured her, "unless you do something foolish."

Valgerth turned back to Bloodsong. Their eyes met. Valgerth leaned forward, again kissed Bloodsong's cheek. "Bloodsong and freedom," she whispered, saying the battle cry Nidhug's slaves had shouted while fighting their way from Nastrond. "Until I see you again, Freyadis . . ." Valgerth said, choking back tears. Then she turned and walked down the hill.

Thorfinn held Bloodsong's gaze a moment and nodded to her, unable to think of anything to say, then turned with a curse and followed Valgerth.

Thokk stepped nearer the bound warrior-woman. "You are in much pain," she said, "but not as much as earlier. You've grown somewhat numb. Unfortunately, I have promised Kovna to do something about that before I leave."

The Hel-Witch concentrated her will, traced invisible runes in the twilight air, spoke words of power. A purple ray of light shot from Thokk's hands and bathed Bloodsong's body.

Bloodsong gasped with pain and strained against the ropes.

"A simple healing spell," Thokk explained, "to restore your nerves to their full sensitivity. And now I shall increase their sensitivity even more."

More runes were traced, more words of power spoken.

Bloodsong's muscles trembled with the strain, the ropes sinking deep into her flesh as she fought her bonds, her face a mask of pain.

"I'd expected a scream, warrior. I have promised Kovna screams before I depart."

The Hel-Witch spoke another word of power.

The pain searing her nerves increased tenfold.

Bloodsong screamed.

At the sound of the scream Valgerth and Thorfinn jerked

around in the saddles to which they had been bound. Kovna, standing nearby, laughed with approval.

The bound warrior-woman screamed again and again, her cries ragged sounds that tore through the twilight.

"Kovna should be pleased," Thokk noted, then turned and walked down the hill. Before she reached the bottom, the screams behind her stopped, Bloodsong hanging unconscious in her bonds once more.

"Jalna! No!" Tyrulf hissed, grabbing the young warrior by the arms, pulling her back.

"Release me, curse you!" Jalna demanded. "Those screams! It's Bloodsong!"

"Keep your voice down!" Tyrulf urged in a harsh whisper. "You can't help her by rushing into the open."

The screams stopped. Jalna ceased struggling.

"After dark I'm going to try to reach her," Jalna vowed.

"As you've already told me over and over."

"Don't try to talk me out of it."

Tyrulf shook his head negatively. "I haven't and I won't. I've been thinking about it myself. No one knows what happened to me. We killed the ones who saw me helping you. Kovna and the others probably think I was slain. If I simply walked up to those guards around the hill, perhaps they would believe that I am still one of them. I could possibly reach Bloodsong without arousing suspicion."

"Why would you do that? It would make more sense for you to claim ignorance of all that has happened, tell them you were knocked unconscious while killing me, and then return to your former place in Kovna's army. Or perhaps you're planning to trick me, make me Kovna's prisoner after all, earn yourself a promotion," she suggested, touching the hilt of her sword.

"Jalna, I would never betray you. I never would have ridden with Kovna after Nidhug's fall if I'd known that you were still alive. I would have searched for you instead."

"Why should you have done that? It makes no sense."

Tyrulf laughed. "Is my behavior any stranger to you now than it was in Nidhug's dungeon? Why do you suppose I wanted to help you then? I had seen many women brought to Nidhug to die before you were chosen. Why did I feel differently about you?"

"I'd never thought about it."

"Somehow that does not surprise me . . . but *I've* thought about it for seven years."

Jalna looked quizzically at him, frowning. "And what answer did you find?" she finally asked.

"If I help you free Bloodsong, will you begin to trust me?"

Jalna was silent a moment. "Aye. If you helped me free her, I *might* believe that you had changed allegiances."

"Then let's start making our plans. It will soon be dark."

"But if you try to trick me . . ."

"You'll kill me first, I suppose? I think you already trust me a little. And by the Hammer, by dawn you will either trust me or we will no doubt *both* be dead."

Some distance from where Jalna and Tyrulf stood hidden among the trees, another pair of eyes watched the hill where Bloodsong was tied.

Beside the watcher, a dagger had been driven halfway to its hilt into a tree at the sound of Bloodsong's screams and the blade snapped off before she fell silent.

The man continued to watch. Soon the black-clad riders disappeared into the forest to the north. Then a man he recognized walked up the slope and stood near Bloodsong.

Kovna, the watcher thought, fists clenched. There were blood debts already owing between them, and now there were more.

The watcher's fists remained clenched until Kovna walked away from Bloodsong, then he turned to a massive black stallion standing nearby and began digging in a leather saddle pouch. The man's height and powerfully muscled body almost made the huge stallion seem to be an average-size steed. Nearby two other stallions were tied, nearly twins of the first.

He found what he sought and removed from the saddle pouch a jewel-hilted dagger he'd taken from a rich merchant's corpse. He examined the decoratively carven, highly polished, but badly balanced blade with disdain, decided that it would have to do, and slipped it into the empty dagger sheath on his belt. Then he turned back to face the hill, unstrapped the circular shield from his back, drew his double-edged broadsword, and set himself to await the night, his eyes holding steadily on the hill where Bloodsong was tied, trying to pierce the deepening darkness, the memory of her screams still tearing raw his mind.

After Thokk, the Death Riders, and their four prisoners had vanished into the forest to the north, Kovna looked up the slope of the hill at Bloodsong. She had not moved since Thokk made her scream. He assumed her to be merely unconscious, but the Hel-Witch could have tricked him and cheated him of his full revenge.

He walked up the hill, grunted with satisfaction upon seeing her breasts still rise and fall with her labored breathing, and examined the ropes that held her to make certain all the knots were still secure.

Kovna glanced back to where Thokk had disappeared. He would not have regretted never seeing the Hel-Witch again, but when Bloodsong was dead, he and his men were pledged to rejoin Thokk at her castle. He frowned, thinking of that horrid place, but then reminded himself that allied with Thokk, distasteful as that often was, more victories would be in his future—perhaps, in time, even a throne.

He turned his attention back to Bloodsong. She had escaped suffering long enough. He slapped her face and was rewarded with a faint groan.

"Wake up, curse you," he commanded and slapped her again.

Bloodsong opened her eyes and fought to clear her vision, noting gratefully that the pain of her bonds was again somewhat numbed. Her gaze focused on Kovna.

"How long did it take you to die before?" he demanded.

Bloodsong said nothing. He slapped her again.

"Three days? Four?" he went on. "Perhaps I will help you to die sooner this time."

Kovna laughed at her continued silence. "No need to wait for dawn," he told her. "After I have eaten and rested I will return. Torches can be brought for light, and, of course, their flames can also be used to sear flesh," he said, suggestively running a hand over her sweat-slicked breasts. "Yes," he said with a grin, "I believe I shall be merciful and help you to die." Laughing, he drew back his hand and slapped her yet again. Then he turned and walked away down the hill.

Bloodsong strained against her bonds, hoping for a knot that might have slipped, a rope that might have loosened after supporting her weight all day, searching for some hope that she might free herself before Kovna returned, but all the ropes remained tight, all the knots secure, and she finally stopped struggling and hung unmoving against the tree once more, fighting the hopelessness that was threatening to destroy her spirit even before Kovna returned to begin destroying her flesh.

10
Vafthrudnir

Huld struggled back to consciousness. She lay in the darkness, confused, shivering with the cold, hugging her nakedness for warmth. Then she began to remember. . . .

"Norda," she whispered. Tears stung her eyes, but an instant later, anger replaced grief.

She moved her legs experimentally, found the pain less, and climbed slowly to her feet. She rubbed at her wrists, found that some numbness still remained in her hands, wondered how long she had been unconscious.

The young Witch concentrated her will, intoned an incantation. Her slightly slanting green eyes began to flicker with yellow-gold light as a night-vision spell, which allowed her to see in the dark, took effect. Her surroundings became visible, illuminated to her eyes by a pale yellow light. The cell's stone walls, ceiling, and corners were clogged with spiderwebs. The dark shapes of rats watched her from here and there.

Huld felt relief that the spell had worked. She had feared that in Thokk's castle her magic might not work, even if free of the spell-chains. But her eyes and head began to ache almost

at once from the spell, exhaustion and lack of food taking their
toll.

Norda had said that Thokk had imprisoned Guthrun in the
castle above. Therefore, that was where she must now go.

The Freya-Witch hurried to the cell's iron-banded wooden
door, the dirty stone floor icy beneath her bare feet. She focused
her concentration on the lock, intoned a spell. Yellow-gold
light flickered like heat lightning over the lock. It clicked open.

Outside the door she saw a narrow stairway leading downward to her right, upward to her left. She turned left and began
to climb the crumbling stone steps, her toes sinking into chilled
dust as she brushed spiderwebs out of her path, avoided rats,
tried to ignore the other crawling things beneath and around
her naked feet.

Up and up she climbed, her head throbbing from sustaining
the night-vision spell as she mounted higher and higher into
the castle of Thokk, straining her physical and magical senses
to search for danger.

She had hoped that the cold would lessen as she went higher
into the castle, but it did not. *I can never survive the icy
mountaintop outside the castle without clothing*, she thought,
but I will worry about that after I find Guthrun.

Huld came to the top of the stairway and found a long
hallway leading off in both directions. She closed her eyes and
concentrated, reaching out with her thoughts, searching for
Guthrun. At first she found nothing and began to fear that her
weakness might keep her from detecting Guthrun's location.
She struggled harder, persisted, pushed farther with her Witch-
senses, and suddenly jerked back from a powerful inhuman
consciousness.

Freya! she thought, her senses reeling from the brief contact.
*What manner of creature was that? Something gigantic, no
doubt one of Thokk's guardians. She shuddered.*

She concentrated again, detected the monstrous consciousness, avoided touching it, strained to push farther, and at last
felt Guthrun's mind.

Huld set off to her left, moving fast, worried that the alien consciousness she had touched might have thereby also sensed her. *What other monstrosities infest this house of Hel*? she wondered as she ran along the cobweb-strewn hallway. *And is Thokk here too*? *Surely I would have sensed her magical aura at once if she were. If, Freya willing, she is not here, we must get free before she returns. Weakened as I am, I could not hope to win a duel of Witchcraft with her.*

The corridor ended in yet another stairway. Huld began to climb once more. Her already strained leg muscles burned with every step.

Other questions filled Huld's mind as she moved up the stairs. She had deduced that the nightmare from which she had not been able to awaken before her capture must have been a spell sent by Thokk to make her helpless so that . . . what? *How did Guthrun and I get here*? *Who brought us*? *But perhaps that does not really matter. Norda said that Thokk intends to awaken the dark power we sensed within Guthrun and that I must not let that happen. For now I must concentrate only on finding Guthrun and getting her away.*

Torchlight flickered through an archway at the top of the stairs. Huld slowed her pace, revoked her night-vision spell, felt her headache abate slightly.

The torchlit corridor was empty. She took a torch from a wall bracket, moved to the right, the direction in which she sensed the presence of Guthrun, thinking that not only did the torch provide light and some meager warmth, but also that it could be a crude weapon should the need arise.

The stone floor of the corridor was covered with a soft grayish substance which reminded Huld unpleasantly of mold, and the musty scent in the hall suggested the same. But the faint odor of decayed flesh was always there too, beneath the mustiness.

The ceiling that arched high overhead was lost in shadows, and occasionally from the darkness above came faint whispers and the soft whir of wings, though Huld's Witch-senses detected no living presence there. From behind some of the doors that lined the hall came other sounds—footfalls, sighs, more whispers—but again her searching mental powers detected no associated consciousnesses. Guthrun's mind, however, was becoming effortlessly easy to detect.

A dark corridor led to the left off the torchlit hallway. Huld hesitated, walked a few steps more down the main hall, felt Guthrun's presence weaken slightly, returned to the darkened corridor, and entered it.

More doors lined the narrower hallway, and again she occasionally heard sounds that her Witch-senses detected as nothing living as she followed the hall in a turn to the left. Then she heard no more sounds save her own until suddenly a familiar voice cursed behind a door just ahead.

Huld approached the door warily, reached out with her mind, and made certain that it was not a trap. Satisfied, she focused her concentration on the door's lock.

Yellow-gold light flickered. The lock clicked. Within the room Guthrun's cursing stopped.

The Witch pushed open the door, saw no one within. A small lamp flickered on a polished table. An uncovered bed and a chair completed the room's contents.

"Guthrun?" Huld called, mentally sensing her friend's presence, though visually there was still no sign of her.

"Huld?" Guthrun's voice asked after a moment's silence.

Huld edged into the room, looked to her right.

Pressed against the wall next to the door, holding a large square of shiny red cloth as if it were a net in which to catch prey, stood Guthrun.

"Huld!" Guthrun cried. She dropped the red bed covering, rushed forward, and threw her arms around the naked Witch.

It was the woman he had chained below, the Freya-Witch whom Mistress Thokk intended to convert to the ways of Hel. He could tell it from her scent, unmistakably identifying her to his inhuman Jotun senses. But how had she gotten free? He was not worried about her escaping the castle, but Thokk would be angry with him if she returned and the blond-haired human was not chained as intended, and those who angered Thokk she either punished or destroyed.

Uttering a Jotun curse older than humankind, Vafthrudnir stood in the torchlit corridor, looking into a dark hallway. He sniffed the air. Yes, the one from below had gone down the dark way.

He stepped into the darkness, waited until his Jotun eyes adjusted, faint purple fires now flickering deep within them, then hurried forward to recapture the escaped human and to make certain that the younger one remained a prisoner in her assigned room, angered that they were causing him such trouble, wishing that he did not have orders neither to harm nor to kill either one.

"Enough questions, Guthrun!" Huld cried, pushing her young friend away and scooping up the red cloth. "We haven't time now for talk. I sense danger coming our way!"

Guthrun grabbed the oil lamp which never ran dry. Huld bundled the cloth under one arm. Then they rushed into the hall, Huld leading the way, holding the torch high.

Sensing the inhuman presence she'd detected earlier approaching now from the direction she'd come, Huld headed the other way, but their pursuer was gaining on them, the air growing colder and colder as whatever followed them neared.

"Run!" Huld whispered.

The dark hallway curved to the right and then stopped, a brick wall blocking the way.

"Freya's teeth!" Huld cursed.

Guthrun tried a nearby door, found it locked. "Huld," she whispered, "maybe if your magic can open this door, we can hide in here."

Huld shook her head negatively and headed back the way they'd come. "Too near the dead end," she explained as she ran toward the nearing guardian, whom she felt would be upon them in a few more heartbeats. In front of a doorway along the curved passageway she intoned the spell to open locks, pushed Guthrun inside, followed, and closed the door.

They waited, muffling their rapid breathing, listening.

The cold kept getting worse, and then it was joined by a

pungent aroma neither could identify. Outside the door, heavy footfalls rumbled by.

Something touched Guthrun's leg. She glanced down and stopped the scream that nearly escaped. Something vaguely human with a grinning corpse-face lay upon the floor, looking up at her, a questing tendril covered with gray mold caressing her bare leg beneath the hem of her sleeping shift.

Huld opened the door a crack, peered into the hallway, and saw that it was empty, the guardian having passed on toward the dead end.

Guthrun pulled away from the thing on the floor and eagerly followed Huld back into the corridor.

They ran toward the lighted hallway, reached it, hesitated, Huld reaching out with her Witch-senses. The presence that had followed them suddenly seemed to be gone instead of headed back their way, which worried Huld even more.

"Huld," Guthrun whispered, "in that room I saw . . . there was a thing . . . it touched my leg . . . it was horrible. . . ."

"I heard sounds behind some of the doors," Huld said as she draped the red cloth around herself and knotted it at one shoulder, "but my Witch-senses could detect no living presences."

"I'm not surprised." Guthrun shivered. "It couldn't have been alive, not like you or me. It had the face of a human corpse, but it was covered in mold, had tendrils like a plant, a maggotlike body . . ."

"It may have been a Hel worshiper who has come to live in Thokk's castle. I have heard that when they give themselves to Hel, she transforms them. They can look human at times, but their true appearance is otherwise. Come on. We have to keep moving," the Freya-Witch said, still unable to detect the inhuman consciousness that had pursued them. She started off down the hall, Guthrun following closely.

"I came the other way," Huld explained. "I was chained in a lower level. Thokk used spell-chains. I couldn't work magic to get free. But Norda—"

"Huld, Norda is . . . dead," Guthrun said, interrupting.

"She is . . . now," Huld agreed. "You see, she—"

An icy wind suddenly whipped at them, a whirling cloud of snow and ice exploding into existence all around. The inhuman presence crowded Huld's perceptions, nearly close enough to touch. Huld's torch and Guthrun's lamp were blown out. They both fought to breathe and felt the warmth and consciousness being swiftly drained from their bodies.

Through eyes squeezed nearly shut to avoid stinging slivers of ice, Huld saw a gigantic shape reaching for her. She jerked back, swung at the thing with her dead torch, missed, and grabbed Guthrun by the arm. She staggered shakily back until she could turn, then ran, Guthrun beside her. Glancing back, Guthrun saw a humanlike form through the swirling snow, something towering twice a human's height.

"It's gaining on us!" Guthrun cried.

Huld thought furiously as she ran and decided that only one thing might help, fought to concentrate, intoned a spell, and threw the force of her will backward toward the pursuing giant, praying to Freya that its mind would be receptive. Then suddenly there was a deep, hoarse cry from behind, the sound echoing from the walls of the corridor, pounding at their eardrums. The icy wind stopped. Huld and Guthrun ran on.

"What happened?" Guthrun cried as they passed the archway through which Huld had emerged from below.

"Frost Giant!" Huld gasped, pushing her legs to run faster, fighting to ignore the exhaustion her exertion was rapidly making worse. "I sent it an illusion of its body turning to flames. It won't stop it long."

"Frost Giant? A Jotun?" Guthrun asked, running slower than her top speed in order not to leave Huld behind. A stairway lit with candles led upward on their right. Huld took it.

"Yes." She was panting, her legs burning as she forced them up the steps. "A Jotun, just like in the old tales."

"I didn't know they really existed."

"Shut up and run!"

"It's not me who's going slow!"

"Then go on ahead! I mean it, Guthrun. Find a way out for

yourself. Thokk wants to make you into a Hel-Witch. She must not succeed. It's more important for you to escape than for me. I'm too exhausted and weak from what I suffered below to keep up. I'll follow later if I can. I can find you with my Witch-senses." She gasped, reeling as they reached the top of the stairway.

"I won't leave you behind!"

"Do as I say! Trust me, Guthrun. Get out of here! I can sense the Jotun coming! Hurry!"

Bloodsong's daughter hesitated a moment more. "I'll be back for you. Just don't let him catch you."

"Wonderful advice. And don't you *dare* come back! Now go!"

Guthrun ran away down the corridor, found another staircase, and headed up it.

Huld leaned against the stairway railing, head swimming, fighting to catch her breath. The giant reached the foot of the stairs and stood looking up at her for a moment. Its skin was a bluish hue. It had thick, long black hair, a long black beard, and more black hair covering its chest, arms, and legs. It started up the stairs.

Huld cursed and staggered away down the hall, the air growing colder as the Jotun neared, her heart pounding in her ears, every breath an agony, sweat streaming.

The Jotun reached the top of the stairs before she'd taken three steps. She tried to concentrate on another desperate spell but felt the giant's massive hand close around her waist before she could complete the incantation.

"Thokk doesn't want you covered," the giant said, lifted her above the floor with one hand, and tore away the red cloth with the other.

Naked, Huld struggled against the giant's imprisoning grip, her bare feet flailing the air above the floor, freezing cold searing her flesh where the giant's hand touched her flesh, the black hairs on the Jotun's huge fingers stinging her like needles.

The Frost Giant turned and headed down the steps.

Huld fought to stay conscious, felt herself losing the battle, used the last of her rapidly fading strength to try focusing on another spell, failed, slumped unconscious in the giant's grip.

Vafthrudnir glanced down at the blond-haired human when she stopped struggling, saw that she was unconscious, and felt new anger boil within him for the trouble she and the other one were causing him. Once she was chained again below, he would have to find the younger one and return her to her assigned room. Using his power to dematerialize into wind and snow had angered him too. It was a great effort and left him feeling sick for days. Then there was also the trick these humans had played upon him, making him think for several horrible moments that he was aflame.

The Jotun race's hatred for humankind seethed within him. *It would be so easy to jerk her blond-haired head from her weak white shoulders*, he thought.

No, Vafthrudnir reminded himself, *I must not. I am pledged to do Mistress Thokk's will. I will fulfill my pledge and preserve my honor. But someday, when my term of service is ended and I'm free of her, perhaps I will return and add Thokk's own head to my trophies*.

The thought cheered him as he continued down into the depths of Thokk's castle. Taking several steps at a time, he soon reached the cell in which the human had been chained, and placed the manacles around her wrists and ankles once more. Then he studied the cell, his eyes of purple fire piercing the darkness, seeking clues, wondering how the human had escaped. In two places he saw piles of something dark heaped on the floor. They had not been there before.

The Jotun examined the nearest one. *Ashes*, he thought, shuddering and jerking back from them. *Human ashes*. He moved to the other pile of ashes, sniffed at them, detected a Jotun scent, the scent of his friend, Thrym, a young Jotun whose bones had not yet grown a complete covering of flesh.

"No!" Vafthrudnir roared, whirling to face the human, thoughts seething, his massive hands hooking into claws. Dying by fire was the most horrible death possible for one of his race. It did more than destroy their flesh. It also seared their soul, mutilated their spirit, gave them pain in the next world, unending agony, kept them from ever again forming new bones and growing new flesh.

Vafthrudnir approached the chained female, trembling with rage, intending to rip her flesh from her bones. He reached out, touched her left thigh, closed his grip upon the white flesh...

No, he thought, stopping himself, and withdrew his hand. *I must not harm her. I must not break my pledge to Thokk.* His curses echoed from the walls.

"I do not know how," his voice rumbled at the unconscious human, "but in some way you were responsible for Thrym's fire-death, and for that you will pay. I will revenge my friend in time. This I vow upon my Jotun honor." *But for now I must keep my patience and find the younger human*, he added in his thoughts, then looked again at Thrym's ashes. *I will return when I've found the younger human and see that your ashes are properly honored*, he silently promised his dead friend, then with a final curse left the chamber and locked the door, leaving Huld chained naked in the darkness once more.

11
Grimnir

From where Bloodsong hung she could see the fires of Kovna's camp beyond the outskirts of the ruined village. Here and there fires still burned in the village itself within blackened husks of cottages and longhouses. From time to time weak screams came from the few captives still alive. Silhouetted against the scattered firelight, guards stood watch around the base of the hill.

Her hands and feet were numb. The muscles in her arms and shoulders ached and throbbed. Waves of nausea swept through her. The night air was cold against her sweat-dampened nakedness.

Her ordeal had begun to give rise to hallucinations, images from that other time she had hung from the tree to die, memories of Eirik and her son being tortured, the helpless horror of feeling her own life slowly ending, weakening, knowing that both she and her unborn child would soon be dead. Her unborn child . . . her daughter . . .

"Guthrun," she whispered through parched lips. "Guthrun . . ."

* * *

"The moon will rise soon," Jalna whispered. "You must have cut her free by then or —"

"Jalna, I know the moon's habits at this time of the month. And we've already been through the plan many times. You have to trust me just a little. I won't disappoint you. Bloodsong will soon be free if luck is with us."

"Not if you crouch here whispering all night long."

"Curse it, woman. You're the one who—" he began, then stopped himself. "Wait for my signal. You've given your word to do that."

"I will wait for the signal."

Tyrulf nodded, bent close to her in the darkness, and touched his lips lightly to her cheek before she understood what he meant to do. Then he hurried away toward the camp fires, grinning at the stream of curses Jalna whispered behind him.

The watcher had drawn within a bowshot of the nearest guard at the base of the hill. He waited a moment, noting the distance of the guards to either side, then started forward again, crouched low to the ground, moving steadily and silently toward the hill, sword and shield gripped tightly, closer and closer. . . .

Bloodsong heard someone speaking with a guard, fought to clear her blurred vision, heard laughter then the sound of someone moving up the slope toward her. She strained against the ropes, thinking that it was Kovna come to begin her torture.

"Bloodsong?" a man whispered. "I'm a friend. I've come to help you."

Bloodsong said nothing. She did not recognize the voice, and there was not enough light to see his face, even had her vision been clear.

"Are you awake?" he asked. "I'm going to cut you free. Jalna is waiting for my signal."

"Jalna?" Bloodsong responded. "I thought her dead. She probably *is* dead. Tell Kovna that his trick won't work. I will not—"

"Keep your voice down!" the man hissed. "Jalna is not dead."

Bloodsong heard the sound of a blade sawing rope. Suddenly her feet were free. She tried to put her weight on them and gasped at the agony of returning circulation.

The last rope came away from her body. The man caught her and eased her to the ground.

"My feet and hands are numb," she said between gritted teeth as she rubbed at her wrists.

The man began gently rubbing the circulation back into her ankles and feet. But then, beyond the base of the hill, he saw men approaching with torches. Bloodsong saw them too.

"Give me a sword," she whispered, "or a dagger! Some weapon! Kovna is returning!"

Tyrulf cursed. "Why is he returning? We thought you'd be left alone, at least until dawn."

"Your dagger!" Bloodsong demanded, fumbling at his scabbard with fingers still half numb.

Tyrulf cursed again and gave her his dagger, his thoughts racing. Kovna and his men were nearly to the base of the hill. Within moments they would be able to see that Bloodsong was free. He counted seven men with Kovna. *Perhaps, with surprise on my side*, he thought, but he knew that all the odds were against it.

"Hide the dagger," he whispered.

Bloodsong understood, tried to stand, and shakily managed to regain her feet by leaning against the tree.

Tyrulf leapt, caught a low branch, and pulled himself into the tree. *Now, if only that guard doesn't mention seeing me*, he thought.

"Tyrulf?" Kovna called, starting up the slope.

Tyrulf cursed under his breath, saw that Bloodsong had raised her arms above her head as if still bound, the dagger hidden behind her crossed arms.

It's not going to work, Tyrulf thought, *and as soon as the fighting starts, Jalna will join the battle, no matter the odds. I'll have saved her life for only one day. Gods! She'll probably think that this is a trick of mine and try to kill me first!*

Kovna stopped several steps away from Bloodsong, the torchlight revealing that she was free. The shock on his face changed to fury. "Traitor!" he shouted. "Find Tyrulf! He has cut her free!"

Four of the seven warriors started searching the perimeter of the hill.

Bloodsong had kept her eyes closed, hoping that the trick might work until he was closer, but now she opened her eyes and gratefully found that her vision had cleared. Had her hands not still been partially numb, she would have chanced throwing the dagger at the exposed flesh of Kovna's throat where it emerged from his mail shirt.

"He's not here!" one of the torchbearers shouted.

A body hurtled downward from above and crashed into Kovna. Tyrulf rolled and came to his feet with his sword in his hand, gutted a surprised warrior, and chopped the legs from under another with his return stroke. His blade came up and parried a stroke from Kovna, who had regained his feet.

Bloodsong staggered forward, dropped the dagger, picked up a slain warrior's sword, and cursed with frustration as her tingling fingers closed awkwardly around the hilt. Holding the blade with both hands, she swung at Kovna's neck while his attention was still on Tyrulf. But she was unable to properly control the angle of the stroke and hit his steel battle-helm instead.

Kovna reeled and slumped earthward.

Bloodsong and Tyrulf both started to aim killing strokes at the fallen leader but were forced to parry the blades of other warriors instead.

Tyrulf thrust into a man's throat and whirled to parry another's stroke.

Bloodsong clumsily parried stroke after stroke, aware that she would have already been slain had they not been trying to take her alive once more. But now the guards from the base of the hill had joined the fight, and others, half drunk on plundered wine, were coming from the camp.

Bloodsong's arms were grabbed from behind. She kicked

back, trying to reach the man's instep, failed, and felt her arms wrenched up until pain coursed through her. But suddenly a familiar voice screamed a war cry behind her. Warm blood spurted onto Bloodsong's back as her arms were released.

"Bloodsong and freedom!" Jalna screamed again, her sword flashing in the torchlight as she blocked cuts with her shield. Another warrior cried out and fell to her blade, a crimson fountain shooting from his ruined neck.

Bloodsong parried another stroke and noticed with relief that with each moment more control returned to her muscles, more accuracy to her feints and thrusts. But she also noticed that more and more warriors were joining the fray.

"To the tree!" she shouted, feinted to the right, dipped low, thrust upward, and jerked her blade free as a warrior screamed and fell at her feet.

Bloodsong, Jalna, and Tyrulf backed up the slope to the highest ground available, fending off blades from all sides until they had the tree at their backs. Her battle skills now nearly completely returned, Bloodsong fought on, not allowing herself to think of the hopelessness of the battle, thinking only of the next parry, the next kill.

Suddenly a bellow like that of a wild beast ripped through the clangor of battle. Near the base of the hill away from the camp men began to scream death cries. In the flickering torchlight Bloodsong saw a red-bearded warrior standing heads taller than most of Kovna's men cutting his way up the hill toward the tree, men falling on all sides as he moved among them.

"Grimnir!" Bloodsong shouted. "It's Grimnir! Cut your way down to him!" she ordered, and started fighting her way down the slope, Jalna and Tyrulf following as they continued to fight off blades from all sides.

"I will hold them!" Grimnir shouted when they had reached him. "Run for the forest!"

Bloodsong continued to fight by his side.

"Run, curse you! Find Bloodhoof! I can hold off these drunken louts!"

Bloodsong hesitated a moment more, killed one more man. "I will return for you!" she cried. "Jalna! To me!"

Jalna and Bloodsong cut free of the last warriors blocking their way to the distant edge of the forest and began to run through the darkness.

"Bloodhoof!" she shouted as she ran, calling the name of Grimnir's stallion, wondering if he would come to the sound of her voice, praying to Freya that he would.

Tyrulf and Grimnir backed down the slope, killing as they went. A blade sliced a shallow cut in Tyrulf's left leg. He cursed, crashed through the warrior's defense, and killed him. Beside him, Grimnir, he noticed, was killing twice as many as he, fighting with nearly a Berserker's frenzy against which Kovna's half drunk men were all but helpless.

Some of Kovna's warriors started to circle around, meaning to follow Bloodsong. Grimnir and Tyrulf cut them off, kept backing toward the forest, side by side, until suddenly there came from behind the thunder of hooves.

Tyrulf whirled, saw Bloodsong mounted naked atop a massive black charger, raised sword gleaming in the torchlight.

Bloodhoof crashed into Kovna's men, trampling and slaying with his flashing hooves as Bloodsong's sword slashed downward again and again, spilling brains from split skulls. Kovna's men broke and ran. Grimnir bellowed a laugh.

"Now *you* run," Bloodsong commanded, and waited until the two men were well out of sight in the darkness, then wheeled the stallion around and galloped laughing in their wake.

12
Crimson Veins

Bloodsong's laughter was short-lived. The battle over, and death on the tree escaped, other thoughts rushed in upon her. The horrors of the day returned in full force, the screams of the villagers and her warriors, seeing all that she had worked to rebuild destroyed, learning that Guthrun was Thokk's captive and that her son's corpse was being made into—

No. Bloodsong stopped the thoughts. *I must concentrate on staying free and finding a way to free Guthrun. Nothing else matters for now.*

The moon was just breaking the horizon. In the brightening moonlight she saw pines rearing blackly against the stars. She reined the galloping stallion to a halt, looked back toward Kovna's camp, neither heard nor saw any mounted warriors in pursuit, wondered how badly she had wounded Kovna, hoping that it might prove fatal.

"Bloodsong!" Jalna called.

Bloodsong saw the young warrior hurrying toward her through the moonlight. She slipped to the ground. Her bare feet came down on sharp rocks. She cursed, wishing for boots, armor, her own weapons, and glanced back at the camp, seeing that there was still no pursuit. Behind Jalna, Tyrulf and Grimnir hurried from amongst the trees. Grimnir led two horses. He placed their reins in Bloodsong's hands. "They were to have been surprises," he quickly explained, "for you and Guthrun. Bloodhoof is their father. They'll make fine war stallions with training. I've named them Freehoof and Frosthoof. Freehoof is yours."

"Grimnir, I . . . my thanks. Such gifts are . . ."

Grimnir laughed. "Not often are you unable to find words."

"Guthrun is a captive in Thokk's castle. Huld too," Bloodsong told him. She looked at Kovna's camp but still detected no pursuit.

Grimnir reached up, jerked a bundle from behind Freehoof's saddle, unrolled a cloak, and hastily placed the soft fabric around Bloodsong's bare shoulders. "Another gift," he explained.

Bloodsong reached out and gripped his hand. "I will ride on Bloodhoof with you," she said, "until we can get another horse."

They mounted the stallions, then moved off through the trees as fast as was safe in the moonlight.

"I saw blood oozing from beneath Kovna's helmet," Tyrulf said as they rode. "Odin willing, he will die."

"What is your name, warrior?" Bloodsong asked.

"Tyrulf."

"My thanks for helping to free me."

"He was one of Kovna's men," Jalna added.

"What changed your allegiance?" Bloodsong asked suspiciously.

"Jalna," Tyrulf answered. "I was sent to kill a spy Thokk had detected watching our camp. It was Jalna. I had thought her dead."

"He was a soldier in Nastrond," Jalna explained. "He knew me from before."

"Ah, you were friends," Bloodsong reasoned.

"No," Jalna quickly disagreed. "It's hard to explain. I don't really understand, myself."

"I think she understands more than she will admit, even to herself," Tyrulf replied.

Jalna did not respond, and Bloodsong decided that it was not important to their present situation. If he proved untrustworthy or acted suspiciously, she would deal with it, but for now other matters concerned her more.

"If Kovna is as badly wounded as we hope and can't lead men in pursuit of us, will someone else see that we are followed?" she asked Tyrulf.

"There is one man, Styrki, who is very loyal and was next in the line of command after me. Kovna saved his life once, years ago. He will send men after us, though perhaps not until dawn. If Kovna is as badly wounded as I think, however, Styrki won't lead them himself. He will stay by Kovna's side to protect and help him. Kovna, himself, would lead men in pursuit immediately, if he were able."

"And since we were not immediately followed, we can assume that Kovna is indeed badly hurt," Bloodsong finished. "Freya willing, by morning our trail will be too cold and, if we are clever about the way we travel, too confusing for any to follow. Now I am going to set my mind to thinking about how to free my daughter. The rest of you are to do the same. There must be a way, and we are going to find it."

Guthrun had stopped running shortly after leaving Huld. She had retraced her steps, seen the Jotun carrying Huld away. Following silently, she had noted the dark archway through which the Frost Giant took the blond-haired Witch. She dared not try to follow farther in the darkness, and a torch would have given her away.

I'll be back for you, Huld. I promise, Guthrun had vowed, then turned and ran back the way she had come, ascending higher and higher into the castle of Thokk, becoming more and more uneasy as the whispers in the shadows overhead became more numerous, the sounds from behind the doors louder.

As Guthrun mounted higher into the castle her thoughts

returned again to the Frost Giant. Old tales said that the Jotun race was older than the race of Aesir Gods to which Odin and Thor belonged.

Legends said that at the beginning of Time, ice and fire met in the yawning Abyss of Chaos called Ginnungagap and gave rise to an Ice Giant called Ymir. The ice and fire also produced a gigantic cow named Audhumla, whose milk nourished Ymir. One day, while licking salt off an ice block, Audhumla's tongue uncovered first the head and then the body of the God Buri, freeing him from the ice.

Descendents of Buri and Ymir waged war upon each other, a war which lasted until Buri's son Borr married a giantess named Bestla, daughter of the giant Bolthorn, the Thorn of Evil. Bestla gave birth to the Gods Odin, Vili, and Ve, who at last put an end to the war by slaying Ymir himself.

The blood gushing from Ymir's death wounds produced a vast flood in which all of his race perished, save for the Jotun Bergelmir and his mate, who escaped in a boat and from whom more Frost Giants were eventually descended.

Using Ymir's corpse, the victorious Gods then created the Earth, which they called Midgard, the Middle Garden. Ymir's eyebrows became Midgard's ramparts, his blood and sweat the surrounding ocean, his bones the mountains and hills, his flat teeth the cliffs, his curly hair the trees and vegetation, the inside of his skull the vaulted sky overhead, his brains the fleecy clouds. Or so the old tales said.

Guthrun had grunted at the memories. Old tales were one thing, a living Jotun another. Thinking of Huld in the Frost Giant's clutches, she had stopped and started to turn back, but then she'd cursed at her frustration and headed up another stairway, knowing that Huld's best hope lay in her continuing to search for a weapon with which to fight the Jotun and finding a means of escape once he had been slain. That it might not be possible to either slay him or escape Thokk's castle had also loomed in her mind, but she'd pushed the weakening and frightening notion down with another curse and kept climbing the stairs.

Finally she reached the above-ground levels of the castle and crouched, hidden, on a thick-walled window ledge, studying the castle's courtyard through the tall, narrow opening. The light outside had grown stronger as the sun rose, but the sky was heavily overcast, an iron-gray blanket of clouds keeping the day as gloomy as deep twilight. The icy air outside the castle clutched at her warmth through her thin sleeping shift, and the crimson-veined black stones chilled her bare feet. But she took comfort from the sword she held, the hilt gripped tightly with both hands, a blade she had taken from a wall in a deserted hall through which she had passed.

She had seen no one, even though the sounds behind the doors had grown ever louder, the whispers overhead clearer, until she had expected those who made the noises to emerge at any moment. The courtyard, too, was empty.

Guthrun eyed the tall, closed gateway cut into the outer wall of the courtyard. Ice-encrusted iron spikes, angled downward to prevent their being used for climbing, covered the thick wooden gate. Similar spikes covered the courtyard's walls. No stairways led upward along those walls, and atop them, instead of battlements, were more of the jagged iron spikes. Everything about the courtyard spoke of a desire to keep the inhabitants in, as well as invaders out.

Bloodsong's daughter continued to study the courtyard with impatience and frustration, seeing no way out unless she could single-handedly draw back the massive bolt that locked the gate and push open the thick, heavy door. No, it would take the muscles of a Jotun to open the gate. She could never hope to do it alone. Her only hope was to free Huld and pray that the Freya-Witch's spell to open locks would work on the gateway as well. But to free Huld might well mean confronting the Jotun again, and if she were not careful, she could end up a prisoner herself once more.

Guthrun looked down at the sword and cursed softly at its small size compared to the Frost Giant's bulk. But she had seen no better weapon than the sword and could not take time to look for one. The inhabitants of the rooms might yet emerge, and the Jotun himself was no doubt looking for her at that very moment.

A wave of hopelessness swept over her. She lowered the sword until the point touched the window ledge and shook her head at the overwhelming odds against her. But then she thought of her mother and remembered the tales about Bloodsong winning over supposedly unbeatable odds in Nidhug's arena and, later, against the sorcerer-king himself.

Guthrun raised the sword, peered around the corner of the window to make certain that no one was in sight, then slipped down to the floor and began running down a flight of stairs.

One thing at a time, she told herself as she hurried downward. *Don't think so far ahead that the task seems hopeless. First find Huld. Concentrate only on that for now.*

A loud creaking sound outside the castle interrupted her thoughts. She stopped, ran back up the stairs, and pulled herself back into the window.

The odds weren't bad enough? she thought bitterly.

The Jotun was in the courtyard, opening the gateway. On the other side she could see black-clad warriors atop skeletal white steeds waiting to enter. Below her in the castle she heard new sounds, peered around the window's edge, saw black-robed and hooded forms emerging. *The inhabitants of the rooms?* she wondered. *Now in human form?* She looked back at the courtyard.

The Jotun finished opening the gateway, then stepped back and went down on one knee in the snow, his head bowed.

The black-clad warriors moved aside, forming a pathway down which a pale woman with long, glistening black hair rode. As she entered the courtyard the black-robed ones emerged from the castle, crowded around her, went down on their knees with bowed heads, and from all came the same chant, echoing through the icy air.

"Hail, Thokk! All power to Hel!" they chanted over and over while the tall woman smiled coldly, exulting in their submission.

And from the crimson veins in the black rocks of the window where Guthrun hid, scarlet drops suddenly oozed forth, hung glistening wetly for several heartbeats, then vanished.

13
Witchcraft

The nine black-clad warriors rode into the courtyard, bringing four prisoners with them.

Valgerth! Guthrun thought, recognizing her. *Thorfinn! And their children. But not my mother?* If Thokk had been to Eirik's Vale and captured those four, why not also Bloodsong?

She's either free, or dead . . . Guthrun realized, fighting to control her fear. *She's alive,* she thought, reassuring herself. *I must believe she's alive. But I . . . cannot depend on it, nor on her freeing me and slaying Thokk. I must believe that she's alive, but also that I have to free and revenge myself. First I must free Huld, then together we must free Valgerth and Thorfinn and slay Thokk. And I won't think of the odds against me but only of victory.*

Guthrun watched the courtyard a moment longer, decided to make a run for Huld while the castle was yet deserted, slipped out of the window, and sprinted down the stairs, holding tightly to the stolen sword, noting that the castle was now as silent as a tomb.

* * *

"Take the prisoners into my throne room and hold them there for me," Thokk ordered.

Vafthrudnir finished closing and securing the gateway, bowed his head in assent, then hastened to obey, worrying silently about the escaped human. If only Thokk had arrived later in the morning, everything would have been as she desired. He had tracked the girl into the upper reaches of the castle and had been within moments of recapturing her when Thokk's mental summons to open the gateway had called him away from the hunt. The Hel-Witch was certain to be very angry. How would she punish him? He would not allow her to kill him, but there were other things she could do, things that he had witnessed firsthand. . . .

Thokk breathed deeply of the icy air in the courtyard. Her gaze swept the towering black walls of her castle. Feelings of pleasure swept through her. She was home. She turned to the Death Riders. "You have done well. I will request of Hel that your pain be diminished. Resume your castle duties."

The Death Riders silently guided their gaunt mares away toward the stables.

Thokk looked down at the black-robed Hel-worshipers surrounding her, still on their knees in the snow. She laughed softly. "You may rise," she told them. "Assume your duties."

One of the robed ones came forward and took the reins of Thokk's Hel-horse. Another aided her descent to the snowy ground. The others hurried into the castle to the duties assigned them when Thokk was within the walls.

The Hel-Witch walked beneath the arched portal that led into her castle. *Time enough later to deal with the prisoners*, she thought, and turned her steps into the lower reaches of her castle where more interesting and exciting matters awaited her amusement and attention.

Down high-ceilinged corridors thick with shadows, Valgerth, Thorfinn, and their children were herded by the Jotun. Even if their children's safety had not been in danger, the two warriors could have done nothing against the giant, hands bound behind their backs as they were. All four of the prisoners shivered in the icy air spawned by the Frost Giant's presence.

They entered a vast chamber, the walls hung with rich tapestries depicting the ecstasies of the grave, scenes that chilled and sickened the captives. At the far end of the chamber stood a bone-white throne.

The Jotun forced them against a wall behind the throne, then stepped back and watched them almost casually, knowing that there was nothing they could do.

The children stood near their parents, Thora glaring defiantly at the Jotun, younger Yngvar turned with his face against his mother's leg.

As the moments stretched out, Vafthrudnir's thoughts turned more and more to the escaped human and Thokk.

Where is Thokk? he wondered. He had assumed that she would come straight to the throne room to deal with the prisoners. Why else have him bring them there? He would have then found some way to tell her about the escaped girl. But if she had gone elsewhere, perhaps into the lower reaches of the castle, and if she found the girl's room empty before he had a chance to tell her . . .

The Jotun's eyes flicked more and more often to the door through which Thokk would enter.

"Why is he so nervous?" Thorfinn whispered to Valgerth.

"I've noticed it too," she replied. "He seems almost frightened, a strange thing for one nearly twice our height."

"Perhaps there is some way we can exploit his fear?"

"We must not endanger the children."

"No, but perhaps—"

"Silence!" Vafthrudnir roared.

Yngvar began to cry. Thora ran forward and aimed a vicious kick at the Jotun's shin.

"Thora!" Valgerth cried, and ran forward, jerking at her bonds.

"Get her back to the wall!" Vafthrudnir ordered, "or I'll twist her head from her shoulders. I've no love for humankind."

"Thora, do as he says," Valgerth commanded.

"But, Mother! We have to fight him!"

"Thora, please . . . perhaps we can fight him later."

Vafthrudnir laughed at the suggestion.

"Skadi's bow," the six-year-old cursed, and stomped back to the wall beside her brother. "Stop crying, Yngvar," Thora ordered. "What would Allfather Odin say, hearing you cry?"

Yngvar didn't care what Odin thought and continued to sob while Vafthrudnir continued to worry.

Guthrun grabbed a torch and plunged through the archway the Jotun had used to take Huld below. At the foot of the long stairway she looked in both directions down a long corridor, wondering which way to go. The Witches had not taught her any spells in the short time she had been with them and had only begun to give her instructions on the potentials of the mind and philosophies of Freya's magic. But Norda had told her that most people used mental powers without knowing it when they followed hunches and intuition. Guthrun had always been good at that. Perhaps . . .

Freya guide me, Guthrun thought, then turned to her left and ran down the corridor, the torch held high, the flames streaming behind her as she ran.

Another archway loomed, and more steps going down. Guthrun turned and hurried into the farther depths of the castle. Another corridor, another intuitive choice, another stairway, down and down she went into the darkness, encouraged by the broken spiderwebs across the paths she's chosen, evidence that her hunches might have been correct so far.

Suddenly she was tearing through spiderwebs, black eight-legged shapes gliding away on the shredded silken strands. Guthrun cursed and frantically brushed the clinging webs and spiders from her face, hair, and shift, imagining that she could feel crawling things all over her body. Controlling her revulsion, she retraced her steps, ascended to the last landing where the webs had already been broken, found an iron-banded wooden door, and tried to open it. It was locked. She placed the torch in a wall bracket and began hacking at the lock with her sword, hoping that she wasn't wasting precious time trying to open the wrong cell.

Hanging in her chains within the cell, Huld was jarred back to consciousness by the clangor of metal on metal. She struggled to clear her thoughts, cursed to find herself chained as before, gasped at the returning pain, and strained futilely to get free, fearing that the noise that had awakened her might portend new horrors, unless—

"Guthrun!" Huld shouted, taking a chance, seeing nothing to lose.

Guthrun hesitated, frowning. It had seemed that—

"Guthrun!" Huld shouted again.

Guthrun grinned. "Yes, Huld! A moment more!"

Bloodsong's daughter began hacking at the lock again, the stolen sword's blade now badly notched. Then suddenly her efforts were rewarded. She grabbed the torch and pushed the door open.

"How did you find me?" Huld asked as Guthrun rushed into the cell.

"Witchcraft," Guthrun said, grinning as she worked to pull out the locking pins to release the manacles around Huld's wrists and ankles. "Thokk has returned," she continued, opening the last manacle, "and she has prisoners—Valgerth, Thorfinn, and their children."

"Freya's teeth. She's been to Eirik's Vale. But why only bring those four as prisoners, unless—"

"My mother's alive and still free," Guthrun said, interrupting. "That's what I'm going to believe until I discover otherwise."

Huld nodded. "I don't know how much I'll be able to do against Thokk, Guthrun. I'm still exhausted. They haven't fed me since we've been here, so I'm frustratingly weak."

"I'll go first," Guthrun said, "with what's left of this sword. You carry the torch," she added, handing it to the Freya-Witch. "Right now I'm more worried about that Jotun than about Thokk."

Suddenly both Guthrun and Huld screamed in pain, hands flying to their skulls, sword and torch falling to the floor.

"More worried about the Jotun?" Thokk laughed, stepping into the cell. She walked to the two sprawled forms lying unconscious on the floor and prodded them with her foot. The Hel-Witch cursed, thinking of the Jotun's obvious carelessness, feeling again the fury she'd felt upon finding Guthrun's room empty, and deciding that Vafthrudnir must be severely punished for his carelessness—and soon.

Thokk bent down, grasped Huld's wrists, easily jerked the Freya-Witch upright as if she weighed nothing at all, and clamped first Huld's wrists and then her ankles back into the spell-imbued manacles.

She picked up the torch, crushed it out, invoked a night-vision spell, and waited until she could see in the darkness, her eyes flickering with purple fire. Then she turned to Guthrun and effortlessly lifted the young woman into her arms and strode from the cell.

Time to begin, child, the Hel-Witch thought, gazing down at Guthrun as she carried her up the long flight of stairs. *Time to begin awakening the powers slumbering within you. Time to introduce you to yourself.*

14
The Teacher

Guthrun opened her eyes and rubbed her throbbing temples. She was back in the room from whence she'd escaped. Beneath her the shiny red fabric again covered the bed. Again the lamp burned upon the carved table. In the chair sat Thokk.

Guthrun jerked to a sitting position, winced, and cursed as pain shot through her body.

"I apologize for the pain, child," Thokk said soothingly, watching from the chair. "It will soon pass. I did not intend for you to know pain in my house—only joy."

"Don't call me *child*," Guthrun ordered, squinting at Thokk through her pain.

Thokk nodded. "Quite so. You will soon become a woman. Your body is nearly that of a woman now, and soon your first blood will flow."

The pain began to fade. Guthrun lowered her hands from her temples, stood and faced the Hel-Witch. "Where is my mother?" she demanded, thankful that her voice did not sound as shaky as she felt.

"Bloodsong, you mean? How would I know?" Thokk asked innocently.

"Valgerth and Thorfinn and their children are your prisoners. You must have been to Eirik's Vale."

"From your thoughts I detect that you witnessed my return and that you think I attacked Eirik's Vale. Why should I have done that?"

"I can't read thoughts," Guthrun answered, "but I can sense when people lie to me."

Thokk shook her head sadly. "You think I'm lying because you have been taught to think badly of those who serve Hel. You might as well know about Valgerth. She has had dealings with Hel for many years."

"More lies."

"No. Valgerth secretly made a pact with Hel, in exchange for being allowed to have children. As you may know, when she was a slave in Nastrond, she had an unpermitted child, which Nidhug killed. Then he used sorcery to keep her from having a child ever again."

"Yes, but once he was destroyed, his spells lost their power and Valgerth was able to have children."

"If not for the pact she made with Hel, Valgerth would still be childless, I assure you."

"Lies on top of lies."

"I am telling you the truth."

Guthrun laughed sarcastically.

"You should thank me, Guthrun. I saved Bloodsong's life."

Guthrun laughed even louder.

"Listen to me, Guthrun. Hel is still grateful for the service Bloodsong performed in returning the War Skull to Helheim and destroying the Hel-traitor Nidhug. And those whom Hel treasures, she protects. When Valgerth made her pact with Hel, she agreed that the first two children she birthed would be given to Hel to become Hel-warriors. In an attempt to get out of that pact Valgerth made a second pact, with Odin. But in order to aid her against Hel, Odin required that Valgerth perform a service for him.

"Odin was the God who stole the War Skull from Hel in Time's dawning. Bloodsong became Odin's enemy when she returned it to Hel. So Odin agreed to help Valgerth against Hel only if she would slay Bloodsong."

"Valgerth would never agree to—"

"Old friends are one matter, Guthrun; children another. For her children's sake Valgerth indeed would have slain Bloodsong, her oldest friend. *That* is why I captured Valgerth, her mate, and her children. Bloodsong remains safe, as Hel desires, while Thora and Yngvar will yet become Hel-warriors, as Valgerth promised. As for Valgerth and Thorfinn, perhaps in time I will let you execute the traitors yourself, after you have come to accept the truth and after I have let my Jotun amuse himself with them. He does so hate humans, especially ones who've made pacts with one-eyed Odin. The Jotun's name is Vafthrudnir, you see."

"The same as—"

"Yes, a descendant of the Jotun who lost his head to Odin when that God of Lies cheated to win a riddle-game."

"Do not speak ill of Allfather Odin," Guthrun warned. "The Jotun race are enemies of humankind. Odin and his son Thor protect us from them. And if that means having to cheat and lie, Odin does so better than any other, praise him!"

Thokk laughed. "How delightful you are! How loyal! And how deluded. You've been warped by lies, Guthrun, but in time you will learn truth. There is nothing but truth in my house."

"*Your* house is the place of lies, Hel-slave," Guthrun countered. "What of Huld? What have you done with her? Why did you chain her below? If you've harmed her, I'll—"

"Enough!" Thokk shouted, rising to her feet. "I bear you no malice, Guthrun, but I will not suffer your concern for that Freya-slut. Norda Greycloak was my oldest enemy. She escaped me by dying, typical of her cowardly ways—"

"Norda was not a coward! She—"

"Ah! You think not? But you know so little of the truth," Thokk said, calming now. "No, as I was saying, I cannot now revenge myself upon Norda, but I *could* upon her disciple, Huld, if I wished her harm, which I do not. She was misled by lies, as were you, and if she allows me, I would like to become her teacher and lead her to the truth. That is what I want for you, too, Guthrun, to become your teacher and your friend, for whether you believe it or not, I am quite possibly the best friend you've got, and more."

"Friends do not keep each other prisoners. You must think me a complete fool!"

"No, Guthrun. Not at all. Just a victim of monumental lies. All I do has a purpose. Even when my actions seem harmful, they spring from motives of love and caring. You will eventually come to understand—"

"I understand all I need right now, Hel-slime. *You* are the fool if you think I will succumb to your lies."

Thokk sighed wearily. "I have other duties to perform, Guthrun. But I will return as soon as I can. We have so much about which to talk. When you accept me as your teacher and friend, you will no longer be kept a prisoner and will become my honored guest, as indeed you already are in my heart. Think on this, however, while I'm away, for of all the lies in your life, this one is the greatest and must be the first you unlearn. *Bloodsong is not your true mother."*

Rage filled Guthrun. Without thinking, she sprang for Thokk's slender throat. Pain shot through her. She staggered, crumpled to her knees, gasping for breath, and when at last the agony passed, she was alone, a prisoner in the room once more.

"Over there, Jotun," Thokk ordered, pointing to a set of manacles dangling from the ceiling of the high-roofed chamber. She and the Frost Giant had just come from the cell in which Valgerth, Thorfinn, and their children had been imprisoned. Around the torchlit room in which Thokk and Vafthrudnir now stood were scattered various ugly devices, all designed for but one purpose: the giving of pain.

Vafthrudnir hesitated, eyeing the manacles. "I will not let you kill me, Thokk," he said in warning.

"You would violate your oath? I thought you an honorable

Jotun. Perhaps the dishonor with which your father shamed his family cannot be redeemed by your services to me after all. Perhaps you are no better than he."

The Frost Giant tensed his massive body, hatred in his eyes, fists clenched at his sides.

"What you are thinking is true." Thokk laughed mockingly, probing his thoughts. "You could, with only a minor effort, pull my head from my shoulders. But an *honorable* Jotun would even allow himself to be slain if that was the wish of the mistress to whom he had sworn obedience. Are you an honorable Jotun, Vafthrudnir? Well? Are you?" she said tauntingly, knowing that redeeming his family's lost honor meant more to him than life itself.

"I am," Vafthrudnir growled.

"And am I your mistress until the agreed-upon term of service is over?"

"You are."

"And was part of your oath of honor to obey me without questioning, no matter what I desired?"

"It was."

"It was, *what*, Jotun scum!"

"It was, *Mistress*," Vafthrudnir hissed, trembling with repressed rage.

"Very well. Position yourself for punishment. Perhaps the next time I leave you in charge of two weak human females, they will not get the better of you and escape."

Vafthrudnir started to protest that it had not been his fault and that he had recaptured one and was about to recapture the other when Thokk had returned. But instead he remained silent and walked to the hanging manacles.

"Lock them on your wrists," Thokk ordered.

Two locks clicked.

"You are thinking that you can break the chains if need be," Thokk noted, "but you are wrong. These bonds have been specially prepared, just for you. The spell with which they are treated will weaken you the harder you struggle to get free. Struggle too much and you may well weaken to death."

Thokk walked to the wall and worked a mechanism to raise the chains. Soon the Jotun was dangling suspended above the floor. The Hel-Witch came closer and tore away the dark blue breechclout that was his only covering.

"I gave great consideration to your punishment, Jotun coward," she said, running her pale, slim-fingered hands over his cold, bluish-hued flesh. "I can give you agony of many sorts, even mutilate you if I desire, then heal you either wholly or partially with my magic so that you can return to your duties unimpaired."

Thokk moved to an assortment of torture devices hanging on hooks along one damp stone wall and selected a whip with three ugly iron barbs attached to the tip. Without a word she stood behind the hanging Jotun and cracked the barbed whip across his tightly stretched back.

Vafthrudnir's massive muscles bunched into knots beneath his bare skin, pain lancing through him, but he did not make a sound.

Again and again Thokk wielded the whip, soon moving around to face him so that the front of his body would also receive attention.

Vafthrudnir jerked against the chains, forcing himself to keep silent in spite of his growing pain as he dangled from the manacles, his struggles causing him to swing helplessly back and forth before his tormentor, his body being torn by more and more ragged-edged cuts as Thokk continued lashing his defenseless, bleeding flesh.

Finally Thokk laughed, threw the whip to the floor, and approached him, smiling sweetly. "Did you enjoy your whipping, Jotun oathbreaker? Since you did not cry out," Thokk mused, digging a sharp fingernail into a bleeding whip cut upon his muscled chest, "I can only assume that you enjoyed my whipping you. Is that true, Jotun scum?"

Vafthrudnir glared hatefully down at her but said nothing.

"Well," she said with a laugh, "if you didn't enjoy that, I'm sure you will *this*."

Slowly, teasingly, she removed her clothing until she stood

naked before him. "From time to time, Vafthrudnir," she said, moving closer, "I've detected lust for my flesh swirling in your mind. How long has it been since you've been with a female, Jotun or otherwise? Shall I be kind to you now instead of continuing your punishment?"

The Frost Giant remained silent.

Thokk concentrated her will and whispered a word of power. Her form began to change before Vafthrudnir's eyes as she worked a spell of illusion, which made her seem to become a beautiful Jotun maid. She moved forward, pressed herself against him, smearing her breasts and belly with his blood, began kissing him, making desire build steadily within him, feeling her own lust burning hotter by the moment.

For a long while, then, in that chamber of screams, the only sounds were ones of intense pleasure, Vafthrudnir, unable to resist her caresses, hung helplessly in his chains until finally he exploded with long-denied passion, his cries of pleasure and Thokk's echoing together from the chamber's stone walls.

Thokk stepped away from him, let the illusion of a Jotun maid dissipate, smoothed back the glistening black coils of her hair, and stared at him a moment, smiling to herself, her bare flesh glistening with sweat and his blood in the torchlight. Then she walked closer and spat on him.

"You shall now pay for your lust, Jotun," she hissed. "Expect no more pleasure this day."

She picked up the whip, looked thoughtfully at it for a moment, then reached up on tiptoes and hung it around Vafthrudnir's neck. "I believe I know just what is needed. I will let pain still be part of your punishment, but humiliation and dishonor will be part of it, too, hurting you even deeper than physical pain and unable to be erased by my physical healing magic, so that you will remember for all time what happens to you here today. You will burn with shame each time you recall what a cowardly, dishonorable Jotun you proved yourself to be while hanging in these chains."

"My father dishonored my family. I will not."

"You are wrong. And I am going to prove that to you.

Afterward, perhaps you may well *beg* to stay in my service
after the agreed-upon time has past. Where else will you be
able to go, once you know yourself for the coward you truly
are? And perhaps, from time to time, I will bring you here for
more . . . pleasure?"

"Get on with your games, Thokk. I grow weary of hearing
your empty threats."

Thokk laughed. "There is a guest whose presence I have
concealed from you with magic," she told him, "someone
perfectly suited to humiliate you and teach you the cowardly
truth about yourself. Let me introduce you to him."

Thokk traced runes in the air and spoke a word of power.
A sphere of purple light appeared nearby, then vanished, leaving in its place a well-muscled, bearded man with a wild mane
of red hair. Battle scars crisscrossed his tanned flesh.

Vafthrudnir stiffened in his chains, then a look of utter hatred
spread over his face.

"Yes, Jotun," Thokk said, "he is a Berserker, a shape-shifter,
one of your race's oldest enemies, a warrior devoted to the
Berserker God, Odin, who helped slay your ancestors in times
dawning."

Vafthrudnir fought for control of himself. "This is a trick!
It has to be! A follower of Odin would not do the bidding of
a servant of Hel!"

"I assure you that this one would, and does, and will. Perhaps he will explain his reasons to you. Perhaps not. I leave
you in his care, Jotun scum. Don't be too gentle," she commanded the grinning Berserker. "I expect you to make him beg
and crawl before you're done. And don't forget that a Frost
Giant's greatest fear is of fire." Then she walked out and closed
the door, smiling to herself.

The Berserker was, as the Jotun had suspected, a trick, a
sorcerous illusion given enough mind and strength by Thokk's
magic to conduct itself as a real Berserker would until she
revoked the spell. But the important thing was that the Berserker would seem completely real to the Jotun.

She probed back into Vafthrudnir's mind as she continued

on down the corridor and laughed softly at the raging terror she found there, the terror of the torch the false Berserker was holding near the Jotun's flesh, singeing his hair, blistering his skin, all the while hurling insults and derisive laughter at the suspended giant, who, she was delighted to discover, had been gagged so that he was effectively mute, unable even to curse or cry out to relieve his fear and pain.

Perhaps, Thokk told herself, *he actually will beg and crawl, though I doubt it. But if he should, he may well do as I suggested and stay in my service past the agreed-upon time. If, on the other hand, today's punishment should turn him against me, I will detect it in his thoughts and destroy him before he can harm me. But whatever the result, it was an amusing and enjoyable interlude. I should bring him down here more often, and perhaps I shall, once Hel's plans are well under way and my present concerns no longer consume all my time. But for now I must concentrate upon another useful and amusing illusion*, she thought, reminding herself with a cold smile as she continued on her way toward the cell where Huld was chained.

"But how did you get free again, Guthrun?" Huld asked, drinking hungrily from the water skin being held to her parched lips.

"Just keep eating and drinking," Guthrun said, placing another piece of cheese in Huld's mouth, "while I figure out how to get you out of these chains. That Hel-Witch changed something when she rechained you."

Huld gratefully chewed the piece of cheese. Never had food tasted so good. But then, never before had she gone so long without eating.

Suddenly Guthrun's image changed, blurred, re-formed. Thokk stood before her, grinning with delight. "I knew you would not accept food from my hand," Thokk explained, "and I wanted you to be strengthened for what lies ahead."

Huld stopped chewing and spat the remains of the cheese onto the floor with a curse.

Thokk's laughter rang from the damp, cold walls. Slowly

she swept her gaze over Huld's chained nakedness. "Your thoughts tell me that you've wondered at the manner in which you're bound, that you've thought of the X configuration in relation to the rune of sex magic. It's a shame that the lover who came to you was not allowed to give you pleasure, Huld. You would have experienced ecstasy such as you've never dreamed. Norda can't suffer for destroying him, but you can, and will, unless—"

"Don't play games, Hel-Witch. Norda was your enemy. I am . . . was her apprentice. You would hurt me even if she had not saved me from that . . . that—"

"He was a young Jotun whose bones had not yet grown flesh. His name was Thrym, a friend of Vafthrudnir's."

"Vafthrudnir? The Jotun who—"

"Yes. You met him. If you would like, I could let him show you how upset he is over Thrym's destruction. I wouldn't let him kill you, and I could always use magic to heal you afterward."

Huld said nothing but kept her gaze locked with Thokk's.

"But you need not suffer, Huld. I would enjoy teaching you the ways of Hel more than hearing you scream. Norda was a fool, but she wouldn't have chosen to teach you Witchcraft if you did not have potential. Hel can always use talented, young . . . recruits."

"What have you done with Guthrun?" Huld demanded.

"Be concerned about yourself, Huld. Accept me as your teacher or I will become your executioner."

"I do not fear death."

"No? But then you know so little about it, while I have savored its terrors and rewards for over a century. And after death, of course, I will see to it that your soul flies to Helheim instead of to Freya's pretty Folkvang, where you will become Hel's plaything to torment for eternity. She does so love to acquire the souls of Freya-worshipers. Perhaps she will reintroduce you to the Hel-traitor, Nidhug. I understand he's a maggotlike dragon now, forced to feast on the flesh of corpses."

Thokk reached out and gently stroked Huld's hair, letting

the long, silky golden strands slip through her fingers. "Your hair is quite lovely, Huld. Like any woman, you treasure it, of course. Then, too, as you know, much of a Witch's power resides in her hair. I think we shall start by getting rid of it."

The Hel-Witch saw Huld's body tense, muscles tightening, searched deep within Huld's widening eyes, probed into Huld's mind, and laughed at the emotions she found raging there. She stepped back and ran her hands luxuriantly through the glistening black coils of her own hair. "One more chance, Huld? Willingly turn away from Freya and toward Hel?"

Huld fought to keep herself from straining against the chains, determined to deny Thokk the spectacle of her futile struggles.

Thokk shrugged, concentrated her will, traced runes in the air and whispered a word of power.

Countless pinpricks covered Huld's head as one by one the soft strands of her hair began to drift downward, slowly pooling around her bare feet on the filthy stone floor.

"Go ahead and weep, Huld," Thokk said encouragingly. "The emotions I detect raging within you tell me that is what you really want to do."

Huld spit at Thokk instead.

"Your chains really are much too comfortable," Thokk noted, lightly running her slender fingers over the strained muscles of Huld's raised arms. "Perhaps I will have Vafthrudnir visit you later and adjust them so that your feet no longer touch the floor. I could let him do . . . other things to you too."

"Monster! You only want to make me Hel's slave because of your hatred for Norda. I myself mean nothing to you!" The last golden strand drifted to the floor.

"I hope you don't catch a chill," Thokk said with mock concern, studying Huld's denuded scalp. She reached out and stroked the newly bared flesh. "You look doubly naked now, poor thing."

Huld threw her head back and forth, trying to escape Thokk's mocking touch.

The Hel-Witch laughed with delight at Huld's reaction, then took the torch from its wall brace, came close to Huld, and used her foot to gently push the fallen strands of hair into a golden mound in front of the chained Witch.

Slowly, watching Huld's eyes, she lowered the torch nearer and nearer to the mound of hair, then suddenly thrust the flames into the silken strands.

Laughing again, Thokk turned and left the cell, taking the torch with her.

The acrid odor of burning hair filled Huld's nostrils and stung her eyes as the fire near her feet continued to burn. She threw herself wildly against her chains as the flesh of her lower legs became uncomfortably hot, but before the skin could be damaged, the fire suddenly died away and left her hanging helpless in darkness once more.

I won't let her win, she promised herself, tears streaking her cheeks. *No matter what she does to me, she is not going to win!*

Mocking laughter came from beyond the open cell door. Thokk, having crushed out the torch, had waited there, probing Huld's thoughts, enjoying her reactions.

Thokk stepped back into the open doorway, eyes now flickering with purple fire.

"Your will is strong, Huld, but mine is stronger. You will eventually kneel at my feet and *beg* to serve Hel."

"Never!"

"What an interesting time we two are going to have," Thokk mused. "Tell me, have you ever slept with the Dead? No? The fascinating thing is, sometimes they wake up. Perhaps I will show you what I mean. Would you enjoy that, Huld?"

Laughing once more, Thokk pulled the door closed and invoked a spell that restored the lock Guthrun had earlier broken. Then the lock clicked tight, and Huld was again left alone in the dark.

15
Berserkers

In the forest clearing sat a woodcutter's cottage. Bloodsong stood a few paces from the door and clasped hands with an aging but still powerfully built man. A woman and two children stood by his side. "My thanks, Ghunthar," Bloodsong said. "You have my promise that you will be paid for this steed, the clothing, and the food."

The woodcutter shook his head. "Payment enough if you avenge our friends and family who were living in Eirik's Vale," he said, making the sacred sign of Thor's Hammer to their memory with his clenched fist. "Were I younger, I would ride by your side. I was once a warrior myself, you know." He patted the neck of the horse he had just given to Bloodsong. "His name is Oakstorm, a faithful steed, an old friend. I am only sorry that he is not younger and more suited for a warrior such as you."

"And I am sorry that my husband's spare clothing is not finer," his wife added, eyeing the loose-fitting breeches and long-sleeved tunic of soft brown doeskin that Bloodsong now wore. "If you would but wait here a short while, I could take some tucks, make them fit you more snuggly."

"Thank you, Agetha," Bloodsong said, "but we are probably being followed and must keep moving. Besides," she added as she mounted Oakstorm, "they are much finer clothes than those I wore, or rather *didn't* wear, when I arrived."

"That's a matter of opinion," Grimnir objected, grinning.

"Men would prefer us never to dress at all," Agetha replied, giving the red-bearded warrior a scathing glance.

Grimnir laughed. "Aye," he agreed, "that we would." He jerked the bejeweled dagger from his sheath and offered it hilt first to the woodcutter. "Payment," he explained.

Ghunthar refused with a negative shake of his head, folding his arms on his chest.

Grimnir drew back his hand and threw the dagger. It thunked into the door of the woodcutter's cottage. The two children ran to the door and examined it curiously.

"Remove the jewels and melt the hilt down for the gold, lest you be taken for the one who killed its former owner," Grimnir warned.

"I do not want you or your family harmed, Ghunthar," Bloodsong said. "We have done all we can to disguise our trail, but our tracks may still lead Kovna to your door. Best you go into the forest and watch until our pursuers, if there are any, pass by. How long that will be, I don't know."

"Thor protect you," Ghunthar said, making the Hammer-sign again.

"And Freya give you victory," Agetha added.

Bloodsong raised a fist in salute, then wheeled Oakstorm around and led the way from the clearing.

When they were out of sight of the cottage and had reached the forest trail once more, Tyrulf called a halt and dismounted. "I will ride the woodcutter's steed," he announced, offering his stallion's reins to Bloodsong. "Freehoof is yours."

"No, Tyrulf," Bloodsong responded.

"Better you should escape than I, should there be a chase," Tyrulf insisted. "Besides," he added with a grin, glancing at Jalna, "I must do all I can to impress Jalna with my bravery and loyalty. Dismount, Bloodsong. Take the stallion Grimnir meant for you. Or do you value the woodcutter's gift more than Grimnir's?"

Grimnir bellowed a laugh.

Bloodsong hesitated, then dismounted, took Freehoof's reins, and patted the beast's neck. "My thanks, Tyrulf, and again to you, Grimnir. He's a fine stallion." Then she mounted Freehoof and set off down the trail at a canter, Grimnir beside her, Tyrulf and Jalna riding behind them.

"The solution is simple," Grimnir said later as he rode along. "You need an army, Bloodsong."

"Maybe the next woodcutter we find will have one of those too," she replied.

"I know a place where there is an army that might stand a chance against Kovna's."

"Even if that is true—"

"I do not lie," Grimnir interrupted, his expression darkening.

"Freya's teeth, Grimnir, I wasn't implying that you were. Let me continue. I *had* a small army of my own at Eirik's Vale. All are now dead. Would another band of warriors follow me now? Would anyone trust me now? Would people come to live in a place I vowed to protect now? Would I *allow* any to now? No. No one would, and I would not. Bands of warriors are no longer mine to lead, nor villages mine to rebuild and protect."

"Yet *we* are warriors, and we are following your lead," Grimnir quietly pointed out.

"It was the Death Riders!" Jalna protested. "The warriors of Eirik's Vale could have beaten Kovna's men, but those dead things . . ."

"Would an army follow me into battle against sorcerous creatures like those Death Riders, then?" Bloodsong countered.

"I would," Jalna quickly answered.

"Then you would die," Bloodsong responded, remembering the battle, her friends and comrades falling and becoming rotted corpses before touching the ground. "No, even if an army would follow me now, I would not let them."

"Not even for your daughter's sake?" Grimnir asked.

Bloodsong glanced angrily at him, started to speak, changed her mind. She shook her head negatively. "I must save Guthrun, but I can ask no one to fight against Thokk and the Death Riders except myself. Against Kovna and his men, yes, if we had a chance at victory. But against sorcery . . ."

"Valgerth and Thorfinn have told me," Jalna said, "about how you tried to get them to turn back all the way to Nastrond, because of Nidhug's sorcery. They did not turn back then, and I won't now."

"Nor I," Grimnir added.

"I've no intention of letting Jalna out of my sight," Tyrulf said, "so neither will I."

"There were only four of you against Nidhug," Jalna commented. "Four were enough then."

"Four?" Tyrulf asked.

"The Freya-Witch, Huld, was the fourth," Jalna answered.

"And the Death Goddess, Hel, was the fifth," Bloodsong added. "I had her aid through the Hel-ring she gave me. That ring allowed me to wield limited Witchcraft. If not for that, Nidhug *would* have slain the four of us with his sorcery before we reached Nastrond."

"Then we need a way to fight magic again," Tyrulf decided. "Maybe the next woodcutter's wife will be a Witch."

Grimnir laughed.

"It would do no good if she were," Bloodsong said, ignoring his attempt at humor. "Thokk's magic killed a Witch in Eirik's Vale, Gerda Snowmeadow, who tried to disperse the clouds before the attack. And the most powerful Freya-Witch I knew was Norda Greycloak, who obviously could not protect my daughter against Thokk. Even if Huld were here, I am sure she could do little to aid us, though she would try to the death. Thokk's power has evidently grown since I returned the War Skull to Hel. The powers of the Death Goddess that helped me defeat Nidhug are now arrayed against me."

"Then what we need," Jalna responded, "is the aid of a God or Goddess, powers as strong or stronger than those Hel has given Thokk."

"An excellent suggestion, Jalna," Bloodsong answered, "but I know of nothing to give me hope of obtaining such aid. Prayers in sacred groves might strengthen our resolve, if it needed strengthening, but that is hardly enough to——"

"The army about which I spoke has Odin's magic in them," Grimnir interrupted. "We may not be able to obtain a God's or Goddess's help directly, but indirectly is another matter."

"All warriors who hope to see Valhalla after death have Odin's magic in them," Tyrulf scoffed.

"Yes," Grimnir agreed, "but these are not ordinary warriors, Tyrulf. I am talking about an army of true Berserkers. *Shape-shifters*."

No one spoke.

"I'm not lying," Grimnir growled.

"I once saw a Berserker imbued with Odin's blood-fury kill several men after he himself should have been dead from his wounds," Tyrulf said, "and he was not a shape-shifter. Berserkers of any kind are deadly enemies but also powerful allies."

"Is it possible that a Berserker might be able to slay a Death Rider even after being death-touched?" Jalna wondered.

"I do not know," Grimnir answered.

"An *army* of shape-shifting Berserkers, Grimnir?" Tyrulf asked. "Not even in the old tales have I heard of such a thing. I'm not saying you are lying," he quickly added, "only that I've never before heard of this army. How is it that you——"

"What I said before still stands," Bloodsong cut in. "I won't ask anyone, not even a Berserker, shape-shifter or not, to fight against Thokk's magic and the Death Riders."

"Then *I* will ask them," Grimnir said. "They owe me a favor or two."

"What dealings have you had with shape-shifters?" Jalna asked, echoing Tyrulf's unanswered question. She had been intrigued by the red-bearded warrior ever since he'd first wandered into Eirik's Vale during a blizzard and somehow managed to gain an invitation to Bloodsong's bed before the spring thaw. No man had done that since the death of Bloodsong's husband many years before. But Grimnir never stayed long during the warm months of the year; sometimes did not even return during the winter. If Bloodsong knew what he did during his absences, she had never told anyone, not even her own daughter, whom Jalna had tactfully questioned upon the subject more than once.

"But if the Berserkers are going to fight for your purposes, Bloodsong," Grimnir continued, ignoring Jalna's question, "they will have to be assured of your worthiness. And they won't approve of your having worked for one of Odin's enemies in returning the War Skull to Hel. You may not survive their test."

Bloodsong looked thoughtfully at Grimnir. "Did *you* survive it, Grimnir?"

Grimnir slowly nodded. "Yes, but only barely," he answered, his eyes haunted by the memory, "and I had not aided Hel. They may make your ordeal even more severe. Perhaps I should not have mentioned this at all," he went on. "If something should happen to you, if you should die because of my mentioning the Berserkers . . ."

"I am sure I could survive their test," Bloodsong said, "*if* I agreed to ask for their help. For Guthrun's sake I would have to survive it. But I have *not* agreed to ask for their aid."

"You won't have to ask them," Grimnir replied. "I told you that I will. . . ."

"Nor will I allow you to ask them for me."

"You won't *allow* me? Curse it, woman! I have vowed to help free Guthrun and take revenge on the destroyers of Eirik's Vale. Do you think I make oaths lightly? I will do whatever I have to do, whether you want me to or not, to fulfill my vow, and I have decided that only with the Berserkers aid can I—"

"And *I* have decided that—" Bloodsong began, then stopped. "Freya's teeth! Listen to us. If Kovna doesn't catch us or Thokk's sorcery slay us, we'll argue each other to death."

Grimnir was silent a moment, then grinned. "Aye. That we might. Very well. It's settled. We'll seek the Berserkers' help," he went quickly on, heading off her reply, "unless you can think of another way to do what we must?"

"I will think on it," Bloodsong promised, and fell at once to doing just that.

16
Mountain and Mound

The sun stood in mid-sky when Bloodsong and her companions emerged from the forest. The road stretched away across a rolling grassland. Lost in thought, Bloodsong had said nothing since mid-morning.

"Here," Grimnir said, offering Bloodsong some bread and cheese the woodcutter's wife had given them. "You must be starved after all the thinking you've been doing."

Bloodsong took the food. "I haven't given up thinking of another way."

"Of course not," Grimnir replied, and bit into a thick hunk of yellow cheese, then winked at her as he chewed.

Bloodsong finished the bread and cheese, accepted a water skin Grimnir passed to her, drank long and deep, and passed it back to him. She ran a hand through her long black hair, grimaced slightly as her shoulder muscles, strained by her bondage to the tree, ached with her movements.

She smoothed her hair behind her shoulders, took a thong from her saddle, used it to tie the raven tresses back out of her way. *I should simply take my sword and hack my hair off short,* she told herself. *I've been meaning to for years, and this might be a good time.* She'd worn her hair short when she'd been an arena warrior in Nidhug's slave pens, but after her escape she'd let it grow, at first hoping to disguise herself, later because Eirik had preferred it that way. *Would Grimnir mind it short?* she wondered, then cursed herself for such trivial concerns. All that mattered was finding a way to free Guthrun.

"How long will it take to reach the Berserkers?" she asked.

"Less than a week."

"And double that to return with them," she noted, "*if* they agree to help, which means leaving Guthrun in that Hel-Witch's castle for nearly two weeks or more. It's unacceptable. There must be a quicker way. In two weeks Thokk could—"

"If you attack unprepared," Grimnir cut in, "your death would leave Guthrun without *any* hope of help."

Bloodsong cursed with frustration.

"I have thought of something that might be helpful," Tyrulf suddenly said from behind, "and it is only a three-day ride to the west, if the story I once heard is true. I've not been there myself, only heard a warrior talk of it. He claimed that he was born near there."

"Tell us," Bloodsong replied.

"There is a large earthen mound at the foot of a mountain. Both mound and mountain are said to be places of magic. The people who live nearby don't go there except to worship and never speak of the place to outsiders."

"Then why did that warrior tell you?" Jalna asked skeptically.

"You still think I might be plotting a trap?" Tyrulf replied, watching Jalna's eyes.

She looked away and shrugged.

"Please continue, Tyrulf," Bloodsong said.

"The man who told me was drunk," Tyrulf said to Jalna, ignoring Bloodsong. "He would not have told me otherwise."

Jalna shrugged again but did not look back at him.

"Hodur's eyes," Tyrulf cursed. "I was told that the mound is charged with Freya's magic, and the mountain with Thor's.

At the summit of Thor's Mountain is said to live the Keeper of the Lightning's Blood, and within Freya's Mound is buried a golden nugget, a tear from Freya's eyes that turned to gold upon touching the Earth."

"I have *seen* the Berserkers with my own eyes, talked with them, lived with them," Grimnir pointed out. "We would be fools to put all our trust in a drunken warrior's story."

"We might also be fools to place all our hope in the Berserkers," Tyrulf answered.

"Is there any reason why all four of us need seek the Berserkers?" Bloodsong asked Grimnir.

"None," he replied. "Should they decide to help us, it will be only because of you and your surviving their test."

"I won't leave you, Bloodsong," Jalna insisted.

"According to the tale I was told," Tyrulf said, "men are not able to approach Freya's Mound. Only a female can obtain whatever magic is there."

"He could just be making that up!" Jalna exclaimed. "He could be lying, inventing the whole tale, to split us up and to—"

"*To what?*" Tyrulf demanded. "Curse it, Jalna. I deserted Kovna's army, killed men I'd known for years, risked my life to save Bloodsong, am willing to do so again, and to fight by your side to the death. Why must you persist in mistrusting me, in fearing me?"

"I do not fear you."

"Jalna," Bloodsong said, reining to a stop and turning Freehoof to face the young warrior, "I don't fully understand your feelings about Tyrulf, nor his for you, and I don't intend to try. But if there's a chance of finding something to the west to help us free Guthrun..."

"I will go," Jalna quickly said, holding Bloodsong's gaze, "for you and for Guthrun, if you wish it. I did not mean to act a fool. It's just that..." Her voice trailed away.

"No need to explain," Bloodsong said, gripping Jalna's shoulder. "I trust Tyrulf. Perhaps you will learn to do so too."

"Freya has cursed me with feelings for you, woman," Tyrulf

told Jalna. "The Gods know such things do not always make sense."

"I have no feelings for you."

"Of course not," Grimnir agreed. "That is why you avoid Tyrulf's eyes, don't want to be alone with him, pretend you dislike him—"

"That's enough, Grimnir," Bloodsong interrupted.

"I have not actually said that I *dislike* him," Jalna said to Grimnir.

"Jalna's feelings or lack of them are her affair, Grimnir," Tyrulf growled, locking gazes with the red-bearded warrior.

Grimnir looked from Tyrulf to Jalna to Bloodsong. He started to say something more, then cursed and shook his head instead.

Bloodsong turned Freehoof and headed down the road again.

"We will take the fork to the right at the next crossroad," Grimnir said to Bloodsong a short time later. "Then, when we reach Sword River, those two can cross it and head west to their goal while we follow the river road southward to the coast."

"Coast?"

"The Berserkers live on an island. Didn't I tell you?"

"No. Do you know how to handle a boat?"

"We'll be using a longship, not a boat. And, yes, of course I do. Don't you?"

"I never had to learn."

"Have you ever even seen the sea?"

Bloodsong shook her head negatively.

Grimnir reached over and clasped Bloodsong's hand. "We'll free her," he promised. "I have never broken a vow. And Guthrun is a strong young woman. She has a warrior's soul, like her mother. That Hel-Witch is the one who should beware."

Bloodsong glanced into his eyes and saw the concern for her there. "I will be all right, Grimnir," she assured him. "It's just that there's this need in me to do something more, to do something quicker, *now*, not weeks from now, not—"

"We'll free her," he promised again.

Bloodsong nodded, watching the road ahead, fighting to

stay calm and to keep her thoughts clear in spite of the impatience churning within her.

Huld heard heavy footsteps growing louder, felt the air growing colder, fought her chains, panic rising within her as she remembered Thokk's suggestion that the Jotun might come to torture her.

A key clicked in the lock. The door opened.

A blast of freezing air lashed her nakedness. Huld drew in her breath sharply, shivering.

The Jotun stood in the doorway, eyes boring into hers for several heartbeats, then entered, and closed and locked the door behind him.

There was a bundle of objects under his left arm. He dropped the bundle on the floor at Huld's feet. Metal and leather gleamed in the torchlight. Her eyes widened at the sight of the knives, spikes, clamps, and whips. Her thoughts raced as she tried desperately to think of some way to avoid what was about to happen to her.

Vafthrudnir placed the torch in a wall bracket and came back to face her. "Vafthrudnir," Huld said, keeping her voice steady, "Thokk said the one who died was your friend. I did not kill him."

"It does not matter. You are responsible."

"That's not true."

"It is to me."

"But . . . you're wrong. If Thokk had not brought me here and told your friend to do what he was . . . doing to me, he would still be alive."

Vafthrudnir reached down into the bundle at Huld's feet and selected a whip with three ugly iron barbs on the tip, the very whip Thokk had used on him. He had not broken under the pain the Berserker had given him, had not succumbed to the attempted humiliation. When Thokk had returned, she'd healed his many wounds and laughingly revealed that the Berserker had been but a sorcerous illusion.

Where Vafthrudnir had previously disliked Thokk there now

burned. hatred, but he had vowed to obey and serve her to redeem his family's honor, and he had no intention of breaking that vow merely to satisfy a need for revenge. Perhaps, however, some of the hatred he felt for Thokk could be vented on the human woman chained naked before him. Had it not been for her escape, the punishment he had suffered would not even have occurred.

The Jotun held the whip close to Huld's face so she could clearly see the iron barbs. When her widening eyes told him that she understood that those barbs would soon be tearing her flesh, he hung the whip around her neck, walked to the wall, and began working a device which controlled the tension in her chains. The pain in her wrists increased as her feet left the floor and she hung suspended.

"Are you Thokk's slave?" she asked as he kept increasing the tension, racking her between the chains above and those that held her feet spread below. "Free me and I'll help you get free of her. I promise! Thokk is your real enemy, not me. I'm a Witch, too, and I can—" Her voice broke off in a ragged sob, pain shooting through her as her joints began to burn with the strain.

Vafthrudnir locked the device, satisfied, then returned to her. He took the whip from around her neck, stared deep into her eyes. "I made a vow to serve Thokk for a certain period of time, to atone for a crime against Hel my father once committed. To redeem his honor and mine I will fulfill my vow. I am not Thokk's slave but her servant. Do not worry so, little human. Thokk has ordered me not to kill you, and I shall not, though I hope to make you wish it were otherwise."

The Jotun stepped back three paces and kept his eyes on Huld's as he raised the whip and drew back his arm.

"Have you ever been whipped before, little human?" he asked.

"I . . . of course not . . ." Huld replied, her voice breaking slightly, her pulse pounding in her ears, still trying to think of something to prevent her torture as her muscles involuntarily tensed for the first blow. Vafthrudnir drew his arm back farther.

"No!" she cried. "Wait! Please, just listen to me for a few moments. Let me talk to you, try to convince you that—"

The whip hissed through the cold air, sliced into the tightly stretched bare flesh of Huld's abdomen. She held back the scream of agony that wanted to escape her throat. Her muscles reflexively bunched into knots beneath her naked skin as she unthinkingly strained to escape her bonds, but she scarcely managed to move at all.

"Even if you *had* been whipped before," he told her, eyeing the crimson drops seeping from the wound across her belly, "it would not have prepared you for the strength with which my Jotun muscles can wield this whip. That first cut was for Thokk, little human. The rest of your whipping, and the other things I shall soon do to you, will be for Thrym and for me, and they will not be so gentle."

"Please . . . don't . . ." She sobbed brokenly, but then felt her fear and panic recede slightly as anger began to push them away. "I have no wish to see harm done to you, Vafthrudnir," she said, her voice suddenly strong again, "but I have made a vow, too, a vow of revenge against Thokk. If you do this to me now, I will include you in that revenge, in Freya's name, I swear it!"

Vafthrudnir remembered the gag to which he had been subjected during his punishment. He smiled coldly and came forward to Huld, hung the whip around her neck again, reached down and picked up a leather-and-steel gag from the floor, brought it to her face, and began working it into her mouth. When he had it strapped tightly in place, he took the whip and stepped back again. "Thokk said to stop hurting you if you changed your mind about joining her, so if you change your mind, tell me at once, but be certain to speak loudly and clearly if you decide to cooperate with her. I might not hear you and keep giving you pain if you do not speak loudly and clearly."

The Jotun stood looking into Huld's eyes for a long moment, well satisfied with the horror and hatred he saw there, grinning at the mixed sounds of anger and pleading she was making through her gag, then his whip hissed again.

17
Separation

The Sword River sparkled before them in the late-afternoon sunlight. It was time for them to part.

"Skadi protect you," Bloodsong said to Jalna, invoking the Huntress Goddess for whom the young warrior had a special fondness as she reached out and gripped Jalna's shoulder.

"If there's anything to the west that can help free Guthrun and defeat Thokk, I will find it," Jalna vowed. "But I still think that if I find something of obvious power, something that could free Guthrun before you return..."

"You have promised to wait until two weeks from today in the forest east of Eirik's Vale," Bloodsong reminded her. "If Grimnir and I still live, which I fully intend us to do, we will meet you there, hopefully with the army of Berserkers."

"Yes, but if it were in my power to free Guthrun the sooner—"

"Jalna, I want to say yes to you. I want Guthrun free this very moment, not weeks from now. But we will only get one chance to attack Thokk's castle, and that attack must not fail. Whatever aid you may discover in the west must be combined

108

with whatever aid Grimnir and I acquire to give us the best chance at victory."

"I won't break my promise to wait," Jalna finally said.

Bloodsong gripped Jalna's shoulder again, then glanced at Tyrulf.

"I'll *see* that she waits," he said.

"I trust Jalna's word," Bloodsong replied, "and at the moment I trust you, Tyrulf. If, however, I discover that you were indeed playing some game of your own to separate us, if you should harm Jalna in any way, I will hunt you down and—"

"If he tries to harm me," Jalna interrupted, meaningfully touching the hilt of her sword, "there won't be anything left for you to hunt."

Grimnir laughed. "If you're both through threatening Tyrulf, I think we should all be on our way."

Bloodsong and Grimnir watched as Jalna and Tyrulf guided their horses through the shallow water at the crossing point. On the far side of the river Jalna looked back and raised a fist in salute.

Bloodsong and freedom, Jalna thought, and saw Bloodsong return her salute, then she turned Frosthoof west, Tyrulf riding at her side.

"I can see why he cares for that woman," Grimnir said as he and Bloodsong began their ride southward along the river road to the coast. "She's a lot like you."

"I care for her too," Bloodsong replied. "We will eat and sleep in our saddles to reach the coast sooner."

"It will soon be dark," Grimnir answered. "I will take your reins and lead Freehoof while you sleep."

"And you will wake me at midnight?"

"Of course."

"I mean it, Grimnir."

"Of course."

"You are as tired as I, need rest as much as I."

"Of course. Don't you trust me, Bloodsong?"

"Of course," she answered. "That's the problem."

He could not even recall his name at first, did not know where he was, had no idea why his head was throbbing with agony. Then his mind began to clear. *Bloodsong*! She had been freed!

He was lying upon a blanket near a camp fire. Overhead, the sky was a dark, deep blue. *Sunset or dawn*? he wondered. Men stood nearby with their backs to him.

Kovna struggled to a sitting position, cursing at the pain. His hands flew to his skull, found it heavily bandaged. A wave of weakness and nausea flooded through him. He fell back, gasping for air.

"He's awake," he heard a familiar voice say. A warrior detached himself from the group of men, walked quickly to Kovna, squatted down beside him.

"Styrki," Kovna groaned. "Bloodsong . . . is she . . ."

"She escaped. We tried to stop her after you fell wounded, but she had unexpected help. Some of the men who survived said they recognized one of her rescuers. It was our old friend, Lieutenant Grimnir, curse his bones."

"Grimnir! I will execute him yet one day, just as I did his wife and children in his absence. But Bloodsong . . . why aren't you leading men in pursuit, Captain? If you've just let her ride away . . ."

"I sent men after her. They have not returned. It was dark. I doubt that they'll find her trail. Your two trackers were killed during our attempt to stop her escape."

"Odin's curse," Kovna growled.

"You are lucky to still be breathing, General. It will be a while before you are strong enough to wield a sword again."

"I am strong enough now, Captain. I don't suppose that traitor Tyrulf was slain or captured?"

"No. I've known him for years. What could have possessed him to help Bloodsong? Perhaps she still has those Witch-powers she is said to have used against Nidhug," he suggested, making a Hammer-sign against the thought.

"Thokk assured me that she no longer has those powers."

Styrki shrugged. "I am glad you've regained consciousness, General. There was talk of desertion. The men do not care to serve Thokk, as you know. If you had died, I could not have kept them together for long."

Kovna nodded. "I will speak with them."

"You should rest. It is nearly sunset. I will tell them you are well. You can talk with them in the morning."

"And how many will slip away during the night? No. I must talk with them now," he decided, and began struggling to stand. Styrki reached to help him. Kovna pushed him away.

"Has just the one day passed?" Kovna asked through gritted teeth.

"Yes, General," Styrki answered, watching with concern as fresh blood oozed through the bandages around Kovna's skull.

Kovna gained his feet, drew himself to his full height. "Assemble the men," he ordered.

Styrki saluted, turned, and began shouting commands.

"Jalna," Tyrulf said, "it is nearly too dark to see. We should make camp."

"We will sleep in our saddles," Jalna announced, "or at least that is what I intend to do. You can make camp if you wish and try to catch up with me in the morning."

"You will never find the mound and mountain without my help."

"Then give me the directions."

Tyrulf hesitated.

"Afraid I'll leave you behind if you tell?"

"You ride a much younger and faster horse," he noted, "but, no, I do not believe that you would endanger our quest by outdistancing me. Two stand a better chance of success than one."

"That may or may not be true. But you're right. I won't leave you behind unless I have good cause. You should still tell me the directions, however. We could be attacked. You might be killed."

"We might both be killed if we don't stop and make camp. This road is not as well traveled as the one Bloodsong and Grimnir are following along the river, and ahead lies a forest where people have been known to disappear. Years ago I was in a patrol that went looking for another patrol. We found the remains of their camp fire but nothing else, not even signs of a battle. I do not think we should ride among those trees at night."

"I do not intend to stop because of your fears. I have heard stories about the forest ahead, but I am not afraid."

"You could be endangering our mission by entering there at night. You wouldn't ride into an ambush about which you knew. Caution does not necessarily mean fear, though healthy fear has led many a warrior to victory over foolishly over-confident opponents."

Jalna rode in silence a moment, then cursed softly. "Perhaps you are right," she finally said. "Your irritating presence keeps me from thinking clearly, and that is dangerous."

"I think we should camp here, well away from the trees," he said after a moment, deciding to ignore her comment. "If someone attacks during the night, they would have a greater open space to cross, giving us more of a chance to see them once the moon has risen."

"And the farther from the trees we camp," Jalna added, "the less chance of drawing unwanted attention from any forest dwellers. Very well, Tyrulf. I will agree to camp here. Will you agree to tell me the directions to the mound and the mountain?"

"I would have done that, anyway," he replied, reining to a stop.

"We need not build a fire," Jalna said as she dismounted. "It might attract the attention of forest dwellers, if there are any."

"And we'll leave the horses loosely saddled in case we need them in a hurry. As soon as we've eaten, I'll take the first watch."

"We'll gather twigs and *draw* for the first watch," Jalna

countered, but when bread and cheese had been eaten and twigs drawn, it was still Tyrulf who was to stand guard first.

Jalna drew her sword and laid it beside her on the ground. "I sleep very lightly," she warned.

"I won't ravish you while you sleep."

"No, you won't," she assured him. "But before I sleep, I will have the directions you promised."

Tyrulf gave them to her, then began his watch, listening as her breathing deepened with sleep.

Sleep well, lovely one, he thought, then grinned at the thought of the curses calling her that to her face would earn him. His mind rushed back over the events of the past two days, then beyond to the first time he'd seen her seven years before. He remembered again his outrage at seeing her in Nidhug's chains, his frustration at being unable to help her, his haunted thoughts of her ever since, imagining her dead.

And now she lay sleeping but a few steps away, strong and alive. Alive! *And she's going to stay that way*, he silently vowed, then set himself to watch, physical senses and warrior instincts straining for the first sign of danger as they never had before.

18
Visitors

The towering crystal War Skull of Hel loomed before her, throbbing with purple light, rumbling like a thunderous heartbeat, the empty chains embedded in its surface waiting to clamp her wrists again. Closer and closer she was carried toward it. She struggled against the hard-muscled arms of the soldier who carried her but could not get free. They reached the Skull. He lifted her up and held her in position while another soldier locked the manacles around her wrists. The soldier who held her then lowered her until she hung above the floor, the surface of the Skull freezing cold against her bare back and buttocks.

She looked wildly down at the soldier who had carried her to the Skull, saw something in his eyes she could not fathom, and watched as he turned away.

"Tyrulf!" she cried. "Help me! Come back! Tyrulf!"

Another man was approaching, a man with the face of a corpse. Nidhug. In his hand glowed a venomous green wand. He brought it slowly toward her, touched her with it. She screamed, saw Tyrulf stop and turn at the sound of her pain.

"Help me!" she begged. "Tyrulf! Please help me! No more pain . . ."

The wand touched her again....

"Jalna!" Tyrulf shouted, gripping her shoulders, gently shaking her back and forth. "Wake up, Jalna!"

Slowly the dream began to fade, her thoughts to clear. The last thing she had wanted was for Tyrulf to learn of her nightmares. "Skadi's bow," she cursed. "Did you enjoy my performance?"

"Jalna, I . . . heard you call out my name, and came nearer. You screamed, begged me to help you. . . ."

"It was only a dream."

"A nightmare."

"Perhaps. I don't remember," she lied. She got to her feet, smoothed down her sweat-soaked hair, saw that the moon had risen. "I might as well take my watch. I've slept long enough. Weren't you going to wake me?"

"At midnight, yes."

"Go on to sleep," she said, stretching. "Nothing to report, I gather?"

"I thought I saw movement near the edge of the forest just after moonrise, but it wasn't repeated, and I've begun to think that it was a trick of moonlight and shadows."

"If I see it again, I'll wake you," she promised.

Tyrulf lay down, looked up at the stars overhead, and remembered Jalna's scream—the way her voice had sounded begging for his help, reminding him of seven years before.

"Jalna," he quietly said, "about the dream. It was a nightmare from what you suffered in Nastrond, wasn't it? That is why you were calling for my help, because I am in the nightmare, doing nothing to stop what Nidhug did to you. Do you . . . have you had such nightmares often since then?"

"I told you I don't remember anything about the dream," Jalna said tightly. "Now go to sleep."

"I just wanted you to know that I . . . I am so very sorry. I've been sorry for a very long time."

"There was nothing you could have done to stop Nidhug," she answered after a slight hesitation. "I know that now. He was too powerful a sorcerer. He would have slain you, and I still would have suffered. Forget it. I have."

"You haven't learned to lie as well as you'd like," Tyrulf commented. He waited, expecting an outburst of denial, but there was none. "You *haven't* forgotten, Jalna, and neither have I. And what I said is true. I *am* sorry, not just for not helping you then but also because any of it had to happen at all, sorry the Norns placed that fate in your path, made you Nidhug's slave, sorry we could not have met in a different situation, sorry we can't put those horrors behind us and start fresh. But we're both scarred by what happened. In the last seven years I've had dreams . . . nightmares too. We must find a way to enjoy life in spite of our memories."

"I've already done that," Jalna answered a little too quickly. "Perhaps you will, too, in time."

"Perhaps, now that I've learned that you're alive."

"Sleep," she ordered. "An army could approach without my knowing it if you keep talking." *And I just hope my nightmare's screams have not already attracted unwanted attention from the forest*, she added to herself, then began concentrating upon watching for danger.

It was not far from dawn when she saw them. Suddenly they were all around, standing motionless and silent in the gray predawn light.

"Tyrulf!" she hissed, nudging him with her boot as she drew her sword and made ready her shield.

He sat up, saw them, scrambled to his feet, drew his own sword, stood with his back to hers, ready to fight.

"They were suddenly just there," she said. "I don't know how they got so close without my noticing, not in this growing light. I should have seen them easily, but—"

"I recognize them," Tyrulf interrupted. "The Gods help me, but I know them. I've finally found those men of Kovna's who disappeared in the forest, or rather they've found me."

"They must have deserted," Jalna reasoned, wondering why they did not attack. "They knew the stories about the forest, decided to use the superstitious tales to get out of Nidhug's army."

"I don't think so. See how their images waver? The brighter it becomes, the more unstable they seem."

"Skadi's bow. You are right."

Then, as suddenly as they'd appeared, the ghostly warriors were gone. The grassland leading up to the forest was empty once more. But Jalna and Tyrulf did not relax, stayed back-to-back, ready for battle, until the sun broke the eastern horizon. Then Tyrulf sheathed his sword. "I'm for breakfast," he said with a nervous chuckle, and went to search a leather pouch on his saddle.

"Tyrulf, look." Jalna pointed with her sword. "That patch of dead grass there, and there, and over there too."

"Yes. I've noticed. I judge that those spots mark where our visitors stood watching us."

Jalna sheathed her sword. "I've always heard that horses shy at the supernatural, yet ours acted as if nothing were happening."

Tyrulf shrugged. "Here," he said, offering her some cheese. "Maybe nothing did happen. I know that doesn't make sense, but neither did what we saw. I never saw one of them move in the whole time I was watching them, not even to breathe."

Jalna took the cheese and began to eat. Later, as they rode nearer the edge of the forest, she drew her sword and unstrapped her shield from her back. "Just because I'm cautious doesn't mean I'm afraid," she told him, throwing his own words back at him.

Tyrulf laughed, then made ready his weapons too. "Perhaps nothing will happen during the daylight hours. I made it in and out of the forest without trouble the time I came searching for those lost men. But they had camped within the trees during the night."

Side by side, senses straining for danger, they rode into the dark shadows of the forest.

The halls through which he walked were coated with black ice. Cold penetrated him to his bones. His legs were shaky with exhaustion, as if he had walked for days and days to arrive at his destination. The soles of his boots were worn through, scarcely protecting his feet at all from the ice over which he walked.

An arched portal towered overhead. He passed beneath it and entered a vast ice-shrouded cavern, in the center of which loomed a black throne. A hooded figure sat there, many times the size of a human, hunched slightly forward toward him. No face was visible within the shadows of the hood. He felt an unreasonable fear that the hood might be pulled back.

He became aware of others in the throne room with him, saw rotting gray forms huddled here and there in the shadows, silently watching as he neared the hooded one on the throne.

You were wise to ally yourself with me, a woman's voice suddenly whispered within his mind.

He did not reply but stood numb with fear at the foot of the throne.

The enthroned one raised its hands to the hood. One hand was that of a young woman, the other the skeletal claw of a corpse. The hood fell back.

You are dying, *General Kovna*, Hel whispered within his mind.

"No!" he cried, staring up at the face of the Death Goddess, half her face that of a beautiful woman, the other half that of a decaying corpse.

Die Hel-praying, Hel urged, *and I will resurrect your flesh after death, make you into a leader of Hel-warriors, let you ride at the head of my army behind Lokith and his Death Riders as you conquer the Earth. You will have power, Kovna. Power! You lust after it. Take it! Take what I offer. You need only die Hel-praying and it shall be yours*.

"No!" he cried again. "No!" he repeated, staggering back from the throne, his feet like lead, each step an exhausting effort.

"General Kovna!" a man was calling. Kovna felt himself being gripped by his shoulders. He opened his eyes. Styrki was bending over him.

He pushed Styrki's hands away from his shoulders. "It was only a dream, Captain. You need not be concerned."

Pain was everywhere, radiating through his body from his head wound. *She told me I was dying*, he thought, his heart beating wildly, *but I'll prove her wrong. I will use her own magic against her. Thokk has the power to heal wounds. If I can only last until we reach her castle, I'll not die.*

The sky was bright overhead. Kovna forced himself to defy his pain and rise to a sitting position. "Bring me food," he ordered, "and wine. Lots of strong wine to dull this cursed pain. Then make the men ready to travel. We are riding at once to the castle of Thokk."

For the first time since entering the dark forest, Jalna allowed herself to relax. She sheathed her sword and slung her shield on her back.

"Don't you hear it?" she asked, glancing at Tyrulf. "A bird," she explained, "the first I've heard since entering this cursed forest. And don't you feel a change in the air? Whatever haunts these woods is behind us now. I'm certain of it."

"You must have the ears of a wolf," he commented as he sheathed his sword. "I'd not heard that bird until you mentioned it. And you're right about the air feeling different. It's easier to breathe now. Are you disappointed that we didn't solve the mystery of this forest, Jalna?" he asked with a grin.

"Not enough to go back," she said, laughing. Their eyes met. She looked away quickly, her smile fading. "I judge it to be nearly noon. We've ridden tensed all morning, ready for a fight that never came, thank Skadi. My stomach feels as if I haven't eaten for a week. Let's have at some more of that woodcutter's rich cheese and bread."

"And also perhaps a bit of the wine?" he suggested, "in celebration of our not vanishing into thin air or worse?"

"Aye. But only a sip or two. Other danger is certain to lie ahead."

19
Persuasion

A sound in the hallway made Guthrun stop pacing the small room and turn toward the door. A key clicked in the lock. She considered attacking, remembered what had happened when she'd tried to attack Thokk before, remembered Vafthrudnir's size, and decided to conserve her energy instead.

Thokk entered, smiled sweetly at her. "Have you rested well, Guthrun?" she asked with concern.

"You know I have not. Every time I try to sleep, someone I knew from my days in Helheim materializes and starts to plague me, to talk to me, urging me to give in to you, to become something I'm not. You said you would be right back. It must have been days! And there's been no food. But it won't work, Thokk. It won't! I'm not going to break. You're not going to get your way. Starve me, keep me from sleeping, torture me, but—"

"Guthrun! I knew nothing of this! I'll have Vafthrudnir punished for not bringing food. I'll go and get some for you this instant myself."

Thokk turned and quickly stepped into the hallway.

"You can't trick me, Hel-slave!" Guthrun shouted at the closing door. "You're just playing games, trying to confuse me, to change my thoughts!"

The lock clicked. Guthrun began pacing again, hugging herself against the cold, head aching from lack of food and sleep. *She won't win*, she vowed over and over, chanting it silently in her mind, focusing her fraying concentration upon the thought, determined to win the mental battle she was waging with the Hel-Witch and the minions of Hel, ruthlessly crushing the traitorous thoughts that were rising more and more often in her mind, thoughts that urged her to give in, to think of Hel as her true mother and of Thokk as a misunderstood woman who wanted only to teach Guthrun the truth about herself and to awaken the powers within her, which were her birthright.

She won't win! Guthrun repeated over and over in her mind. *I won't let her win. I am Guthrun*! *Bloodsong is my mother. Thokk won't win. She won't*!

Guthrun kept pacing, not surprised when Thokk did not keep her promise and immediately return with food.

Sleep pulled at her, made her stumble against the table. She cursed weakly, slumped down on the bed, tried to keep her eyes open, knowing what would happen the moment they closed and started drifting to sleep.

Her eyes closed.

"Guthrun?" called a familiar voice. "Wake up, please? I can't stay long."

"I'm awake, curse you," Guthrun growled, eyes still closed.

"If you're not going to look at me..."

The image of a young boy's corpse appeared in Guthrun's mind.

With a startled cry Guthrun tried to open her eyes but now found that she could not.

"Leave me alone!" she commanded. "My thoughts are my own! It's not like the others have said. Hel is *not* my true mother. Bloodsong is my mother! I am *not* a Hel-born Witch-child! I have no special powers slumbering within me. I—"

"Don't fight the truth, Guthrun. We're friends, aren't we? I would not lie to a friend, Guthrun. Remember all the times we played when you lived in Helheim? We shared secrets, were close friends. Friends, Guthrun. Friends. When you used to cry, after the woman you thought was your mother went to fight Nidhug for Mother Hel, I would comfort you, bring smiles back to your face. Remember, Guthrun? Friends. Friends . . ."

"Curse you, Orm!"

"So you do remember my name. I'd begun to wonder."

The image left her mind. Guthrun opened her eyes. Orm stood nearby, gray flesh tattered with decay, his skin rippling here and there where maggots crawled just beneath the surface.

"It hurts when you curse at me, Guthrun," Orm said. "Mother Hel is unhappy with us, your friends, when we return without convincing you of Thokk's good intentions. I will be punished if you don't say you'll cooperate. Give Thokk the chance to show you the truth. Accept Hel as your true mother. Inga was punished when she couldn't convince you, Guthrun. She screamed a long time. It was your fault."

"Lies!"

"Don't make Mother Hel mad at me, Guthrun. Promise to let Thokk teach you the truth? Save me from punishment? Don't force Mother Hel to make me scream too. We're friends, Guthrun. Friends. Agree to cooperate—for me? For friendship's sake? Please?"

"No!"

"For all the times I cheered you when you were crying, Guthrun? Please? Don't you owe me that much at least? Agree to cooperate—for me? Please?"

Guthrun gripped her throbbing head between her hands, tried to keep her thoughts her own, reminding herself to keep fighting, not to give in. But she didn't want to cause Orm pain. She *was* his friend, wasn't she? She had been, once. She must still be. And she didn't want Mother Hel to be angry with him . . . Mother Hel, her true mother . . .

"She's *not* my mother!" Guthrun cried, fighting the traitorous thoughts, exhausted and weakened from lack of sleep and food. "Get out!" she yelled at Orm. "Go back to Helheim! I don't *care* if she makes you scream! I hope she does!"

Tears sprang to Orm's sunken eyes, and fear settled upon his face. He began to dematerialize. When he was gone, Guthrun heard him begin to scream, the sound faint but distinct, as if it came from deep within the bowels of the Earth.

Guthrun returned to her pacing, breath coming in panting gasps, holding her hands over her ears but unable to shut out the agonized screams that went on and on and on.

Huld heard the sound of footsteps coming nearer, opened swollen eyes, found the cell still totally devoid of light. She stiffened in her chains, thinking that Vafthrudnir might be returning. The Jotun had visited her three times, and each time she had been ready to beg for death when he allowed her to lose consciousness. But the air was not growing colder as it did when the Frost Giant neared, and the footsteps were not as heavy as his.

Hanging suspended above the floor as Vafthrudnir had left her, Huld struggled to concentrate through her pain. It sounded like more than one person was approaching. The lock clicked and hinges creaked as the door to her cell was opened. Torchlight flooded inward. Several figures entered.

"I see that Vafthrudnir accepted my invitation to visit you, Huld," Thokk purred, sweeping her gaze over the suspended Freya-Witch. She reached out and lightly touched the dried blood caked on one of Huld's thigh wounds. "I detect from your thoughts that you've entertained him three times. And that he . . . gagged you to keep you from stopping the torture by agreeing to cooperate with me. That does not please me, Huld. He will be punished for that in time. And I meant for him to visit you only once, but for the last few days other matters have occupied my attention, and I momentarily forgot that you were down here alone in the dark. Do you believe that, Huld? Do you believe I might just forget about you, leave you to slowly die and rot in your chains?"

Huld looked down at the Hel-Witch but kept silent.

"No," Thokk said with a laugh, "your thoughts tell me you do not believe I would forget you. Perhaps you are right. Perhaps not. But Vafthrudnir will not forget. Be certain of that. Agree to be my student, Huld, and Vafthrudnir will never harm you again. Are you ready to agree?" Thokk asked, experimentally touching other wounds on the Freya-Witch's body, smiling as Huld winced and grimaced in pain. "But I promised to heal you if Vafthrudnir amused himself at your expense, and I shall."

Huld ignored Thokk's taunts and struggled to clear her pain-blurred vision, trying to see the others who'd entered the cell. There were two adults and two children. They looked familiar. Her vision cleared a bit more.

"Val—gerth?" Huld asked in a hoarse whisper. "Thorfinn?"

"Aye," Valgerth said, gazing up at the ruin of Huld's body. "Yngvar and Thora are here too. We would help you if we could, but—"

"But if they attempt to escape or harm me," Thokk interrupted, "or to go against my will in any way, their children will be the first to suffer. Let me show you how cooperative they are."

She turned to Thorfinn. "Thorfinn, I am going to remove your bonds. When I do, I want you to take Valgerth to that wall over there, untie her, and clamp manacles around her wrists. When you have done that, you will also chain yourself. Do you understand?"

Thokk placed her hands suggestively on Yngvar's shoulders and slowly slid them toward the boy's neck.

The war raging within Thorfinn was evident in his expression, but with a glance at Valgerth and then at their children, he finally gave a quick nod of agreement.

Keeping one hand near Yngvar's neck, Thokk traced runes in the air with her other hand and spoke words of power. Thorfinn's bonds fell away.

He rubbed his wrists for a moment, reluctant to do what he'd promised. Both of Thokk's hands again rested on his son's shoulders near the boy's slender neck.

"With but a thought I can make your son scream," Thokk said, "perhaps blind him for life, paralyze him, twist his face into a mask of horror. . . ."

Thorfinn took Valgerth's arm and led her to the wall.

"Don't do it!" Huld cried. "Don't give in! Try to overpower her!"

"Would you have their children suffer?" Thokk asked Huld.

"There isn't any choice, Huld," Thorfinn explained. "There hasn't been any choice since Eirik's Vale fell."

"They destroyed it all, Huld," Valgerth said numbly as Thorfinn removed her ropes and clamped the manacles on her wrists to hold her arms above her head against the wall. "Kovna and his army, along with Thokk and her Death Riders, attacked and destroyed it all. Everyone is dead except we four and Freyadis, who may well be dead by now too."

Huld groaned. It was worse than she had imagined. And with Norda also dead there no longer seemed to be any hope at all. She could well understand Thorfinn's and Valgerth's surrender to the inevitable.

"I didn't know," she said to them, watching as Thorfinn now clamped manacles around his own wrists, the locks clicking with a sharp finality as they snapped into place. "But we can't give up all hope. Bloodsong may yet live. She may—"

Thokk's laughter cut her off. "Tell the Freya-slut how you last saw Bloodsong."

Neither Valgerth nor Thorfinn spoke.

Thokk's hands moved closer to Yngvar's neck. Thora whirled around and started to kick at Thokk's legs. Thokk hissed a word of power. Thora screamed and fell unconscious to the floor.

"Thora!" Valgerth cried.

"She's not badly harmed," Thokk assured them. "And now I believe that one of you was going to tell Huld about Bloodsong?"

"Freyadis was tied to the death tree," Valgerth quietly said. "Kovna and his army were standing guard, waiting for her to die slowly."

Huld did not reply, struggled to keep the last of her determination to resist alive, to believe that there still might be hope.

"And now let me tell you why I brought you to my castle," Thokk said, smiling coldly at Valgerth and Thorfinn. "Guthrun is being taught to see things . . . differently. When her awakening to her true self is completed, I shall have her kill the two of you as proof of her allegiance to Hel."

"And our children?" Thorfinn asked.

"I will not kill them. You can die knowing that your cooperation saved their lives. After you're dead they will stay on here as my servants."

"Your slaves, you mean," Valgerth growled.

"My *servants*. If they please me, I will in time let them do other things, give them more responsibility. They might eventually aid Hel in her struggle for domination over the Earth."

"Better you should kill them," Thorfinn whispered.

Yngvar began to whimper.

"Of course," Thokk continued, "if you should choose to die Hel-praying, you can return to ride by their side and help in Hel's coming conquests."

"Never," Valgerth quietly said. "Hel will not get my soul."

"Oh? But you're wrong," Thokk countered. "The souls of all those who die in my castle are Hel's to do with as she pleases. Didn't you know?"

Thokk laughed at their expressions, then she spoke a word of power, touching Yngvar's head. The small boy slumped to the ground and lay still.

"Merely a sleep spell," Thokk assured his parents.

The sound of heavy footsteps grew louder, and the air became colder. Huld tensed in her chains, recognizing Vafthrudnir's approach.

The Jotun entered the cell and frowned down at the humans within it.

"Take the children to their rooms," Thokk ordered.

Thorfinn and Valgerth strained against their chains as the Jotun lifted the children from the floor.

"You shall not see them again in this life," Thokk told Valgerth and Thorfinn as the Frost Giant carried the children from the cell. "I meant to let you say a last good-bye"—she smiled coldly—"but I have so many things on my mind that I forgot. You understand, I'm sure?"

Thokk walked to the wall and worked a mechanism to lower Huld's chains. The Freya-Witch groaned as her feet again touched the floor, pain shooting through her body. Thokk stopped the mechanism, walked nearer, traced runes in front of the bound woman, spoke words of power. Rays of purple light shot forth from Thokk's hands, bathed Huld's body, healing her wounds, restoring her strength. The glow faded. Huld's flesh was again whole, unmarked, her hands and feet no longer numb. She stood in her chains and stared into the Hel-Witch's eyes.

Thokk detected one of Huld's fleeting thoughts and laughed. "No, Huld," she said, "the healing spell did not give you back your hair. I have grown rather fond of you bald. However, if you should agree to become my student, I *do* have a spell that could make your golden tresses return. So I will ask you again before continuing your . . . persuasion: Will you become my student?"

Huld said nothing, merely stared defiantly at the Hel-Witch, her chin arrogantly raised.

"Your choice," Thokk said with a shrug, "but you're not going to enjoy what happens to you next. Think it over, Huld. As soon as Vafthrudnir returns I will have him take you to another chamber, a quiet place that will encourage you to think and change your mind. You have until he returns to prevent that from happening, to prevent a visit to the Chamber of Decay."

20
The Chamber of Decay

Huld felt stronger than she had since awakening in Thokk's castle. The healing spell had swept away her exhaustion and pain. Huld knew that Thokk meant her to be as receptive as possible to whatever new torments awaited. But she also knew from experience that a healing spell drained a great deal of a Witch's energy.

The Freya-Witch studied Thokk in the flickering torchlight. How much had the Hel-Witch been weakened by the healing spell? Enough to give Huld a chance against her in a duel of magic, should the opportunity arise?

The air grew colder as Vafthrudnir returned. Huld steeled herself, determined to watch for signs of weakness in the Hel-Witch. But when Vafthrudnir entered the cell, he ignored all but Thokk, bent low, and whispered in her ear.

Thokk's expression darkened. She cursed, turned, and strode from the chamber, motioning for the Jotun to follow.

"What could have happened?" Huld wondered aloud, relieved to have gained a respite.

"The Gods know," Thorfinn growled, pulling at his chains. "What a fool," he went on, "to have chained myself."

"For our children's sake you had no choice," Valgerth reminded him. "I did not struggle, either, when you chained me."

Thorfinn jerked on his chains in response.

"Huld," Valgerth said, "before Thokk comes back, I must tell you something. Freyadis told us that Thokk claims to have taken the corpse of her son. It's supposedly in this castle and has been made to grow older. Is such a thing possible?"

"For a Hel-Witch like Thokk, practiced in death magic, yes, it is possible. But why would she want to do it?"

"To awaken him and have him lead Hel's Death Riders," Thorfinn answered.

"And Guthrun is to become a Hel-Witch," Valgerth added.

Huld nodded. "As am I, if I give in, which, Freya willing, I won't. And I doubt Guthrun will, either, unless..."

"Unless?"

"As you know, Norda and I were just starting to teach Guthrun the ways of Freya's magic. But I sensed something dark in Guthrun, a slumbering power. I did not have time to discover more, had hoped to teach her how to control it before telling her about it. Norda was worried about it too. We attributed it to the first six years of Guthrun's life spent in Helheim. If that power is stronger than Guthrun's will to resist, Thokk might indeed succeed in turning her into a pawn of Hel."

"Tell me what happened," Thokk ordered, looking down at Kovna's unconscious form on her throne room floor.

Styrki drew himself to his full height and pushed down his fear of Thokk as best he could. "General Kovna was wounded trying to prevent Bloodsong's escape. He had us return here, to you, knowing that you had the power to heal wounds. I fear he will die if you do not help."

"Bloodsong escaped?"

"Yes, Mistress Thokk."

"Unfortunate, but of more importance to Kovna than to me. She could, however, cause problems later, after her children are serving Hel, so I will send Death Riders to slay her," she decided, and turned to go.

"Wait!" Styrki called, his tone more commanding than he'd intended.

Thokk whirled on him, anger glinting in her green eyes.

"The general needs your help," Styrki said, holding his voice steady, fear clutching at him.

"Let him die," she said, laughing. "*You* can lead his men."

"The men are loyal to General Kovna. Not to me."

"Kovna's so-called army is nothing but a gang of thieves. They will follow you."

Anger pushed away some of Styrki's fear. "The men with whom I serve General Kovna are honorable warriors for the most part. If some were once thieves, it was to survive in the aftermath of Nidhug's fall. Many served the general before the collapse of Nidhug's power and serve him again now. Their loyalty is *only* to him. They will desert if the general does not live, myself included. None wish to serve *you*."

Some of the anger drained from Thokk's face as she probed Styrki's thoughts and learned that he was speaking the truth. "Very well. I will heal him. I could force his men to stay in my service with magic, but it is not worth the effort if there is an easier way, and a healing spell drains less energy." *Though two in such a short time will weaken me more than I prefer*, she added in her thoughts.

She traced runes in the air over Kovna's body, concentrated her will, and spoke words of power. Purple rays from her outstretched hands bathed Kovna's body. Within moments his head wound was healed. He opened his eyes and saw Thokk standing over him.

She turned and strode away without a word.

Styrki squatted by Kovna's side. "She did not want to heal you, General, curse her," Styrki told him. "But she still needs your army, and I was able to change her mind."

Kovna nodded, sat up, and tore the bloodstained bandage from his head. "My thanks, Captain, for bringing me here after I lost consciousness on the trail. And for convincing her to heal my wound."

"She is going to send Death Riders to find and slay Bloodsong."

"I had wished a slower death for Bloodsong," Kovna replied, "but I will comfort myself that Thokk's magic shall find her where I could not and that the Death Riders will execute her for me." He got to his feet. "I will speak to the men now, show them that I'm all right. We will rest here in the castle for now. I don't trust Thokk. I want to stay near her, study her. If she's keeping secrets from me, I want to find out what they are before they can bring us harm."

Kovna walked from the castle into the courtyard where his warriors were uneasily waiting.

"Care for your horses and yourselves," Kovna commanded. "And," he added softly so that only Styrki could hear, "pass the word to listen and watch and report anything of importance to me at once."

Guthrun's eyes had closed again, and again a familiar voice had called her name. She opened her eyes. Orm again stood before her, now bearing ghastly wounds.

"You caused this to happen to me," he accused, tears streaking his decay-ravaged face. "You caused Hel to punish me."

Guthrun nodded. "Yes. I am sorry. But it won't happen again. I have decided to cooperate."

"You will have to prove it."

"I know."

"Thokk will ask you to kill the prisoners, Valgerth and Thorfinn."

"I will do it."

Orm studied her expression. She seemed sincere, but it was not long ago that she had seemed determined to fight stubbornly on.

"I'm not stupid, Orm. I could keep on fighting, but for what? Sooner or later I'm bound to break. No one can go without sleep and food and maintain the strength to fight. Better to give in now and save my friends in Helheim further pain. Can you open the door of this room, Orm? Open it if you can, and we will go in search of Thokk to tell her the news."

Orm began to vanish; within moments he was gone.

Guthrun remained seated on the bed, waiting. The next move was Thokk's.

"Take her to the Chamber of Decay," Thokk said, watching as Vafthrudnir unchained Huld's ankles. New spell-imbued manacles were then clamped around her ankles before her wrists were freed. Several links of hobbling chains joined the ankle manacles, which, unlike the manacles she had worn till now, would require a key to open, the key the Jotun was using to lock them on.

"You will never be free of spell-chains," Thokk explained, "until you agree to let me teach you the ways of Hel. And in addition, the hobbling chain on your ankles will prevent you from running very fast should you be foolish enough to try."

Vafthrudnir slipped a length of heavy, rusted chain around Huld's slim waist and locked it in place so tightly that it became hard for her to take a deep breath. Behind her, attached to the waist chain, hung spell-imbued manacles on short lengths of glossy black spell-chains. Then the Jotun freed her wrists, violently twisted her arms behind her back, locked her wrists into the waiting manacles, and roughly lifted her from the floor until her naked form hung doubled over his massive, icy-skinned shoulder.

"Don't injure her," Thokk ordered the Jotun. "You've already had your revenge for Thrym's death."

She has not suffered nearly enough, Vafthrudnir thought to himself, but said nothing as he carried Huld from the cell and turned to descend the stairs.

Thokk took a torch from a wall bracket and began to follow, but suddenly stopped and stood frowning thoughtfully. Into her mind had come Hel's voice, telling her that Guthrun had agreed to cooperate. *I expected her to resist longer*, Thokk mused. *It's no doubt a trick, but I will probe her thoughts and find out soon enough, once Huld is enjoying her next ordeal.*

Down and down they descended over crumbling stone stairs, breaking through spiderwebs as they went, the silken strands clinging to the Jotun and to Huld.

The Freya-Witch was struggling hard to keep her fear under control, determined not to shame herself in front of Thokk. She concentrated on remembering the signs of weakness and fatigue she'd detected in the Hel-Witch when Thokk had returned to the cell. Whatever had called Thokk away had obviously drained even more of her energy. *If only there was a way to get free of these spell-chains*, Huld thought, *I would gather all the strength at my command and attack while she is yet weak and I am still strong.*

Huld tugged hopelessly at the chains that held her wrists behind her back, desperately trying to think of a plan to get free.

There were no longer any passageways leading off from the stairway. The spiderwebs were even thicker now, the stairs more crumbling, the walls pressing closer together. The Jotun bent low as he carried Huld deeper and deeper beneath the castle of Thokk, occasionally, painfully scraping her bare skin against the low ceiling and walls as if by accident.

The cold air grew more and more stale with the stench of decay. Then suddenly the stairs leveled out and the passageway dead-ended at a closed door, its iron-banded wooden surface covered with thick layers of spiderwebs.

Thokk spoke words of power. The lock clicked. Vafthrudnir used his foot to shove the door open, bent lower, and carried Huld inside.

Huld gagged at the stench of decay, the smell overpowering, making it nearly impossible for her to breathe.

Thokk did not enter the chamber, but from the passageway the flickering light of her torch revealed a large chamber containing mounds of countless corpses in various stages of decay. The dirt floor was alive with crawling things. Rats, their eyes red in the torchlight, looked up from their grim feasts and glared at the intruders.

Vafthrudnir stood Huld on the floor. She reflexively cringed as the crawling things tickled her bare feet, but kept herself from giving Thokk the pleasure of seeing her futilely try to escape their touch.

"This is the deepest chamber in my castle," Thokk said from the passageway, her breath frosty in the icy air, "a place for the forgotten Dead. It is very quiet here. A good place for thinking. And since you have much thinking to do..."

Thokk motioned to Vafthrudnir. "Lock her in," she ordered.

The Jotun moved to stand with his hand on the door, grinning with satisfaction at the spectacle of Huld standing chained nude among the mounds of rotting flesh, the horror in her eyes giving her emotions away though she stood with chin held high, keeping all expression from her face. Some of the crawling things were already climbing her bare legs.

"Promise not to let me forget that she's down here," Thokk urged Vafthrudnir, then nodded for him to close the door. The Jotun gave Huld one last grin and obeyed.

Hinges creaked as the door closed, shutting out all light. The lock clicked. Then Thokk and Vafthrudnir started back up the stairs, laughing together, leaving the naked Freya-Witch alone in the decay-ridden dark.

21
Lokith

As soon as the closed door shut her from Thokk's sight, Huld began trying to dislodge the things crawling on her legs. The hobbling chains kept her from kicking, but by stamping first one foot and then the other, she finally managed to shake what felt like most of them off, though others immediately began to take their place.

She began cautiously walking in the total darkness, hoping that by moving around she might keep more of the crawling things off, but the chains on her ankles, clanking mockingly as she moved, forced her to move so slowly and to take such short steps that she found it necessary to stamp her feet every few paces to keep the crawling things from climbing higher than her calves.

How long will she leave me here? she wondered, fighting a rising panic. With every step she felt soft bodies squish beneath the soles of her bare feet. She breathed shallowly to take as little of the filthy air into her lungs as possible. How long could she keep walking? How long could she stay awake? She shuddered at the thought of falling asleep in that place, of lying unconscious upon that floor....

135

But I am freer than before, she told herself. *I can move around. I'm not in pain, not injured, and thanks to the healing spell, my exhaustion is gone. If only I could get free of these spell-chains while Thokk is still weakened from healing me....*

Some of the corpses I saw in the torchlight still wore clothing, she remembered. *Perhaps some still have a weapon upon them, a dagger or sword, something I could use to force open these manacles.*

Huld's mind rebelled at the thought of searching the decaying corpses in the darkness, but it was the only chance she had, and she intended to force herself to take it.

She moved carefully forward until her foot touched cold, rigid flesh, then, her heart racing with repulsion, she squatted down and tried to reach the mound of corpses with her bound hands. But it soon became evident that with her hands chained behind her, the only way she could reach the bodies was to go onto her knees and sit on her heels with her back to the decaying things.

Defying her repulsion and fear, she slowly knelt on the floor and tried to ignore the feel of the crawling things that immediately began swarming over her thighs....

With a cry of disgust Huld struggled madly back to her feet, shook her legs, and stamped her feet as best she could, to get rid of the crawling horrors.

I must kneel, she told herself when the spasm of repulsion had begun to recede slightly. *I must search. It's my only chance. Let them crawl all over me. It won't matter if I succeed in getting free. I have felt no bites. Perhaps they are harmless to the living, are interested only in dead flesh.*

She slowly made herself kneel again and felt the crawling things swarm up her thighs once more.

The naked Freya-Witch pushed down panic, forcing herself to remain on her knees, to sit back on her heels, to reach back to the mound of corpses.

Her questing fingers found cold, bare flesh instead of clothing. She moved on her knees until she could touch a different corpse in the mound but again found only decaying nakedness, the skin so rotten that her fingers suddenly broke through into a mass of squirming maggots beneath.

Choking back tears and gagging with revulsion, Huld moved on to the next corpse, and then to the next and the next, panting with disgust at the things she was touching in the darkness.

The crawling things were now swarming over her upper body, and as she continued the search, some finally reached her face.

Even a piece of metal like a belt buckle might help spring the manacles, she thought desperately, forcing her hands to touch dead flesh again and again and again. Something crawled over her lips and tried to force entry into her mouth. She frantically shook her head back and forth, whimpering deep in her throat, and finally felt the thing fall away from her lips.

Tears of rage and horror streaking her face, the Freya-Witch hesitated, fought to calm herself, to force down the panic that sought to make her scream and scream and scream. Then, her nakedness now covered with crawling, questing horrors, she moved on her knees to the next mound of death and began another search, wallowing in decay, determined to somehow thwart Thokk's plans and gain revenge for all she was being forced to endure.

"I can detect your thoughts, Guthrun," Thokk said, "and I know what you're planning. It won't work. You can't fool me with lies."

"And you can't break me with sleeplessness and lack of food!" Guthrun shouted, overwhelmed with anger that Thokk had so easily detected the trick she'd carefully planned.

"I think it is time you met your brother," Thokk decided after a brief pause.

"My brother is dead."

"More or less." Thokk smiled. "But with your help he can awaken to new life."

"I will make a deal with you," Guthrun said, stalling. "Free Huld, Valgerth, Thorfinn, and their children and I will promise to cooperate. Let them go."

"No, Guthrun. I won't make deals with you, except to give you a promise. Come with me willingly now and do not try to escape or I will instruct Vafthrudnir to torture Huld again."

"Again? What have you done to her!"

"She's not injured now. I performed a healing spell, and at present she is enjoying a restful interlude in a quiet place. But if you do not follow me to your brother willingly . . ."

"I will go with you," Guthrun decided. "For Huld, I must."

Thokk unlocked the door to Guthrun's room and stepped into the hall. Guthrun followed.

"Remember, Guthrun," Thokk warned, "make any attempt to get away or harm me, and Huld will suffer."

Guthrun said nothing, merely stalked along in silence as the Hel-Witch led the way, her head throbbing with pain, her body weak from lack of food and sleep.

Some while later Thokk stopped in front of a closed door. They had descended far into the castle's depths. Thokk held a torch to one side and looked thoughtfully at Guthrun.

"I am the only one who has entered this chamber for the past thirteen years, Guthrun. Your brother lies within, fully grown, a handsome young man in his middle teens. He is special, Guthrun, just as you are special to Mother Hel and to me."

"Hel is *not* my mother. Repeating it over and over makes no difference. *Bloodsong* is my mother."

"Bloodsong gave birth to you, Guthrun. I will not deny that. But she did not give new life to you after you died in her womb, and Hel is ever the Mother of the Dead."

"I didn't die. Bloodsong did, but—"

"But she told you that you had not?" Thokk asked with a sad, understanding look on her face.

Guthrun's head was aching even worse. It was becoming harder and harder for her to think clearly. She wondered if it were only exhaustion and weakness muddling her thoughts or if Thokk might be working some spell.

"You *did* die, Guthrun. Hel gave you *new* life, just as she did Bloodsong. She *is* your true mother. And slumbering within you are dark powers aching to be used. The same is true of your brother, Lokith."

"His name is Thorbjorn, Eirik's son, no matter what you've done to his corpse. And I have no special powers. I . . ."

Guthrun slumped against the wall, head spinning, nausea flooding through her.

Thokk steadied her until the wave of weakness passed, then she unlocked and pushed open the door, stepped inside, and beckoned Guthrun to follow.

Within the chamber Guthrun saw the naked body of a handsome young man lying on a dais. Slowly she walked closer, noticing how like her own were his features. But his hair was blond, not black.

"Your father had blond hair," Thokk said. "You never saw your father, of course, but I did once. Lokith looks much like him, could nearly be his twin."

"But . . . he is dead. He's not breathing. And how can this be my brother? He was . . . only a young child when—"

"Hel's powers flow through me, Guthrun. I healed his decayed flesh. I gave him energy of my own, caused him to grow and develop. Could Norda Greycloak have performed a wonder such as you see before you? No, she could not. But I have! And in time, with my help and guidance, you will be capable of even greater wonders, Guthrun. Think of it! Great power sleeps within you, the Coils of Old Night waiting to be awakened, to be trained, used, wielded by you, Guthrun. *By you*!

"You've felt the pull of your true self. That is why you wanted to study Witchcraft. But it is not Freya's magic for which you lust. It is Hel's! I speak the truth, Guthrun. And as proof of the power within you, the first wonder you shall perform is to bring your brother to life. Even *I* cannot do that. Only your first woman's blood has that power because of who and what you are, a Deadborn, a chosen child of your true mother, Hel, a child born in Helheim of a woman who had herself died."

"My first . . . blood?"

"Yes, Guthrun. And I can cause that to happen whenever desired. It will happen soon now, anyway, but I can hasten its arrival. You need only ask, and once your blood has begun to flow, but a single drop placed upon your brother's lips will awaken him, cause life to flood through him, make his heart start to beat and his lungs to pump air. Only you can do that for him, Guthrun. Only you. Only your blood."

"The dead should—"

"Stay dead?" Thokk completed. "A strange thing for you to say. Would you prefer Hel never to have given Bloodsong and yourself new life? Hel is the Goddess of Death. She takes Life. But, if she desires, she can also restore life to those from whom it has been taken. Will you deny your brother new life, Guthrun? Do you have that right, when it is within your power to do otherwise? If I gave you a dagger, would you use it to slit his throat?"

"No . . . I . . ."

"Accept the truth, Guthrun," Thokk urged. "Accept that you are one of Hel's most precious treasures, a Deadborn, destined to help lead Hel's conquests at your brother's side."

"No! I won't accept it! If I were so precious to her, Hel would not have let me go. She would have kept me a prisoner in Helheim. You would not have to use trickery and lies to gain my cooperation now. I would have known nothing but what Hel wanted me to know."

"Hel *wanted* you to spend these years among the living," Thokk assured her. "Your years in the sunshine make you even more valuable to her. You have learned and experienced many things that will aid you in leading her conquests. You now know the weaknesses of the living and have slumbering within you the strengths of the Dead. No, Guthrun, your years away from Helheim are only further proof that all I've told you is true. Accept your destiny, Deadborn Daughter of Hel! Accept the truth! At long last let your soul be at peace with the truth."

A moan of horror bubbled from Guthrun's lips.

Victory glinted in Thokk's eyes as she sensed the last of Guthrun's mental defenses beginning to crumble.

Guthrun's vision dimmed, her head pounding as if about to explode. She slumped onto her knees, gripped the edge of the dais, then slipped unconscious to the floor.

Thokk looked down at her and smiled. *You were as strong as I'd hoped*, she thought, *perhaps even stronger. But the battle is finally over. You don't know it consciously yet, but you are now indeed Hel's, and you are mine.*

22
Waveslasher

Bloodsong and Grimnir sat atop their horses at the crest of a sandy hill and looked out over the horizon-spanning sea. Morning sunlight sparkled upon the surface of the blue water. Bloodsong turned to Grimnir, wonder in her eyes. "I've never seen its like before," she admitted, looking back at the sea. "It's beautiful but also a little unsettling."

Grimnir nodded, remembering the first time he'd seen that vast expanse of water as a child. "You've done deeds that shall be told and retold long after your passing," he said, "and yet you have never before seen the sea. I am glad I could be by your side for your first sight of Aegir's rooftop."

"Ah, yes. Aegir. I suppose many who live near the sea invoke the Sea God's name."

"And that of his wife, Ran, who catches humans in her net and pulls them down into her coral caves."

"She'll not drag *me* down in her net," Bloodsong replied. "You promised a longship, Grimnir. I see no ship."

"It's not far from here."

"Then let's be on our way. The days we've ridden to get

here seemed to take forever. I hope the voyage to the Berserkers' Isle will be as quick and easy as you have promised."

Grimnir angled his horse away from the beach toward an inlet marked by a thick stand of trees.

Within the trees stood several dwellings, and in the still, deep waters of the secluded inlet rode a longship.

"She stands ready for this year's raiding," Grimnir told Bloodsong. "Her name is *Waveslasher*. I've lived on her decks more than once."

"We two cannot handle such a large ship alone," she commented, eyeing the sleek craft.

"We won't have to," Grimnir replied, then dismounted and roared a greeting.

"Ho! Magnus! Come and greet your old swordmate!"

Bloodsong dismounted, ready to draw her sword, suspicious of the situation until she had reason to feel otherwise.

A huge, barrel-chested, blond-bearded man emerged from a longhouse and bellowed a return greeting as he hurried toward them.

"Come to go raiding with us again?" Magnus asked as he clapped Grimnir on the back. "It's been too long, Grimnir!"

Magnus looked at Bloodsong. "Who is this woman you've brought with you? A companion for my wife while we are away on *Waveslasher*?"

Bloodsong held Magnus's gaze. "I am Bloodsong. I need your ship."

Magnus laughed. "And, of course, I'll just give it to you! A woman!" He laughed again. "Another of your fine jokes, Grimnir? You were always a great one for playing jokes!"

The look on Grimnir's face stilled Magnus's laughter. "We have just come from Eirik's Vale," Grimnir said. "Kovna came, and a sorceress, the Hel-Witch, Thokk. Eirik's Vale was destroyed, all the inhabitants massacred. Did you not hear this woman's name, man? She is Bloodsong. *Bloodsong*! Treat her with the respect a warrior such as she deserves!"

Magnus looked back at Bloodsong. "I meant no disrespect," he told her with a return glance to Grimnir. "Grimnir always liked to play jokes. I had friends who lived in Eirik's Vale, though I never visited there. Are you certain that everyone—"

"Kovna left no one alive save Bloodsong and four others," Grimnir assured him, "and she was also meant to die, but I and two of her friends managed to free her. Now we need aid, and your ship is the way to obtain it. Will you and your crew take us to the Berserkers' Isle on *Waveslasher*?"

Magnus hesitated, looking doubtful.

"Thokk serves the Goddess Hel," Bloodsong told him. "She plans to spread Hel's darkness and ice over all the Earth. What happened at Eirik's Vale will happen everywhere. No one will be safe. I am not asking you and your crew to fight Thokk's sorcery. I intend to ask the Berserkers to do that. We hope that Odin's magic within them will be a protection against the Hel-Witch's magic. Take us to the island and you will have done much to fight Hel's plans."

"Some say," Magnus replied, "that Ran, Goddess of the Sea, is the God Loki's sister. And Hel is Loki's daughter."

"Aye," Grimnir agreed. "Hel and Ran are kin. But we've defied them both many times before, Magnus. Each time a warrior enters a battle or boards a ship, Death is being risked. If you won't help us, I'll have to talk with Njal...."

"Njal's ship is a rotten pile of timber," Magnus growled.

"True," Grimnir grinned, "while *Waveslasher* is the finest ship ever to skim Aegir's rooftop."

Magnus thought a moment more, then laughed. "I thought I'd never return to the Berserkers' Isle. Do you suppose," he added in a whisper with a glance back at the dwelling where his wife waited, "that Zara might still remember me? Understand," he quickly added to Bloodsong, "that I was younger then. I had not met Ulla, my wife. And, well..."

"Berserker women make love the same way they fight," Grimnir explained, winking at Bloodsong. "Magnus thought he was going to die the next morning."

Magnus laughed at the memory.

"When you two are finished telling old tales," Bloodsong

said, "could you trouble yourselves to make ready to sail? Each moment wasted is another which my daughter spends in Thokk's clutches."

Magnus's and Grimnir's smiles faded. "We can be ready to sail by morning," Magnus said.

"By this afternoon," Grimnir corrected.

Magnus started to protest, saw the look on Bloodsong's face, and changed his mind.

"By this afternoon," he agreed, and hurried off to begin preparations.

The mountain reared skyward into boiling black clouds. Thunder rumbled and lightning flashed incessantly around the cloud-enshrouded summit. Though it was near noon, the land was bathed in a twilight gloom, save for the moments when the blinding whiteness of the lightning seared the Earth. Nearer the base of the peak, rain fell in torrents.

"No one could live atop that mountain," Jalna said skeptically, " not even someone called the Keeper of the Lightning's Blood."

"The tales say that the summit is *above* the clouds," Tyrulf replied. "But in order to get there you have to climb through that tempest."

"Skadi curse Thokk and Kovna and all people like them," Jalna growled. "Most people could happily live together in peace, save for the greedy ones who lust for power and more riches than they can ever use."

"And save for those who anxiously follow such leaders," Tyrulf added. "But if not for their kind, Jalna, warriors such as you and I would have to find other work."

"I was not always a warrior," Jalna reminded him. "I became one to make certain that I would never again be made a slave. If not for the Nidhugs and Kovnas and Thokks of this world, I would never have been a slave to begin with."

Thunder crashed overhead.

"Freya's Mound is supposed to be near the base of the mountain, according to the tale you told me," Jalna remembered.

"The drunken warrior who told me of this place said people came here only to worship," he reminded her, "but we'd be fools not to keep watch for danger."

"Aye," Jalna agreed, loosening her sword in its scabbard, "and people who worship here might not approve of our taking away any magic we find."

"No," Tyrulf agreed, "that they might not."

Neither Tyrulf nor Jalna had expected the mound to look as it did. Each had seen grave mounds before, some quite large, towering many times a person's height. But the earthen mound looming before them was massive beyond their imaginings, and high atop it grew an ancient tree, branches spreading protectively over the top of the mound, limbs heavy with leaves, gnarled roots thrusting deep into the mound's rich, black soil.

Three figures stood atop the mound, looking down at Jalna and Tyrulf. One of them beckoned.

"I suppose we should dismount," Jalna said. "We are here to obtain Freya's help, not to insult her and make her our enemy, too, by riding horses to the summit."

"I doubt I'll be allowed to approach," Tyrulf said. "Remember, I was told that only women could worship here."

"We're not here to worship."

Tyrulf nodded. "I will come as far with you as I can. Those three atop the mound are all women," he noted. "They could be the three Norns the way they stand there staring down at us, spinning our fate as we watch."

Jalna and Tyrulf dismounted and tied their horses' reins to stout bushes nearby.

Jalna's eyes met his. She surprised him with a smile and again by touching his hand. "If we die here today, Tyrulf, know that I am grateful for your helping and that I no longer think you are planning a trick. I do not return the feelings of affection you have for me, but—"

"But you may in time?"

Jalna removed her hand from his. "I make no promises."

"My thanks for the smile, the first you've given me."

"But, perhaps, not the last?" she asked, smiling again.

Tyrulf laughed. "Aye, Freya willing. Aye."

They moved forward, reached the base of the mound, and began to climb a pathway that spiraled around the earthen site toward the top. A thick carpet of green grass covered the mound. Brightly colored wildflowers grew everywhere in defiance of the gloomy, storm-ridden skies overhead.

The mound was far enough away from the mountains so that no rain fell upon it, but windblown spray from the nearby tempest filled the air, chilling exposed flesh, while moisture soon collected upon clothing and weapons.

When they reached the top of the mound, the three women there came forward to greet them. All stood naked beneath flowing green cloaks, the hoods thrown back, the aura of power strong around them. One was a girl on the brink of womanhood, one a mature woman, one a crone. "They look even more like the Norns close-up," Tyrulf whispered to Jalna, a chill of superstitious dread flashing along his spine.

"Aye," Jalna agreed, tensed as if for battle.

"We are but reflections of the true Norns," the mature woman said. "Freya has made your quest known to us. You seek her aid against Hel. If you dare enter the mound, and if you survive the dangers there, you may possibly win the aid you seek."

"You say Freya has told you of our mission," Jalna said suspiciously, "but perhaps Thokk's sorcery is at work here. You could be in her employ, or demons sent to trick us."

"Yes. We could be. It is up to you to decide. But know this: If you decide to enter the mound, you must do so without weapons. Your trust in us must be that complete before the Earth will receive you into this, its womb."

Jalna looked at Tyrulf. He shrugged. "Thokk could have attacked before this," he said, "if she knew of our quest. So I assume she does not. But as to whether we can trust these three . . ."

"Do we have a choice, Tyrulf? I suppose that if we used our swords on them, we would never find the entrance."

"You would not live to do us harm should you try," the crone assured them.

"But it would take you a long time to die," the girl promised.

"Freya protects we three," the mature woman explained, "the guardians of her sacred site."

"I am no enemy of Freya's," Jalna told them, "though Skadi is the Goddess I call upon most often."

She hesitated a moment longer, then reached up and began to unstrap her sword and shield. "And may he come with me?" Jalna asked as she reluctantly laid her sword and shield on the ground.

"He not only may, he *must*, if the two of you are to find what you seek."

"In that case..." Tyrulf said, then finished by unstrapping his weapons and laying them on the ground beside Jalna's.

23
Freya's Mound

The three women motioned for Jalna and Tyrulf to follow them. They led the way over the grass, circling behind the massive trunk of the ancient tree. Then they stopped and turned to face the two warriors.

"Weapons of steel would not have aided you within the mound, even had they been allowed," the mature woman assured them. She caught Tyrulf's gaze. "You are the first man to enter the mound in many lifetimes. Even if the woman survives, you may not. Will you still go?"

"You said that I must, if we are to find the aid we seek. I am going. What form will Freya's aid take? For what will we be looking? I've heard that there is a golden nugget. Is that our goal?"

"I cannot say."

"Cannot or will not?"

"It's all the same to you, since either way you'll not be told. Understand, both of you, that Freya is ever Hel's enemy. Though Freya leads the Choosers of the Slain and claims half the dead killed in battle, she is first a champion of Life. I wish you

149

victory within the mound, but if you fail, Freya will in time find others to aid her in the struggle against Hel's plans for conquest, plans which you aided," she said accusingly to Jalna, "by helping the warrior Bloodsong return the War Skull to Hel."

"Freya should have stopped us then," Jalna accused back, "or Odin, or any of Hel's enemies. But no God or Goddess did. I acted to revenge myself against Nidhug and to survive. Whether Hel regained the War Skull or not meant nothing to me . . . until now."

"Freya's not having acted to stop you does not mean she approved," the woman answered. "Your trial within the mound will be more severe because of your part in returning the War Skull."

"And is part of the test to see how long I'll listen to you talk?" Jalna asked, becoming impatient. She then cursed herself for speaking so disrespectfully to one whose good wishes she needed.

The woman smiled coldly. "Very well, since you are so anxious to meet your fate, I'll delay you no longer."

The three women walked to a circle of blood-red flowers that formed a ring in the green grass nearby. They joined hands in a circle around the ring of flowers and began to chant a phrase in the lilting tongue Jalna had often heard Huld use to perform Freya's magic.

From deep within the Earth came a rumbling that made the ground vibrate beneath their feet. The women discarded their green cloaks and began to dance around the ring of flowers, holding hands, dancing slowly at first, then gradually faster and faster, the crone moving as smoothly and gracefully as her younger companions as the chanting and dancing went on and on.

Suddenly the grass within the circle collapsed into a narrow passageway leading down into darkness. The women stopped and stood, still and silent. Jalna glanced at Tyrulf. Their eyes met. He touched her hand and she did not draw away.

"Shall I be polite and let you go first?" he asked with a halfhearted laugh, "or shall I be heroic and lead the search?"

"The woman enters first," the mature woman said.

Jalna strode forward as the women stepped back. She stood on the edge of the opening and looked down. A tunnel from whose walls protruded countless roots yawned darkly. The rich scent of moist earth filled her nostrils. She looked back to the women. "Have any of you three been down there?" she asked.

All three laughed in response.

"What are your names? I want to know them."

They laughed again.

"We will need light," Jalna continued, after a pause in which she controlled her anger and the first hints of fear. "A torch."

Three heads shook negatively amid more laughter.

"Perhaps," Tyrulf said, coming up beside her, "we should forget Freya's aid and start climbing the mountain. Thor's aid may be more easily obtained, after all. This mound and that passageway chills me deeply, and I don't care who knows it."

"I don't relish it, either," Jalna replied, "but I'm going in, unless . . ."

She looked thoughtfully at the three women. "If you serve Freya, and Freya wants to aid us against Hel, why don't you three simply come with us? I assume you all wield magic? You could help us defeat Thokk's sorcery. Perhaps there is no aid within the mound. Perhaps you three are the aid we've come seeking."

The three women laughed yet again. "Leave the mound?" the youngest asked incredulously.

"Easier should the tree leave the mound than we," the crone added.

"Cursed Witches," Jalna said under her breath as she sat down on the grass and swung her legs over the edge into the opening, deciding that she might as well get started before her fear grew any stronger.

"Just one more thing," the mature woman said. "In your impatience to seek your fate I forgot to tell you that you must enter the mound naked. Otherwise you will die at once, buried alive in the darkness below."

Jalna got back to her feet and approached the woman. "I

think you are enjoying this too much," she growled. "Why must we be naked? It's bad enough to voluntarily enter a place of danger without weapons, but to have to do so naked?"

"Save for Brisingamen, her necklace, has anyone ever seen Freya clothed?" the crone asked.

"Has anyone ever seen Freya at all?" Tyrulf grumbled.

"Many times," the girl assured him.

"The opening will close soon," the mature woman told them, "and cannot be reopened for one lunar cycle. Strip naked and enter now, or return to your horses and ride away."

"How will we get out if it won't open again for a month?" Jalna asked.

"There are many ways out of the mound but only this one way in."

Cursing beneath their breath, Jalna and Tyrulf quickly removed their clothes, and then Jalna, leading the way, squeezed into the cold, damp passageway and crawled downward into the Earth. Moments later the opening overhead rumbled shut, leaving them in darkness.

"Many's the time I've wanted to be alone with you naked," Tyrulf commented as he crawled on through the dark. "Shall we stop for a moment and make love?"

Jalna ignored him, kept moving downward, fighting a growing panic, a feeling that she was going to suffocate, be buried alive. Soon they were forcing their way through an ever-narrowing passageway, moist earth pressing closer and closer all around. Jalna heard soft whimpering, realized that it was coming from her own throat, clamped down on her fear, let anger push her muscles to work harder, and crawled on and on through the clinging, close-pressing earth.

The tunnel widened, leveled out. Jalna got to her feet, stood panting, her fear subsiding slightly as she wiped at the dirt clinging to her face and body. Beside her, Tyrulf was doing the same. It was several moments before they realized that they could see again, the earthen walls of the tunnel glowing with a dim green light.

They began to walk forward down the tunnel. It angled

downward, became warmer beneath their bare feet as they kept moving onward. The bare earthen walls began to harbor life until soon, everywhere they looked, they saw growing things in the dim green light, unidentifiable plants, unknown flowers. The warming air grew rich with exotic perfumes.

"How can they live without light?" Tyrulf wondered, studying the plants as he walked.

"They seem to produce their own light," Jalna said. "The green glow is coming, at least in part, from them."

Tyrulf looked closer and saw that she was right.

The warm, moist tunnel turned to the left. A dark opening yawned ahead. Cold air wafted from it, bringing gooseflesh to their bare skin.

Jalna looked closely at the walls, the dirt floor, the root-encrusted ceiling, and was not surprised to find no other opening but the dark one directly ahead.

She walked to the edge of the portal and stopped, hugging herself against the cold, the dirt beneath her bare feet no longer warm but deeply chilled.

"Perhaps," Tyrulf suggested, "Freya would not begrudge us some of these glowing plants to light our way?"

Jalna nodded, bent to start pulling up the glowing flowers, and suddenly stopped. "Wait!" she commanded.

Tyrulf's hand hovered a hair's breadth away from a flower.

"We must risk the dark," she said. "Remember what the woman said about Freya championing Life? I think it would be very dangerous and unwise to kill anything here, even a plant."

Tyrulf withdrew his hand as if from a serpent. He studied the dark opening. "Before we enter, perhaps you might reconsider my proposal to take a few moments to make love?"

"Always joking," Jalna said, eyeing the opening.

"Not entirely," he said, daring to touch her short-cut black hair. "Freya is the Goddess of Love, among other things, and being here with you is affecting me more strongly than usual."

"Than usual?" Jalna asked. "When have we been naked together before? It's just the sight of my exposed flesh that is affecting you, Tyrulf. Ignore it."

"And then I'll stop breathing, too, just for good measure."

Jalna glanced at him, shook her head and gave a quick smile, then concentrated on the darkness ahead. Experimentally she stretched out her foot into the opening and shivered with the cold. Suddenly something unseen in the darkness grabbed her ankle and jerked her through the portal.

"Jalna!" Tyrulf shouted, and hurried forward. The ground opened up beneath him. He plummeted downward, gasping for breath in the icy air, engulfed by total darkness. Faster and faster he fell, but he managed to draw enough air into his lungs to shout Jalna's name, and when he heard no response, he shouted her name again, expecting at any moment to smash into rocks at the bottom of the chasm into which he had fallen. But suddenly his environment changed.

He was surrounded by a thick, warm liquid, which glowed with a ghostly blue light. Serpentine shapes slithered past, ignoring him. He tried to swim through the clinging warmth, made but little progress, felt his lungs starving for air, and knew that if he didn't breathe soon, he would die.

Determinedly he kept swimming in the direction he hoped was upward, finally could hold out no longer, sucked warm liquid into his lungs, and found himself lying on a sandy beach, waves rolling in, bright yellow sunlight warming him from out of a clear blue sky. Of Jalna there was no sign.

Kicking and fighting, Jalna was dragged over rocky ground into a vast cavern. She recognized it at once, the Cavern of the War Skull in which Nidhug had tortured her. She told herself that it was a trick, could not be real, fought with all the skills and strength she possessed to stop the black-cloaked and -hooded men as they dragged her closer and closer to the towering War Skull with its waiting chains. A man with the face of a corpse stood to one side, holding a glowing green venom wand with which to sear and blacken her flesh.

They threw her at the feet of the corpse-faced man. For an instant fear paralyzed her as all her worst nightmares battered her consciousness, then, with a cry of outrage and denial that it should ever happen again, she sprang to her feet in a crouch, kicked out, jabbed her foot deep into the corpse-faced man's abdomen, grabbed away the venom wand he held, then whirled and swung it at the hooded ones.

The wand struck the nearest one. With a scream he burst into purple flames and fell writhing to the ground. Jalna side-stepped the rush of another hooded man, sent him sprawling, thrust with the wand, and found herself engulfed in icy water.

She clawed her way to the surface, breathed in huge gulps of air, saw a sun-drenched beach nearby and Tyrulf standing there. She began to swim, cursing Witches and magic and all the tricks that went with them. *And what was all that about?* she wondered. *Conquering my greatest fear? Proving that I really have changed? Really am strong and free? Proving to whom? To Freya? Or to myself?*

She came dripping from the water still cursing, relishing the warm sunlight after the icy water, and not even minding when Tyrulf embraced her, grateful for his warmth, too, until his embrace started to become something more. . . .

She pushed him away and pointed. "Over there," she said, staring at an earthen mound that was a twin of the one they had entered. At the top stood three figures, hooded in black robes. . . .

Like in the cavern, Jalna thought.

They began walking toward the mound, reached it, and hurried up the pathway to the top. The three black-robed ones were no longer there.

"Curse magic and magic-workers," Tyrulf complained.

Jalna nodded in complete agreement and walked to a ring of blood-red flowers near the trunk of the tree. "Even these are the same. Perhaps if we——" she began, but never finished as the ground suddenly erupted beneath her, skeletal arms emerging on all sides. Bony-fingered hands clawed at her legs, trying to pull her down into the Earth.

She fought to get free, but skeletal talons dug deeply into her flesh and held her fast.

Tyrulf rushed forward, grasped her hands, and began pulling back, desperate to free her. But then the ground gave way beneath them, and both fell into darkness, icy talons raking their flesh.

They cursed and struggled and screamed in rage and pain, felt blood pumping from torn veins and arteries, knew that they were going to die, kept struggling, anyway, feeling weaker by the moment, life ebbing from them in rivers of blood.

But then a new emotion entered their emptying veins, and they no longer felt skeletal hands clutching at their nakedness, but each other's instead, stroking, caressing, beckoning emotions of passion into flames within them, causing them to pant with their need for each other, their bodies demanding fulfillment, demanding that they cling to each other in hungry embraces, speaking each other's name over and over like a chant as they made frenzied love in the womb of the Earth.

When their passion was spent, they lay sweating in each other's arms, aware that their surroundings had changed again. In the distance a towering portal glowed with yellow-gold light.

Tyrulf gently stroked Jalna's sweat-soaked hair. "I warned you that Freya was a Goddess of Love," he said.

"And, in her way, of Death," Jalna added with a shudder. "Those skeletons, tearing at us . . . reminded me so much of . . ." Her voice trailed away.

Tyrulf nodded in understanding, remembering the Death Slaves with whom Nidhug had entombed Jalna.

"But that golden glow looks inviting," Tyrulf said, getting to his feet.

Jalna stood, and together they walked forward toward the towering entranceway. When they reached it, they found that through the opening they could see nothing but the light.

"And what will happen when we step across *this* threshold?" Jalna wondered aloud, then reached out and took Tyrulf's hand. "At least let's not be separated this time."

Together they stepped into the golden light and found themselves surrounded by nine fierce-eyed women in golden armor, gleaming swords and gilt-edged, falcon-embossed shields held ready. One of them tossed two swords and two shields to the golden floor at Jalna's and Tyrulf's feet.

"Valkyries?" Tyrulf whispered. "Freya is said to lead them, after all, when they make forays to battlefields to choose which of the dead are worthy of Valhalla and Folkvang."

"Old tales," Jalna growled, "and more Witch-tricks."

The warrior women were advancing upon them now, surrounding them.

"It would seem part of our test, however," she added as she picked up a sword and shield, "to prove our worth as fighters."

"Aye," agreed Tyrulf, doing the same.

"Bloodsong and freedom!" Jalna screamed, and attacked, Tyrulf by her side.

The nine women fought with weapon skills worthy of Goddesses, their speed and timing and precision awing Jalna even as she fought to defeat them.

On and on the battle raged, sweat streaming from Jalna's and Tyrulf's naked bodies, mingling with streaks of blood seeping from various minor wounds. Then at last Jalna saw an opening, blocked a cut with her shield, and thrust into a warrior's throat. But no blood came from the gaping wound, and the woman simply laughed, raised her sword in salute, then stepped back out of the fight.

Jalna and Tyrulf wearily fought on, beginning to tire, while the eight women who remained were still as strong and fast as when the battle had begun. Then suddenly a Valkyrie's sword cut deep into Jalna's left leg. She cursed at the pain and kept fighting but almost immediately received another serious cut in her side.

Tyrulf was faring little better, now bleeding from several deep wounds, his strength fading fast as more and more blood left his veins. He cursed with frustration, suddenly feeling as helpless as he once had when, as Nidhug's dungeon guard, there was no way to help Jalna escape her torture. Anger boiled through him, bringing a last reserve of strength from somewhere deep inside.

"Bloodsong and freedom!" he yelled, he directed a series of slashing cuts at the Valkyries before him, broke through one's guard and landed a savage cut downward through her collarbone, halfway to her breasts.

She smiled and saluted him then stepped back from the fight, her bloodless, ghastly wound healing, the flesh closing.

Then suddenly the rest of the warriors stepped back, too, saluting Jalna and Tyrulf with swords and smiles.

A rumbling sound filled the golden air. Jalna and Tyrulf stood sweating and panting, holding their swords and shields ready, expecting some new trick, blood pouring from their wounds, their strength rapidly waning.

The nine warriors vanished. In their place a sphere of yellow-gold light began to glow as the rumbling increased in volume to an ear-shattering roar.

Suddenly silence descended, and within the glowing sphere appeared a woman in a chariot drawn by two savage mountain cats. She was naked and breathtakingly beautiful, though little could be seen of her face, the glow too bright near her head to long suffer a direct gaze. Around her neck blazed a necklace of fiery jewels.

Tyrulf felt an overwhelming mingling of fear and sexual desire building within him, making his heart hammer faster and faster in his chest. Beside him, Jalna felt the same. Suddenly their wounds began to heal and their strength return. Within moments they were uninjured and feeling stronger than before the fight.

Their swords and shields vanished, and then, through the glow, they dimly glimpsed the woman smile, nod to them, and raise a golden spear in salute.

A rumbling flash of golden light engulfed them, and when, cursing and rubbing at their eyes, they were again able to see, they found themselves back atop the first mound, their horses calmly nibbling grass at the base, their clothing and weapons lying nearby. Of the three women there was no sign. Thunder crashed overhead, and a gust of wind blew cold rain onto their jnaked bodies.

"Freya," Tyrulf whispered, shaken, awed by the Goddess he had seen with the golden glow.

"Aye," Jalna replied, also whispering, also awed. Then she cursed. "Skadi's bow!" she exclaimed, stamping a foot in frustration. "Was it all for nothing? I thought we would undergo some severe test and then either die or find the aid we sought. But here we stand empty-handed, with nothing to show for our trouble! Nothing!"

Tyrulf shrugged. "Perhaps we will have better luck atop the mountain, if we can reach the summit. But I can't say that I entirely regret the journey we made together into the mound; certain parts of it, at least."

"And I can imagine just *which* parts." Jalna frowned at him, then her expression softened. She shook her head, reached out, and gently touched his face. "I won't forget, either," she softly added.

"I never thought I'd say this to you, Jalna," he said, smiling, "but can we get dressed now? It's cursed cold."

Jalna laughed and bent to her clothing. Soon both were again dressed, then reached for their weapons, but gave cries of surprise when they touched their scabbarded swords.

"My sword feels as if warmed in a fire!" Tyrulf exclaimed.

"Mine too," Jalna said as she cautiously drew her blade. The once smooth blade was now engraved with runes, and the polished steel seemed to give off more light than it received. She slammed the sword back into the scabbard with a curse.

"Mine is like yours," Tyrulf said, sheathing his sword too. "Perhaps we have received Freya's aid, after all?"

"Skadi knows I care little for the ways of Witches," Jalna growled, "whether they owe allegiance to Freya or to Hel. Why can't they do things ordinary folk can understand? No one is going to explain what happened here today. We're going to be left with our questions, the mysteries unsolved. And if those runes on our swords are meant to help us defeat Thokk, perhaps allow us to slay Death Riders, we will probably not know for certain until the moment of truth when we put them to the test."

"Perhaps just because we're out of the mound the testing may not be over," Tyrulf suggested. "Perhaps each time we draw these blades the test will continue."

"And perhaps we could spend the rest of our lives thinking

of other perhapses," Jalna complained. "Cursed Witches," she grumbled, and started off down the trail toward the horses. "I'm for the mountain."

"Aye," Tyrulf readily agreed, walking eagerly down the path by her side.

24
Berserkers' Isle

Bloodsong studied the rocky coastline of the island ahead. Squawking seabirds swooped low over a short stretch of sandy beach. On each side of the beach sheer cliffs reared skyward. The crashing of waves against the rocks grew more thunderous as they neared the isle.

"I once heard a Skald sing a tale of Odin and Thor," she said to Grimnir, who stood by her side watching their approach to the island. "Odin and Thor were trading insults," she went on, "and Odin accused Thor of a shameful act in killing women on some island. But Thor responded that those women were more she-wolves than humans, and that they had attacked his ship with iron clubs. He called them the Brides of the Berserkers."

"I would say that the Skald had been to the isle we approach," Grimnir commented. "But I doubt that *we'll* be attacked. They will recognize *Waveslasher* and know us for friends. Some of our crew stayed with them."

"They preferred she-wolves to ordinary women, I suppose," she suggested, "like your friend Magnus?"

"And like myself," Grimnir agreed. He grinned when Bloodsong stiffened slightly. "That's why I like you."

Bloodsong glanced sideways at him and smiled faintly.

Grimnir laughed, slid a hand around her shoulders, and squeezed her against him. "Are you concerned about the tests the Berserkers will set you?"

"What good would that do? My concern is to acquire aid and free Guthrun. I have not thought much about what sort of ordeals they will require me to survive. Personal combat with the leader perhaps? Or . . . what did you have to do, Grimnir?"

Grimnir looked into her eyes. "Before we were allowed to leave the island that time, we all took a vow not to reveal its existence unless in need of aid only Odin's Berserkers could give. And there was a second vow as well: never under any circumstances to reveal the sacred ordeals we underwent to prove ourselves worthy. I cannot break that vow. Not even to you."

"I understand. The nature of the ordeal doesn't really matter, anyway. I must, of course, find a way to survive whatever test they set me."

"Aye." Grimnir nodded, and squeezed her against him again. "That you must. If you do not, and it was I who brought you here . . ."

"You could always take up with some other she-wolf," she replied, "since the island is full of them."

"My concern for you is real," Grimnir said quietly. He drew back his hand from her shoulder and fell into silent thought, staring with a frown at the approaching beach.

Bloodsong reached over and touched his hand. "I will survive," she promised.

He nodded but did not take his eyes from the island.

Before they touched land, men and women appeared on the low hill overlooking the beach, but none moved downslope to greet them. All held weapons. All the men were bearded, all the women's long-haired, unshorn tresses blowing freely in the sea wind. Men and women alike wore breechclouts and nothing else, their exposed flesh hard-muscled and deeply tanned.

"Something's wrong, Grimnir," Magnus said as they prepared to leave the ship.

"Aye. They should have swarmed onto the beach to welcome us. Something must have happened since last we were here; perhaps other ships have visited and made them distrustful of all outsiders, though what *they* would have to fear, I can't imagine."

"But this is *Waveslasher*!" Magnus complained. "Surely they recognize her and know we are friends!"

"I think perhaps you and your crew should stay aboard until I find out what's going on," Grimnir suggested.

"If you are attacked, you will need our swords to aid you," Magnus responded.

"Grimnir and I will approach them alone," Bloodsong said. "If they've reason to distrust outsiders now, two people approaching them in friendship will upset them less than many storming onto their beach."

"And two will fall the easier should they attack," Magnus protested.

"They won't attack," Bloodsong said. "I know it, sense it. Look at the way they stand, holding weapons but relaxed. They're waiting, that's all. They could have attacked already if they did not want us to land."

Soon Bloodsong and Grimnir were walking up the slope of the hill, carefully keeping their hands away from their weapons.

"The one with the gray beard is Harbarth," Grimnir whispered. "When last I was here, he was their leader. The flame-haired woman beside him is his mate, Ulfhild."

The gray-bearded man stepped forward as they neared. Bloodsong noted that his skin was crisscrossed with scars, recent ones atop those that had long since healed. Warriors who survived to exhibit such a collection of scars were formidable ones indeed, and as she looked, she noticed that Harbarth's scars only slightly exceeded those of the other warriors waiting atop the hill, men and women alike.

"They fight without armor," Grimnir told her as if sensing her thoughts.

Bloodsong nodded. Her eyes met Harbarth's, then Ulfhild's.

"Hail, Harbarth! Ulfhild!" Grimnir said, raising his right hand, palm outward.

"Grijmnir," Harbarth grunted. "I suspected it would be you."

"Suspected?"

"I've been plagued by sleeplessness and visions for nearly a week."

"Odin wants us to help the woman with you," Ulfhild added, "if she proves worthy."

"Odin distrusts her," Harbarth went on, "because she helped his enemy, Hel, regain the War Skull and become more powerful again."

Bloodsong stepped nearer, until almost touching the aging, but still massively muscled, man. She stared into his eyes. "I did what was necessary for my daughter and for revenge against Nidhug. I will not ask Odin's forgiveness. There is nothing to forgive. He did nothing to stop me from returning the War Skull, so he has no right to complain about it now."

Harbarth's expression darkened. "This island is sacred to Odin. I will allow no ill to be said of him."

"Nor I of me," Bloodsong responded.

Harbarth frowned down at her a moment more, then he glanced at Grimnir and winked. "Steel in her soul, eh, Grimnir?"

Grimnir laughed and clapped the leader on the arm. "Aye, Harbarth. Would I ride with any other?"

"Would you *ride* any other," Harbarth added, sweeping Bloodsong's body with an appreciative glance.

Grimnir's smile faded as he saw Bloodsong's expression.

"Freya's teeth," she cursed, "I have come here for aid, not jokes and male glances. Grimnir tells me I must survive whatever tests you set me to. I am ready to begin. My daughter is captive to the Hel-Witch, Thokk, and you stand here wasting time!"

Harbarth nodded. "You may begin at once. But no others may set foot inland, not even you, Grimnir."

"You expect me to return to the ship while she—"

"I *require* it," Harbarth interrupted.

"The island has been specially . . . prepared, for the testing of this woman," Ulfhild said.

"My name is Bloodsong," she growled. "Use it."

"We *know* your name," Ulfhild answered. "Bloodsong, Nidhug's Bane, Arena Warrior, Hel-warrior, Freyadis—"

"Bloodsong will do," she said, cutting Ulfhild off.

"Return to the ship, Grimnir," Harbarth said. "We will come for you when it is over, either to celebrate with us or to carry her body away."

Grimnir's eyes met Bloodsong's.

"It will be a celebration," she promised him, reaching out to grip his shoulder, "but"—she turned to Harbarth—"a *short* one. Then we will sail. Have your visions also told you what it is I want from you? To fight Thokk's sorcery? Her Death Riders? To help me free my daughter?"

"I knew that Hel-magic would be involved."

"And you agree? When I have survived your tests, you will return with us to battle Thokk?" she asked.

"Odin wills it," he answered.

"*If* you survive," Ulfhild added doubtfully. "Many who appeared stronger than you have not."

"Since Odin is Hel's enemy," Grimnir said, "perhaps you should help us whether or not Bloodsong undergoes your ordeals."

"Return to the ship, Grimnir," Harbarth repeated, then motioned Bloodsong inland.

Bloodsong gripped Grimnir's shoulder again, then turned and walked away.

Harbarth and Ulfhild at her side, Bloodsong approached an ancient tree in the bottom of a small, barren, bowel-shaped valley. The tree's branches were bare. From one thick limb hung a rope. Beneath the rope coals glowed red-hot.

"Odin hung on a tree for nine days and nights to acquire the secrets of the runes," Harbarth told her. "Our legends say that he hung upon this very tree."

"Other legends say otherwise, I'm sure," Bloodsong replied,

eyeing the rope, beginning to guess what was coming. "I've little use for legends, and I don't have nine days. Whatever you want me to do, it must be done quickly."

Harbarth took the rope's end and began forming a noose. "This test will last until sunset," he promised. "It is now nearly noon. Will that be quick enough for you, impatient one? Quick enough to die?"

"Or *not* to die," she corrected. "What must I do?"

"Merely survive." Ulfhild laughed. "Any way you can."

Harbarth finished fashioning the noose, reciting runes under his breath as he gave it a final tug. Then he placed it around Bloodsong's neck. Ulfhild lifted Bloodsong's long black hair and smoothed it down outside the circle of splintery rope. Then, without warning, the other end of the rope was jerked upward.

Bloodsong had half expected the attempt to surprise her and was ready. She reached up and grabbed hold of the rope above the spiraled knot as her feet left the ground. *Until sunset*, she told herself. *All I need do is hold on until sunset.* She kept her grip with her right hand, reached up, and managed to wind her left arm around the rope to get a better hold. *I can do it*, she assured herself. *I have to do it.*

Suddenly she felt hands upon her, clawing at her clothing. Within moments she was hanging naked amid the Berserkers, their eyes appreciatively noting her own collection of battle scars. She saw Harbarth lift a spear, its tip engraved with runes.

"Odin hung naked upon the tree," Harbarth told her, "bleeding from nine spear wounds. He wounded himself, sacrificed himself to himself, but since you cannot do that, I will help."

Pain shot through her as the spear tip pierced the flesh of her left thigh. Blood oozed forth. Again and again the sharp steel point sank into her body, the wounds bleeding freely but not deep enough to prove fatal in themselves. The ninth wound pierced her. She had not cried out. Harbarth nodded his approval as he looked up at her sweat-slicked body dangling from the rope, her arm muscles bunched rock-hard as she held on, bare skin glistening in the sunlight, crimson trickles from the wounds streaking her flesh.

"Learn you now, Hanging One," Ulfhild said, intoning the words ritualistically, "the secret name of our island, the sacred heritage of our people. And may Odin give victory to your enemies and destroy you and all your kin if ever you speak of this knowledge to one who has not survived the Gallows Ordeal."

"In the Long Ago," Harbarth intoned, "arose a warrior of our people to fight for our right to live free, unchained, un-collared, without masters, bending the knee to no one, not even the Gods."

"Bending the knee not even to Odin," Ulfhild responded.

"Not even to Odin," solemnly repeated the others.

"Our chains the warrior broke," Harbarth continued, "our people freed, the lost knowledge of our heritage from Time's Dawning restored."

"We are free women and men, the chosen of Odin." Ulfhild spoke sternly, assuming the warrior's part. "We will never again be enslaved. We will never again be treated like beasts!"

"And in time," Harbarth went on, "after many battles and many died in freedom's winning, the warrior led our people to this island."

"And here we made our home," Ulfhild said.

"Home," spoke the others as one.

"Wolfraven," whispered Ulfhild.

"The warrior," said the others.

"Wolfraven," Ulfhild repeated, louder.

"Our home," the others said.

Harbarth handed the rune-engraved spear to Ulfhild. She raised it to her lips, kissed the tapering spearhead still crimson with Bloodsong's blood, then lifted it to Bloodsong's lips.

Bloodsong understood and kissed the offered spearhead.

Ulfhild raised the spear high. "Wolfraven and Odin!" she shouted the Berserker's battle cry.

"Wolfraven and Odin!" shouted the others, raising their weapons skyward.

All eyes turned upon Bloodsong. For several heartbeats there was silence, then Bloodsong guessed what was expected and shouted, "Wolfraven and Odin!"

Smiles broke across the Berserkers' faces. They relaxed and began to talk among themselves.

"Welcome to the island of Wolfraven." Ulfhild laughed up at Bloodsong. "You've done well thus far, Swordsister. Odin willing, there's a slight chance you may survive this ordeal."

"Odin willing or not," Bloodsong growled, clinging determinedly to the rope, "I will survive it."

"Only one more thing needs now be done," Harbarth said, "then we will leave you alone to face Odin and your fate."

Looking down, Bloodsong saw them bring fresh coals and dump them on the fire. Seeing the look in her eyes, Harbarth laughed. "We do not mean to roast you," he assured her. "Herbs will be placed on the coals. The smoke that will rise around you will help encourage visions of Odin."

The herbs were dumped onto the coals. Pungent blue smoke rose around her. Eyes stinging and watering, coughing from the thick smoke being drawn into her lungs with each breath, Bloodsong dangled from the end of the rope, only the grip of her hands preventing the noose from tightening upon her neck.

Through the thick vapors she caught glimpses of the Berserkers walking away. Moments later they were gone, leaving her to hang in the barren valley alone.

25
Odin

Bloodsong hung alone in the small barren valley with none to see if she lived or died, her world reduced to her straining grip on the rope. Drops of blood and sweat fell from her glistening skin, hissing as they touched the hot coals below. The vapors from the herbs were beginning to make her vision swim. She concentrated on staying conscious and holding on to the rope.

Until sunset, she reminded herself, *no rules except surviving any way I can. Who says I even have to stay suspended here? Perhaps if I climb up the rope a short way, I can loop a foot in the rope and give myself enough slack to take this cursed noose from around my neck.*

She decided to try it and began climbing the rope, hand over hand. But suddenly she began sliding downward again, unable to grip the rope as before. Too late she noticed that a short distance above the noose the rope was coated with a colorless greasy substance that now also coated the palms of her hands.

She struggled desperately to regain a firm hold, but not until her hands reached the coiled noose itself did she succeed in stopping her plunge into oblivion.

She cursed, swaying at the end of the rope over the smoking coals. Her palms began to burn. She gasped with pain as the burning grew steadily worse. *Something in that cursed grease*, she realized. *Some sort of acid* . . .

The noose became slick with blood where she gripped it, crimson ooze coming from her burning palms. Her grip slipped farther down the noose, nearly to her neck. The muscles in her arms screamed with the strain. She knew that soon they would begin to cramp, become impossible to control, and when that happened, she would die.

She twisted herself around to face the trunk of the tree, searching for a low branch around which she could wrap her legs by swinging toward it, but no such branch existed, and the trunk was too wide for her to hope to grip it between her thighs.

Her blood-slicked grip slipped a fraction more. Fighting panic, she felt the noose tighten around her neck. She was losing the battle. She was going to die.

"No!" she shouted, forced her trembling arm muscles to heave her upward a short way, risked all at a try to wind her left arm around the rope. It worked. The grip of her left became more secure and also allowed her to extend the grip of her right hand.

Panting with the strain, Bloodsong determined to simply hang as she now was until sunset.

As the afternoon wore slowly on, the herbs stopped smoking on the coals without having given her any visions of Odin. The burning in her palms gradually subsided, leaving the lesser pain of gripping the rope with raw-fleshed palms. Blood stopped flowing from her nine spear wounds. The coals themselves died beneath her, and an afternoon breeze cooled her sweat-dampened skin. With all her concentration focused upon holding the rope from heartbeat to heartbeat, she did not at first notice when the light began to dim, but finally it penetrated her consciousness that the sky had darkened, the sun having dipped below the rim of the bowel-shaped valley in which she hung.

It's nearly over! she thought excitedly. *Whatever else they have planned will have to be an improvement over this stupid, deadly game.*

She began watching the rim of the valley expectantly as the rope twisted back and forth in the breeze. The sky continued to darken. Stars began to appear. It became too dark to see the valley's rim, but still no one came to let her down.

Bloodsong cursed, arms aching, hands growing more and more numb from relentlessly gripping the rope. Her left hand slipped. The noose tightened slightly more before she regained her hold.

Where are they? her mind screamed. *I made it until sunset! I won! Why don't they come and let me down! Curse them all!*

The stars wheeled slowly across the heavens. The air cooled, chilling her nakedness. Far away she heard the rumble of thunder and soon began to notice the distant flash of lightning. The breeze picked up, shifting to the north from whence the storm was approaching, became a gusting wind.

It became even harder to maintain her hold on the rope as the strengthening wind jerked her back and forth, spun her around, swung her in ever-increasing arcs.

Bloodsong sobbed with the strain, cursed with rage. Where are they?! she asked herself over and over again. The storm was swiftly rising. If it got much worse, if it began to rain and the rope became wet...

It began to rain. Soon hail joined the rain, beating against her bare flesh, battering her unprotected skin as the wind lashed her with violent, disorienting gusts.

Her grip began to slip, the noose to tighten. With each new blast of wind the splintery circle of death cut deeper into her neck.

Lightning flashed nearby. The air sizzled. The wind roared as if maddened beasts battled in the clouds. Suddenly she felt new pain as something fluttered against her face, striking her again and again near her eyes.

Another flash of lightning... She saw two black-winged shapes with piercing eyes near her face, beaks darting toward her, trying to blind her.

Ravens! she realized. *Two ravens! And the storm,* she thought, struggling against her ever-loosening grip and the steadily tightening noose. *A storm like in the tales when Odin leads the Wild Hunt! And Odin is said to have two ravens....*

"Begone from me, Hugin!" she shouted hoarsely into the howling tempest. "Begone, Munin!" she cried, using the names she had once heard a Skald call Odin's ravens. "Tell your one-eyed master that he cannot have my eyes this night! Not so long as I live! Begone!"

With loud cawes the two ravens disappeared into the storm.

The fury of the wind increased. The rain fell faster, the hail beat harder. The limb from which Bloodsong hung jerked and shuddered, whipping her back and forth, tightening the noose. She could barely breathe, felt her consciousness going, her grip slipping faster and faster. Then suddenly she was hanging solely by her neck, hands flailing numb and useless as she futilely tried to regain her lost grip. The roaring of the storm penetrated her skull, now came from within her mind now.

The flashing of the lightning seemed to dim, the crash of the thunder to become a mere whisper. She writhed at the end of the rope, kicking and twisting as the roaring in her head became a gentle murmur.

Suddenly light flashed within her mind, searing her consciousness. An orb as bright as the sun burned its way into her brain. Flames hissed as her thoughts burned chaotically, the hungry orb of light consuming her being, probing every corner of her soul, questioning everything, doubting everything, seeking truth, hungry for wisdom. Deep male laughter boomed within her mind, followed by ragged screams and the howls of a ravenous beast.

Odin! she screamed with her thoughts. *Berserker God! Gallows God! Cursed be your name if I die! For Guthrun's sake I must live!*

The orb of blinding light in her mind grew dim and went out. Whispers cold as sifting snow slithered like a serpent at the edge of her consciousness.

She had ceased being able to feel even the rope around her neck, but suddenly it became a ring of pain once more, burning as if aflame, searing deeper and deeper into her throat. The agony of her burning neck spread fire through her veins until every nerve was seared raw.

A scream rent the air, long and piercing, a wail as of a newborn in agony. Dimly she realized that it was her own scream, wondered how she had drawn enough air into her starved lungs to sustain the cry.

Images swirled, formed, changed into others within her mind. Then one began to dominate, a vision of a young woman's face . . .

Guthrun! Bloodsong called with her thoughts.

In the vision Guthrun's gaze focused on her. Confusion, then delight, filled Guthrun's eyes. Her lips formed words Bloodsong could not hear.

Be strong, daughter! I'm coming for you! Be strong!

Guthrun's lips continued to move, but Bloodsong could still hear no sound. Then the image began to fade. Guthrun's eyes swept back and forth as if searching for Bloodsong.

Guthrun!

The image of her daughter's face vanished.

Suddenly she was falling. She hit the dead coals beneath her, lay still, unable to move, gasping for air, her neck throbbing as if it had been branded with red-hot irons.

Rain no longer fell. Overhead she saw stars begin to appear as the storm clouds parted. Lightning flashed faintly in the distance. Thunder rumbled less and less often.

Bloodsong tried again to move, still found that she could not, let her eyes close, and gave herself up to exhausted sleep, not understanding how she had escaped the rope, not caring, remembering only the image of Guthrun's face, so vivid, so real. . . .

* * *

At dawn Harbarth and the others returned and found her lying across the dead coals, her nude body battered but still warm with life. Harbarth lifted her into his arms, glanced up at the rope, the noose dangling broken, its inner surface blackened as if by fire, then he turned his attention to Bloodsong's neck, excitedly studying what he saw there.

Encircling Bloodsong's throat, runes had been branded deep into her flesh. Harbarth's eyes swept over the symbols. Shock rushed through him. He, a master of runes, could not read them.

"What do they mean?" Ulfhild asked at his side as she leaned closer to study the encircling runes.

"I've . . . never seen their like. Odin knows what they mean, I assume, since he must have put them there, but I do not."

"How I envy her!" Ulfhild said, touching her own throat.

"Somehow," Harbarth replied, "I doubt that she will share your enthusiasm." Then he turned and carried Bloodsong's still-unconscious body away from the tree, Ulfhild and the others following behind, gripping their weapons and talking excitedly about the marks on Bloodsong's neck, anxious to follow wherever she might lead and to slay any who sought to harm her or her kin.

26
Alive

Guthrun opened her eyes. Her surroundings confused her. Her head ached horribly. The image of her mother's face was still strong and vivid in her mind.

A dream? she wondered. *No, it was more than that. I touched her mind somehow. She's still alive! But she's not my mother, is she? Not my true mother, she's...*

"Freya!" Guthrun cried, gripping her throbbing head between her hands. "Bloodsong *is* my mother—my *only* mother. A curse on Thokk's tricks and lies!"

She felt as if awakening from a drugged sleep and shook her head to clear her thoughts and vision. *Bloodsong is alive! And she said she was coming for me, said for me to be strong...*

The aching in her head was fading. She felt chilled and noted that she was naked upon a stone slab, the only light that of a flickering torch in a wall bracket. Someone was lying beside her.

She tried to focus on who it was, rubbed her eyes, fought her way as if through a fog, and finally saw clearly.

Beside her lay the corpse Thokk claimed to be her brother's. One of his hands rested upon her bare thigh. He was breathing.

With a startled cry Guthrun jerked away from his cold touch and scrambled down off the slab. She backed away until she was stopped by a wall. She ran to the door, found it locked, and looked back at the slab. Upon the corpse's lips glistened dark smears. As she watched he frowned, licked away the stains, began to awaken.

She felt something warm and sticky on her inner thighs, looked down, saw blood. . . .

It all came back in a rush, a nightmare she now knew had been real; Thokk battering away at her mental defenses, her mind finally giving way, agreeing to what Thokk wanted, asking that the Hel-Witch make her first woman's blood to flow, using her own fingers to place that blood upon the corpse's lips, hearing the ragged intake of his first breath, the creaking of his dead skin as his chest heaved, lungs expanding beneath. . . .

Other memories tore at her. She felt sick as she remembered what had happened next, how she had willingly done as Thokk wanted, had stripped herself naked and stretched out next to the living corpse, taken his cold flesh into her arms, comforted him, strengthened him with more and more of her blood. . . .

Guthrun's breath came in sobs as she crumpled to the floor and buried her face in her hands. *Be strong*, her mother had urged in the vision. But she had not been strong. She had given in. Thokk had won. . . .

"No!" she cried. *Thokk has won a battle. That is all. I am not dead. I am not yet lost to Hel. I will fight back, somehow help my mother destroy the Hel-Witch. And I can begin by destroying the Helish thing before me.*

Guthrun got to her feet, wiped away her tears, felt a cold rage settle on her heart. The corpse was still struggling to awaken. She had to act fast.

She grabbed the torch from the wall bracket, hurried to the slab, lowered the torch . . .

Lokith's eyes snapped open. He saw the torch and knocked it away with blinding speed. "No, *Sister*," he hissed, smiling coldly as he sat up in one smooth motion and stared into her eyes. "You will not harm me."

Guthrun sprang for the torch. Her right hand closed upon it. She whirled to face him. He was not on the slab. A cold hand gripped her wrist from behind. His laughter rang out.

She kicked back, caught him on the instep, kicked again, and connected with his knee. He seemed not to notice the blows and laughed again. She transferred the torch to her left hand, twisted to thrust it into his face, but again he was too fast, gripping her other wrist.

They stood facing each other, Lokith gripping both her wrists, his hands like ice-sheathed steel. Within his eyes flickered embers of purple fire.

"I am not pleased, Sister," he said, "and neither will be Thokk. I am the important one of we two. Your blood was needed to bring me to life, and more is needed until I gain my full strength. But after that, unless you cooperate—"

"My blood did not bring you to *life*!" she cried. "You are not *alive*, monster! You are dead! Dead!"

"Not as dead as *you* will be, if I so choose. I could snap your neck as easily as I can snap your wrist."

Lokith's grip tightened upon Guthrun's left wrist. She heard a crack and felt blinding pain shoot upward along her left arm. She screamed, dropped the torch.

Lokith released her with a laugh. She cradled her broken wrist against her body and glared at him through tear-blurred eyes.

"You won't win!" she vowed. "Your mother will destroy you if I don't first!"

"My mother? You mean Mother Hel? No," he said with a grin. "I can see you refer to that *other* woman. She is not our true mother, Guthrun. Why can't you accept that?"

"Thokk's lies!"

He whipped back his hand and struck her face so swiftly that she had no chance to dodge.

The force of the blow threw her back against a wall. Blood trickled from a split lip.

Lokith picked up the torch and walked slowly toward her, smiling hungrily as his eyes swept over her nakedness. "Your body is nearly that of a woman, dear Sister, and your blood is sweet."

She kicked sideways, catching him in the stomach.

He cursed, then swung the torch at her head.

She ducked, sidestepped, kicked out again, and caught him in the side, sending him reeling.

The purple fires in his eyes blazed brighter. His lips drew back from sharp white teeth. He growled like a beast and crushed out the torch, plunging the room into darkness save for his burning eyes.

Bloodsong had trained for six long years in the darkness of Helheim before riding against Nidhug. She had taught Guthrun the skills needed to fight in the absence of light. Guthrun used them.

A series of lightning kicks drove Lokith back against a wall. She moved closer, gasped with pain as cold fingernails raked her already injured left arm, and struck at where she estimated his throat to be with the edge of her right hand.

Lokith cried out as the edge of Guthrun's hand chopped into his windpipe. His eyes closed, shutting out the purple fires burning within them. She heard him sliding downward along the wall, heard ragged breathing as he lay upon the floor.

Now to finish him, she thought, teeth gritted against the pain of her broken wrist. Though the torch no longer burned, it could still be used as a club to smash open his skull.

Guthrun hurried to the spot where she remembered he'd thrown the torch, searched but a moment before finding it, started to turn back toward Lokith, and cried out as cold hands closed on her shoulders.

Lokith spun her around and hurled her forward.

Pain exploded within her head as her skull struck the stone wall. She crumpled to the floor, clinging to consciousness, dimly saw eyes of purple fire staring down at her, coming nearer, and felt icy hands grip her ankles. Her bare skin scraped against the floor as she was dragged toward the slab. Corpse-cold arms lifted her into the air and roughly dropped her on the slab. The eyes of purple fire came nearer. She tried to move, to fight back. He pinned her wrists to the slab and easily held them there. His icy lips touched hers.

"When I no longer need your blood," Lokith hissed, his breath against her face cold and moist and stinking of decayed flesh, "you will die as unpleasantly as I can devise."

He drew back a fist, struck her again and again and again until satisfied that he had battered all consciousness from her flesh.

Then he began to feed.

27
Ropebreaker

"Guthrun!"

Grimnir's head snapped around at the sound of Bloodsong's cry. He ran to her, knelt beside her. "Bloodsong?" he called, gently stroking her sweat-dampened hair.

The nightmare images she had been experiencing began to fade, images of Guthrun unconscious upon a stone slab and a dead thing who called her Sister, hitting her, battering her without mercy.

"Bloodsong?" Grimnir called again, louder.

She groaned, murmured Guthrun's name once more, and opened her eyes. Grimnir stared down at her with concern. Harbarth and Ulfhild stood nearby.

She was lying by a fire in a cave, naked under animal furs. Her hands and throat were bandaged. A soothing salve coated her other wounds.

Grimnir smiled encouragingly and gripped her shoulder. She winced with pain at his touch and he jerked back his hand.

"I—I didn't mean to hurt," he said, stammering.

"I doubt you could touch a place that *didn't* hurt just now," she told him with a weak smile. Then she glared up at Harbarth.

"You promised to return at sunset," she accused, rising anger giving her strength.

"I did not say *which* sunset," he replied, grinning.

"Cursed Odin-worshiping, word-twisting—"

"You survived," Grimnir cut in. "That's what matters. You have gained the allegiance of the Berserkers."

"Bloodsong," Harbarth said, kneeling beside Grimnir, his eyes searching hers, "what happened during the storm? What did you see? Hear? I . . . *we* must know."

"Go hang yourself and find out."

"I have," he solemnly assured her. "We have all ridden the gallows, Odin's steed. But never before has what happened to you befallen any of us. There have been visions, of course, even visitations, but—"

"Nothing happened."

"Tell him, Bloodsong," Grimnir urged. "It's important."

Bloodsong glanced from Grimnir to Harbarth and back again. "Is my testing over? May things I now do and say allow them to withdraw their aid?"

"The testing is over," Harbarth said.

"Grimnir?" she asked, ignoring the leader.

"It is over."

She looked back at Harbarth. "I couldn't be certain *which* testing you meant, Word-twister."

"What did you see?" Harbarth demanded.

"My daughter, Guthrun," she finally replied, looking at Grimnir again. "Our minds touched somehow, giving both of us strength."

"A gift from Odin," Ulfhild said.

Harbarth nodded. "Aye. And what else did you see, Bloodsong?"

"Two ravens who wanted to gouge my eyes."

Harbarth beamed and looked up at Ulfhild. "Hugin and Munin!" He laughed.

"And did you also see Odin's wolves?" Ulfhild asked. "Did you see Freki and Geri?"

"No, but there were many images inside my mind after I

lost my grip and hung by my neck. I saw a bright orb of light, then deep darkness, felt fire and then ice. I only barely remember. What I *do* remember, all I *care* to remember, is seeing my daughter again, knowing that she's still alive."

Bloodsong reached out and touched Grimnir's arm with a bandaged hand. "I'm certain of it, Grimnir. Guthrun *is* alive." She looked back at Harbarth. "For that knowledge I thank Odin. For everything else I curse him."

Harbarth and Ulfhild laughed. "Curse him all you want, Ropebreaker," Ulfhild smiled.

"Ropebreaker?"

"Odin no doubt now approves of your curses," Harbarth went on. "It is said that the heroes he values most are those who, distrusting him, their very God, refuse to give up their weapons before entering Valhalla. Now that you bear his marks, your curses most likely merely make him grin."

"Marks?" Bloodsong asked, then touched her bandaged throat. "You mean the rope burns. You all bear the scars of the noose, I notice that now. Even you, Grimnir."

"There's more, in your case," Grimnir quietly told her. "The marks on your throat are not entirely like ours."

"It's one of the reasons we wanted to know all that happened to you last night," Ulfhild said.

"I was hoping for a clue," Harbarth explained, "a key by which I could decipher the runes Odin burned into your neck."

There were several heartbeats of silence, then Bloodsong began to curse.

"I'm slipping!" Jalna cried, losing her grip on the rainslicked rocks. "I'm going to fall!"

Tyrulf tightened his own grip, shifted his weight, reached down, and helped her to a more stable position against the rocks. "You can't fall now," he told her between pants. "We're too near the top. It would be bad luck."

"Especially for me," she gasped, pulling herself up as he continued to climb. Thunder crashed nearby, the concussion nearly enough in itself to make her lose her precarious hold.

"I thought you said the summit was *above* the storm," she complained.

Tyrulf kept climbing, glancing down to check on Jalna every few moments. Wind whipped at them, trying to tear them from the side of the mountain. A flurry of hail battered them, then passed. Lightning struck the rocks overhead. The air hissed. Rocks clattered down around them. They clung desperately to the mountainside until rocks no longer fell.

Up and up they climbed, muscles aching and burning, lungs straining in the ever-thinning air. Then suddenly the tempest around them grew less violent. Continuing to ascend toward the summit, the rain soon stopped. Farther, through a rapidly thinning fog, they broke into sunlight.

"I told you so." Tyrulf laughed, helping her onto a narrow ledge to rest. "Look," he said, pointing. "The summit."

"If only we didn't have to climb back down," Jalna growled, rubbing sore muscles.

"They'll be even more sore tomorrow, I'll wager." Tyrulf grinned. "Mine too. It's been years since I enjoyed a good climb."

"A good climb!" Jalna exclaimed, then laughed, glad to have challenged the mountain and still be alive.

Soon they began to climb again, covered the short distance left to the summit, and stood side by side, gazing at the mountaintop.

A chill went up Tyrulf's spine.

"It's beautiful!" Jalna exclaimed. "I never dreamed mountaintops looked like this."

"They *don't*," Tyrulf replied, making the sign of Thor's Hammer, then laughing at the gesture. If it were Thor's magic, as the tales suggested, which ruled atop the mountain, the Hammer-sign would do little good.

Thunder rumbled up to them from the raging tempest below. As far as the horizon on all sides stretched a sea of white clouds, the billowing tops of thunderheads. The air was cold but not as cold as Tyrulf knew it should have been at that altitude. Neither should there have been green, heavily leafed trees, nor a thick carpet of grass sprinkled with brightly colored wildflowers. In many ways it reminded him of Freya's mound, though there should have been nothing there but barren rocks and possibly remnants of the winter's snows.

In the center of the small plateau that formed the summit sat an even more unexpected sight, a thatch-roofed cottage, smoke curling lazily skyward from its chimney.

They glanced at each other, then began walking toward the cottage.

Jalna placed a hand on the hilt of her sword as they neared the closed door of the cottage.

"I think, until we know differently," Tyrulf said, "we had best not show hostility. Nothing is as it should be here, but I don't sense danger. Do you?"

Jalna shook her head negatively. "I feel exactly the opposite, comforted, deeply happy, safe. But I'll leave my hand on my sword's hilt. I'll not be taken by surprise."

The door of the cottage opened, and an old woman squinted out at them. "Who's there?" she called in an ancient, cracked voice. "Who has come to see Mother Groa after all these years? Come closer. My eyes see but dimly."

Tyrulf stepped nearer, then stopped, tension tightening his muscles. He studied the crone and was surprised to be reminded strongly of his long-dead grandmother. Groa wore a tattered shawl over a faded red robe. "I am Tyrulf," he finally said.

"And my name is Jalna. Are you a sorceress? A Witch? We have come seeking Thor's aid against Hel."

"A Witch?" Groa wondered, touching a gnarled finger to her chin. "I was once. Perhaps I still am. I don't remember. Are the two of you in love? Young people should be in love. I was in love once. I've been alone now a long time, such a long time. . . . "

"Mother Groa?" Tyrulf said, walking even nearer as Jalna glanced warily all around, "we have heard that this place is called the home of the Keeper of the Lightning's Blood. Do you know anything of that? We have heard that this mountain is sacred to Thor, and as Jalna has said, we seek his aid against Hel."

The old woman shook her head, frowning as if trying very hard to think. "There is much lightning below. None here."

"We must search the mountaintop," Jalna said, "if you have no objection?"

"Search all you like," Groa said. "You won't find any lightning here. Come in first, children. I so seldom have company. Let me fix you something warm to eat and drink."

Tyrulf glanced up at the sun. They didn't have long until sunset. "We will be happy to spend the night with you, if you like," he said, "but while there is still light we must search for something to aid us against Hel."

The crone nodded, shuffled out of the cottage toward them, and stopped within reach. Jalna's grip tightened on her sword's hilt. "Would you like me to help you search?" Groa asked, peering closely at them. "I know where the best herbs and berries grow. If you're going into icy Helheim, you'd best take food, as much as you can. I've heard nothing grows in Helheim. There's nothing but Death there, of course."

"Make ready the food and drink for later," Jalna suggested. "You need not come with us."

Groa nodded. "I would only slow you down, of course. Very well. A meal will be ready when you return. It's so nice to have visitors again. So very nice..."

The crone shuffled back into the cottage and closed the door.

"I doubt we'll find anything out here," Tyrulf said.

"As do I. The old one is the key, if key there be. But where magic is concerned, where the Gods are involved, logic often leads you astray. So let's search, anyway. We'll have the night to question Groa and search her cottage, if she allows."

"I don't like the thought of spending the night with her. Even if she does remind me of my dead grandmother, I do not intend to fall asleep."

"Grandmother? I never knew mine. She was dead before I was born. But she reminds me of a kind old woman I used to *wish* was my grandmother."

"Magic," Tyrulf grunted.

"Aye," Jalna agreed, "some spell perhaps, trying to convince us to trust her by reminding us of someone we used to trust. I won't sleep tonight, either, by Skadi," she vowed, then together they hurried away from the cottage to begin their search.

28
Thor's Blood

"I told you there wasn't any lightning up here." Groa laughed, grinning a toothless smile. Thunder rumbled below the summit as they sat inside the cottage near the hearth. Outside in the night, flashes of lightning illuminated from within the billowing tops of the thunderheads.

Jalna sniffed at the bowl of steaming stew the old woman handed her. It smelled delicious, much like a stew she'd once loved as a child. Her stomach growled in response.

Tyrulf sniffed at his, too, and glanced at Jalna.

"Eat, children. Go ahead and eat," Groa said, sitting on a rickety wooden chair and spooning stew from her cauldron into a third bowl. "Aren't you hungry?" she asked, sipping from the newly filled bowl.

Jalna sipped at the stew cautiously and found that it tasted even better than it smelled.

"I have remembered something that might be of interest to you," Groa said between sips, "but I won't tell you until you eat your stew."

"What have you remembered?" Jalna asked hopefully.

"First finish your stew, child. Is your hearing as bad as my vision?"

When the bowls were empty and they had refused second helpings, Groa passed around wooden mugs of mead, the strong honey-wine giving off an invitingly sweet aroma.

"Once long ago," Groa said, "when I was much, much younger, I remember that I knew certain spells, spells to heal, to take away pain. Herbs helped, too, of course, but I also knew magic with which to enhance their power."

Jalna glanced at Tyrulf. His raised eyebrows told her that he had also noticed how Groa's voice had subtly changed when beginning the tale, how strong it now seemed, no longer old and weak.

"I'm certain it was me who knew those spells," Groa continued, "or nearly certain. Many of my memories come and go, you see. Sometimes I think I'm somewhere else, that my husband is just outside the door. I can hear him chopping wood. I go to see, and there's no one there, but the wood is always chopped fresh for the hearth," she added, her eyes filling with tears. She took a sip of mead and looked into the fire.

"There is a thing that happened to me," she finally went on, "which may interest you. There isn't any lightning in this story, but he who makes the lightning when he throws his Hammer has a part in the tale."

"Thor is in this tale?" Jalna asked anxiously.

Groa laughed. "Do you know of another who makes the lightning flash and the thunder rumble, save Asa-Thor?"

"No, Groa," Jalna replied. "Please continue. I want to hear the tale about you and Thor."

The old one nodded and took another sip of mead. "Is the mead to your liking?" she asked.

Tyrulf took an exaggerated swallow, grimaced as it burned its way down his throat. "It's excellent. The best I've ever tasted. Now, about Thor..."

"I was younger then," Groa said, "or at least the woman in this story was younger. Sif, Thor's golden-tressed wife, she who helps the summer crops to grow after he has provided spring rains, came to me and told me that Thor had been in a great battle with the Jotun named Hrungnir. Thor had won, but in the struggle a large sliver of stone had become embedded in his forehead. It was giving him much pain, and no one in the realm of the Gods could remove it.

"Sif came to me and said she had heard that on all of Midgard, here on Earth, that I was the only woman who knew runes strong enough to loosen the stone in Thor's forehead.

"Yes, I told her, what you have heard is true, and I am indeed that very woman. I also told her that because Thor had always blessed and protected me, I would do all I could to help heal his wound.

"Sif took me by the hand, and in a twinkling we had passed over Bifrost, the rainbow bridge which leads to Asgard, realm of the Gods. Never have I seen such beauty. But when I saw the God Thor, all thoughts of the beauty around me became insignificant.

"The stone was embedded so deeply, no blood had come forth. I began to recite runes. Soon the stone loosened slightly. Blood oozed out around it. I used my apron to soak up the blood so that I could see to continue working. Farther and farther out came the stone as I continue to chant my runes. The pain began to leave Thor, and he was so happy, he then made a mistake for which I suppose he is still sorry.

"He was so happy that his pain was leaving, you see, that he wanted to reward me before I was finished. He is such an impulsive God, you know, good-hearted but so impatient.

"He told me that he had recently rescued a child of mine, one who had been stolen away in infancy by an evil Jotun. I was so excited by the news that I forgot where I was in my spells, and once my rune spell stopped, nothing could start it again, not for the same wound. And there the stone is to this day, still embedded in Thor's forehead where I had to leave it, still paining him, but not as much as before. I felt bad about having to leave him in any pain at all, but he was still grateful and told me that one day, when my time on Midgard was through, that Sif would come again and take me back to Asgard to live in Bilskirnir, Thor's Hall, forever.

"After that I returned to my home and lived there with my husband for many years. Are you two in love? Young people should be in love."

The tale told, Groa's voice had reverted to its former ancient, cracked tones.

"Yes," Tyrulf answered. "We are in love."

"Perhaps," Jalna corrected. "*Perhaps* we are in love."

"Well, *I* am in love, at any rate," Tyrulf laughed.

Groa laughed with him. "Yes," she agreed. "It is why you were able to survive Freya's Mound."

Jalna and Tyrulf stiffened.

"How do you know about that?" Jalna demanded.

"About what?"

"Freya's Mound," Tyrulf answered.

"Everyone knows about Freya's Mound."

"How did you know we'd been there and survived it?"

"Have you been there? I didn't know. It is good you were in love or you couldn't have survived it."

"But just a moment ago, you said—" Tyrulf began, then stopped when Jalna shook her head negatively, deciding not to pursue the matter since Groa had either actually forgotten or was pretending to do so.

"Is there more to the tale about Thor?" Jalna asked. "Do you have any . . . proof that the tale is true?"

"True?" Groa asked. "Proof? I think I used to have the apron, still stained with Thor's blood. . . ."

Tyrulf and Jalna looked at each other.

"Some might call Thor's blood the blood of the lightning, might they not, Groa?" Tyrulf asked.

"And," Jalna added, "if *you* keep the apron, you might be called the Keeper of the Lightning's Blood."

"I might be, but I don't think I am. Call me what you like, however. It's so good to have company. It's beautiful here but lonely."

"Do you still have the apron, Mother Groa?" Jalna asked hopefully.

"Apron?"

"The apron with Thor's bloodstains upon it."

"Perhaps. If I ever had it at all. The tale might have been about someone else. Didn't I tell you I wasn't sure?"

Jalna resisted the frustrated curses that wanted to erupt from her mouth. "Mother Groa," she said, keeping her voice subdued, "it's *very* important. If you have the apron, could we have just a small piece of it, with Thor's blood upon it, to fight the Goddess Hel? The bloodstains of the Hammer-wielder would be embued with powerful life-affirming magic, magic that could fight the sorcery and death-magic of a Hel-Witch like Thokk."

"If it's here, it's here," Groa said, sweeping her hand in a gesture at the cottage's contents. "You are welcome to look where you like. If you can't find it, perhaps I will be able to remember where it is, if it's here, after a good night's sleep. . . ."

Groa's head sank lower and lower on her chest. Soft snoring came from her throat.

"Groa?" Jalna called.

Tyrulf got to his feet, and gently touched the crone's shoulder. She made no response.

"Skadi forbid she dies before morning," Jalna growled.

Tyrulf lifted Groa into his arms, carried her to a narrow bed of straw and pine needles along one wall, laid her down upon it, and covered her with a worn square of cloth she used as a bed covering.

"Jalna," he whispered, motioning for her to come closer. He pointed to the bed covering. "It might once have been an apron," he suggested, "and those dark stains . . ."

"Yes," she whispered excitedly back. "But perhaps we should take her up on the offer to search the cottage, just in case."

"I *insist*!" Groa said, standing in her doorway, looking out at Tyrulf and Jalna. Jalna held the stained square of tattered cloth in her hands. "Take it! *All* of it! Though I'm certain it's not what you think. Still, I cannot remember where I put that apron, if I ever had it, and you have searched the cottage from top to bottom."

"Our thanks," Jalna said, then carefully folded the thin square of cloth. She reached out and touched the old woman's hand. "You've been kind."

"Come again when you can," Groa urged. "Maybe I will find that apron, if that old cloth you hold is not it and if I ever had it here."

Jalna squeezed Groa's hand, then stepped back.

"We must start down," Tyrulf said, "while there is still plenty of light."

"Down?" Groa asked.

"Again, our thanks," Jalna said, slowly backing away, keeping her eyes on the old woman, remnants of suspicion still hovering in her mind. She waved when she was some distance from the cottage, but Groa did not wave back and went into the cottage and closed the door instead.

"She probably could not see you wave," Tyrulf suggested, "and she'll probably forget we were even here before noon."

Soon after they had left the summit and were climbing back down through the roaring storm, the billowing thunderheads that surrounded the mountaintop began to boil higher, towering over the summit, shutting out the sun. The magic of the blood-stained cloth had been taken away. The natural order was reasserting itself. Rain began to splatter against Groa's cottage. The rain turned almost at once to snow.

Leaves fell from the trees. The grass withered and died. Groa's cottage fell into ruin.

Within the rotting timbers of the cottage, amid the rapidly drifting snow, Groa slept in her chair beside a hearth gone cold. Then, beside her within the ruins appeared a tall woman in a red robe, her long hair shimmering as if made from strands of glowing gold.

The golden-tressed woman bent over Groa and whispered her name.

Groa opened her eyes, looked up, and recognized the Goddess she had seen once long ago.

"Sif!" she cried. "Beautiful Goddess! Has your husband been fighting Jotuns again? I am ready to help if I can."

The woman with golden hair gestured to one side. A man appeared, standing amid the swirling snow beyond the ruins, smiling at Groa, his arms opened wide with invitation.

At first she did not recognize him. He was so much younger than she remembered, as young as when they'd been married. Then recognition came, and tears stinging her eyes, she rose shakily to her feet and started toward him, each step she took becoming firmer, swifter, until she was running on young legs, sobbing and calling her husband's name over and over and over.

Smiling, the Goddess Sif followed and surrounded the embracing couple with her arms. All three vanished from the mountaintop.

The snow continued to fall, piling steadily higher, burying the ruins of Groa's cottage. But, in the chair by the hearth, her soul now free, all that remained of Groa were her bones.

29
Victory

Lokith awoke. The chamber was still without light. His eyes reacted, adjusted, purple fires flaming to life within them. In his sight, objects in the chamber became bathed in a ghostly purple glow.

He looked at Guthrun lying sprawled beside him. She was still unconscious, dried blood caking her swollen face where most of his blows had landed.

Lokith stood, stretched his steely muscles, and inhaled deeply. Guthrun's blood had strengthened him greatly. He would soon have his full strength, then she would no longer be needed.

Thokk will resist my killing her, he realized, *but I'll not share my power with my sister.*

He walked to the locked door. Unbidden into his mind came knowledge of a spell to open locks. *Thokk has imbued me with many powers over the years*, he thought. *I wonder if I already know as much as she? Foolish of her, if that is the case. I believe she thinks too much of Hel and not enough about herself. But she has been useful to me and to Mother Hel. Perhaps there will be a place for her in the new order of things. Perhaps not.*

Lokith considered the lock. Yes, he could open it easily. But for now it might be best not to show his awareness of his powers. Better to let Thokk think him still weak and unsure of himself. She wanted to keep him there in isolation until she was certain that he was at his full strength. Then, he knew, she had planned some grand ceremony to introduce him to the Hel-worshipers who served in the castle.

Very well, he decided, *I will allow her to think I am contented to follow her plans, for now. . . .*

He turned, walked back to the slab, and sat down beside Guthrun. *I could heal you, Sister*, he thought. *Perhaps I should. You're no fun unconscious.*

Smiling coldly, Lokith began to invoke a healing spell.

Bloodsong stood on the deck of *Waveslasher*, watching the shore of the mainland coming steadily closer. She again wore the doeskin clothing the woodcutter had given her. Though the breeches and tunic had been torn from her by the Berserkers during her gallows' ride, she had insisted they also mend the clothing they had ruined, rejecting Ulfhild's suggestion that she be content with a breechclout.

She flexed her bandaged hands, grimaced at the stiffness and pain, thought of Huld. *How I wish she were with me now*, she thought, remembering the young Freya-Witch's ability to magically heal wounds. *Is she even still alive? I have but a few days to heal before we reach Eirik's Vale. But I may well have to wield a sword even before then, bandages or not. Curse the Berserkers and their foolish tests of worthiness!* And yet, were it not for them, she would not be returning with an army capable of challenging Thokk and Kovna, and were it not for her experience at the end of the gallows' rope, she would not have touched Guthrun's mind.

"How long till we reach land?" she asked Grimnir as he came to stand beside her.

"Magnus says before noon, which isn't long to wait. I saw you moving your hands. The salve Ulfhild put on them will speed the healing."

"Freya grant that they will heal quickly enough," Bloodsong replied.

"Or Odin," Grimnir suggested.

Bloodsong touched her bandaged throat. "Aye, perhaps." She had examined the runes burned into her flesh in the reflection of a polished sword blade. She thought of Huld again and wondered if a healing spell would make the runes go away. Somehow she doubted that Freya's magic could banish the effects of Odin's, but if Huld still lived, Bloodsong intended to find out someday.

"I've been having dreams of Guthrun," Bloodsong told Grimnir. "Not like the ones before the testing on the isle but vivid images, as if I were glimpsing things that are happening to her without being able to make her aware of my presence. What I have seen makes me even more impatient to reach the castle and free her."

She flexed her bandaged hands again and cursed. "If only Huld were with me," she said, then fell silent, watching their approach to the shore.

How long has it been? Huld numbly wondered as she forced herself forward again on bleeding knees, began searching yet another mound of the Dead. *Has it been one day? Two? Three? Or only a few hours? How long since Thokk shut me in here? Perhaps it doesn't matter. Nothing matters. There are no weapons here. I can't get free. She isn't coming back. I'm going to die here. My flesh will join all these other forgotten ones, decaying. That's all I am now, flesh waiting to decay. Why even keep searching? Why not give in to sleep, stretch out on the floor, let the rats begin their feast . . .*

With a strangled sob Huld tried to push the thoughts of surrender away. She stopped searching and knelt, sobbing in the darkness. She wejpt for a long while, then slowly pulled herself back together, began searching again, suddenly felt stiff fabric. She probed through the folds of the cloth. Pain shot through her finger as something stabbed her. She jerked back with a cry, thinking of the sharp teeth of rats, pushed down her panic, and forced herself to reach into the cold fabric again.

Metal. It is metal! Something with a sharp point but not a dagger, not a sword, not a weapon of any kind. It was too small for that, a convex, hollowed-out piece of metal with a straight pin attached on a hinge. *A brooch,* she decided, carefully working it free of the fabric. *A brooch used to fasten a cloak or other outer garment.*

It came free. She moved on her knees away from the mound of corpses, trying to decide whether to tjry opening her ankle manacles first or those on her wrists. It was easier to reach the locks on her ankles. Better perhaps to try opening them first, then to use the experience thus gained to open the manacles on her wrists, which would be much harder to maneuver into the proper position.

She swiveled the sharp pin away from the body of the brooch and strained to reach the manacles on her ankles. She began to poke and prod within the locks. *Freya forbid that it should break,* she thought, hoping it was made of bronze or silver and not soft gold. The pin slipped. She moved it until it caught again, and applied gentle pressure.

Her muscles began to ache from the strained position. She straightened to give them a moment's relief, then reached down and back and began again, kept at it without success, refused to give up, straightened and relaxed a moment more, then tried again and again and again. . . .

Suddenly there was a soft click. A lock opened. The manacle on her right ankle came free.

Tears of relief filled her eyes. She tried to calm her excitement, to still her trembling fingers. She moved her freed feet to a more accessible position and began to work on the other ankle manacle, using what she had learned on the first one. After several failures there was another click.

Laughing with victory, Huld got to her feet, stamped her feet, and kicked her freed legs to shake off the crawling things that covered her nakedness. Then she began trying to maneuver the pin into the locks on the wrist manacles behind her. She lost her grip on the brooch. It fell to the floor. She cursed, squatted down, and searched among the crawling things until she found it. Then she stood and started trying again, succeeded in reaching one lock, slowly and carefully used what she had already learned, patiently kept trying and trying until there came another soft click.

With a cry of triumph she tugged the waist chain's lock around to the front, carefully worked on first the other wrist manacle and then the waist chain itself, until finally she was completely free of her bonds.

She started to hurl the waist chain and attached manacles away, decided they might make good weapons if the need arose, kept them instead, gathered up the ankle chains from the floor, and slung them all over her shoulder.

She invoked her night-vision spell. It had no effect.

Her hopes sank. Perhaps a spell had been placed upon the chamber itself. Maybe she would still not be able to use Freya's magic, even when free of the spell-chains.

The spell-chains . . . perhaps as long as they even touch my flesh will they inhibit my magic.

Reluctantly she tossed all of the chains away, tried the night-vision spell again. This time it worked, her eyes soon flickering with yellow-gold light. She looked down at the brooch and laughed at what she saw. It was decorated with an image of the Goddess Freya. *So, I am not the first who honored Freya to have been imprisoned here. Whomever you were who owned this brooch, my revenge shall be for you as well. Thokk probably let you keep this pin to mock you even in death, but it will lead to Freya's victory instead, and Thokk's destruction. I swear it by Freya and by my soul.*

She hurried to the door, and intoned her spell to open locks.

A blast of purple fire flared from the lock, struck her forehead, and hurled her back, stunning her.

With a curse she realized that she would not be opening the lock with her magic, but perhaps with the pin on the brooch . . .

She inserted it into the lock, felt it catch, applied pressure. With a sudden snap the pin broke.

Cursing, Huld started to throw the brooch away, then calmed herself and held onto it instead. *No*, she told herself, *I must keep it always.* She looked around the chamber. Might there be another way out? She had no choice but to look. Thokk had said that the chamber was the deepest one in the castle. It might therefore conceal a secret escape route for its inhabitants in time of siege.

The chamber stretched away into a distant darkness even Huld's night vision could not penetrate. She began to search the nearer walls, satisfied herself that there was no way out there. She moved reluctantly into the darkness beyond, gagging with the stench as the mounds of rotting bodies grew steadily higher, the rats more numerous, the floor thicker with crawling things, until they swarmed ankle-deep over her bare feet.

Looking around, she found that she could no longer see the door. *If Thokk does come for me and I am back here, she might not search, might really leave me here to die. . . .*

A frantic need to return to the door possessed her, but she fought it down and kept moving, clutching tight to the brooch as if Freya's image might give her strength.

Suddenly she stopped, listening intently. Something panted up ahead, a beast from the sound. She slowed her pace, moved cautiously forward, finally saw something crouched on all fours atop a mound of corpses. It was unidentifiable. It moved down the mound toward the floor, its movements at first like those of a serpent, then like a rat, a wolf, a mountain cat.

Fear grew within her as it moved onto the floor and stalked forward toward her, sniffing the air. She could see now that its very form was shifting from moment to moment. Save for its burning purple eyes, it seemed no more than the shifting shadows of many beasts.

Huld stood motionless, searching the spells she possessed, pushed down panic, then concentrated upon a spell to banish wild beasts. The creature stopped and listened to the lilting language of Freya she was chanting. Then it began to growl, to hiss, to howl, and started toward her again, moving faster and faster.

She kept repeating the invocation, concentrating more and more of her energy upon making the spell work, giving it power, force, and strength.

The creature slowed, screamed, gathered its wavering limbs beneath it, and leapt for her throat, its form dissipating even as it jumped.

A cold chill swept through her as the remains of the thing reached her. She hugged herself against the more-than-physical cold. She had won another victory. But had she still been in spell-chains, unable to invoke her own magic...

She shuddered at the thought, then moved forward again, watching for any other danger that might lurk in the depths of the Chamber of Decay.

The walls and ceiling began to lower, the mounds of corpses to decrease in size. Huld kept going, and soon saw no more corpses.

The chamber became more and more tunnellike until she was moving through a narrow passageway angling downward. Encouraged, she hurried forward. Crawling things no longer scuttled upon the floor. The air was steadily becoming cleaner and easier to breathe.

The tunnel turned to the left. Rocks blocked the way. Huld cursed, then began straining to move them. Soon her hands were bleeding as she clawed at the stones, dislodging the smaller ones, slowly making a small passageway.

She worked on and on, sweat streaming down her bare flesh in spite of the cold. Then a whisp of fresh air caressed her face. She revoked her night-vision spell and saw faint light coming through a tiny crack between two small rocks.

She wrenched the rocks out, breathed deeply of cold, crisp air, basked in the meager light thus revealed, began working again, and finally had an opening just large enough to squeeze through.

She ran toward the light, laughing.

Huld reached the end of the tunnel, looked out upon cloudy skies and snow-covered mountain peaks, and saw that the tunnel opening was itself on the side of a steep cliff, too far from the ground to jump. She would have to climb down.

Perhaps there was once a rope here, she thought, *to make climbing down easier. But I can make it. I have to.* An icy breeze bathed her nakedness. *I won't last long after climbing down, though, not naked like this.* And there was no place she could acquire clothes, except...

The Chamber of Decay, she thought, sickened. *I should have thought of it before starting to search, should have prepared for finding a way out. But there is no point in thinking about what I should have done. I must take each step now as it comes, and be wary of new danger. There's no one to help me, not Norda, nor even Bloodsong if she is indeed dead, Freya forbid.*

An emptiness nearly as great as the knowledge of Norda's death fell upon Huld as she tried to imagine Bloodsong dead.

Freya willing, she escaped, Huld told herself, *but I can't count on her to help me, even if she is still alive. When I have enough clothing to keep me from freezing outside, I will find a way to return and destroy Thokk, a way to free Guthrun and the others, a way to revenge Norda, Eirik's Vale, and Bloodsong, if she's dead. But first I need that clothing. I must not make any mistakes. It's all up to me now. I'm all alone....*

She looked down at the brooch in her hand and gazed at Freya's image.

Well, she added, in thought, *perhaps not entirely alone. Freya, give me victory....*

Carefully keeping the brooch clasped tightly in her left hand, Huld turned and hurried back the way she had come.

30
Homecoming

Waveslasher again rode the still waters of the inlet near Magnus's home. The nine longships of the Berserkers rode there too, all empty now, the more than two hundred warriors who had crewed them standing with weapons and shields ready, staring at the ruins of the farmstead.

Magnus emerged from the smashed doorway of his longhouse carrying his wife's body in his arms, tears streaking his bearded face.

"She looks as if she's been in the grave for a year," Grimnir said to Bloodsong as Magnus came toward them, "as do the others," he added with disgust, glancing at the other rotting bodies sprawled here and there on the ground.

"Death Riders," Bloodsong answered, her voice tight with rage. "Thokk must have sent them to find me. They followed my trail here somehow but either lost it at the water's edge or were not able to cross the sea to the island."

"Perhaps," Grimnir suggested, "because the land is Hel's domain, but the sea is Aegir's and Ran's."

"Perhaps," Bloodsong agreed. "But what I do know for

certain is that what you see here is what I saw in Eirik's Vale when my warriors tried to fight the Death Riders. Merely to touch your weapon to theirs is to die. We will help Magnus care for his dead, but quickly. The Death Riders are no doubt still searching for me. They may sense my return and come back."

When oval graves had been dug and filled, then outlined with stones and the burial ceremonies completed, Magnus turned to Bloodsong. "I'm coming with you," he announced, "as are most of my crew. We demand to be a part of your vengeance, for it's also our vengeance now."

Bloodsong started to refuse, not wanting to see more die futilely trying to fight the Death Riders but could not deny Magnus his deserved revenge. She nodded in agreement. "But if Death Riders approach, remember what I've told you. Do not attack them. Try to avoid all contact with them. We will let the Berserkers form a shield wall around us and fight the Death Riders. I just pray that Odin's magic will protect them from the Death Riders' death-touch."

Grimnir gave Freehoof's reins to Bloodsong and she mounted. Their horses, which they had left at Magnus's farmstead, had not been harmed by the Death Riders, nor had any of Magnus's animals.

Harbarth approached, Ulfhild by his side. "Are your legs injured as well as your hands?" he asked Bloodsong.

"Harbarth and his people think it is a sign of weakness to ride horses," Grimnir explained with a laugh as he mounted Bloodhoof.

"It's just as well," Bloodsong answered. "I doubt that any horse would accept them."

Harbarth laughed. "Ride your stallions, then." He grinned. "We will run slow enough for you to keep up."

"Harbarth," Bloodsong said, becoming serious, "you've seen here what Death Riders can do. If you do not want to risk your people's lives, I will understand. Even though I had told you about the Death Riders, actually seeing the aftermath of their attack may have made you have second thoughts."

"It has not."

"If we die fighting them," Ulfhild said with a shrug, "we die. Odin wills us to help you, Ropebreaker, and help you we shall."

Bloodsong and Grimnir guided their horses away from the farmstead, Magnus and most of the crew of *Waveslasher* following on their own horses, the Berserker army jogging along in no particular order.

"Faster, Ropebreaker!" Ulfhild shouted, running alongside Freehoof. "This slow pace is insulting!"

Bloodsong gave the Berserker woman a raised-eyebrow glance, then kicked Freehoof into a canter.

"Better!" Ulfhild called, breaking into a long-strided lope, easily keeping up.

"But how long can they keep up this pace?" Bloodsong asked Grimnir, turning toward him.

"All day and night if Odin wills it!" Ulfhild shouted.

Grimnir laughed. "Ears of a wolf," he commented. "Speak softer, Bloodsong, if you don't want Ulfhild to overhear."

"Excellent advice!" Harbarth shouted from even farther away. "Many's the time I wish I'd heeded it myself!"

Ulfhild laughed and swatted at him playfully with her double-bladed war ax.

"May I ask you something, Wolf-ears?" Bloodsong called to Ulfhild. "I saw no children on the island." Her thoughts had turned again to Guthrun.

"You did not see them, but they no doubt saw you," Ulfhild answered. "They were there, Runethroat. They were there. But not with us. At birth we leave them with the beasts. If they prove worthy and survive, they find their way back when old enough to wield sword and ax."

"But by then, how can you be certain which is yours?"

Ulfhild and Harbarth laughed louder than ever.

"By their scent," Grimnir said.

Bloodsong just shook her head and glanced skyward at the sun. They had arrived at the farmstead near noon. Most of the afternoon had been spent burying the dead. Sunset was now not far away. But she had no intention of stopping to make camp.

"We must watch the sky closely during the daylight hours," she said to Grimnir, certain that Ulfhild and Harbarth would also hear. "If clouds appear, we should start worrying about Death Riders. Their skeletal steeds cannot bear the touch of direct sunlight."

"And they themselves?" Grimnir wondered.

"I don't know. Sunlight does not affect other Hel-warriors, only their Hel-horses. But Death Riders..." She ended with a shrug. "At night, however, we must be wary all the time. And whether night or day," she said, turning to Ulfhild and Harbarth, "we may have warning of their approach by a low moaning sound, the Hel-wind upon which their white steeds tread."

"I will listen for such a sound," Ulfhild promised, "as will all our people."

"And at night," Bloodsong went on, "if they are not riding the Hel-wind, we might have some slight warning by the purple fires that burn in their eyes and in the eyes of their steeds."

"Our eyes are as sharp as our ears, Ropebreaker," Harbarth replied, "and since they are living-dead creatures, our noses may be of help, too, in detecting their death-scent, if we are downwind from them."

Bloodsong nodded and flexed her bandaged hands with a grimace. Her hands became stiff if she did not move them often, and gripping the reins of her horse was only making matters worse. The healing flesh beneath the bandages had also begun to itch. But she did her best to ignore her discomfort as she turned her thoughts to the dangers ahead, trying to think of other ways to insure that the journey ended in victory over Thokk and Kovna and freedom for Guthrun.

The day faded into night as they kept traveling onward, Bloodsong keeping careful watch for specks of purple fire in the darkness and for the first hint of a moaning wind. But the night wore on uneventfully, stars wheeling serenely across the heavens. For a short while thunder rumbled far to the west, and they saw the faint flash of lightning, but the distant storm drifted south without coming nearer.

They gave the horses a short rest at a stream and took the opportunity to refresh themselves as well. Then they set out once more, moving ever northward toward the forests and mountains that were their destination.

At dawn Bloodsong called another short rest, glad to see that the sky was still clear, no clouds in sight. But as they traveled on later in the morning, she saw black clouds forming farther to the north, moving southward with great speed.

"There's a moaning sound, Runethroat," Harbarth said, running alongside Freehoof, "getting louder."

"Form the shield wall," she quietly ordered, flexing her bandaged hands. Then she shouted orders to the others.

The Berserkers formed a double shield-wall around Bloodsong and the others.

"I don't care for being out of the fight," Grimnir growled.

"Neither do I," Bloodsong agreed.

"Nor I," Magnus added.

The Berserkers continued to joke and laugh while waiting for the battle to begin. The moaning sound grew steadily louder.

"I had heard," Bloodsong said to Grimnir, "that their kind worked themselves into a frenzy before battle, even to gnawing on their shields."

"Harbarth once spoke of that to me during our stay on the island years ago," Magnus told her. "He said that it is a hard habit to break, but better that than to break your teeth."

As the moaning grew ever louder the Berserkers grew quiet, weapons and shields held ready. Noses wrinkled at the first hints of the death-stench that surrounded the Death Riders.

They should have shape-shifted, Bloodsong told herself. *They shouldn't try to fight in human form. Odin's magic will be strongest in beastform.* But when she had earlier suggested that strategy to Harbarth, the leader had flatly refused, saying that it was not honorable to use beastforms unless faced by overwhelming odds, and Bloodsong's insistence that the Death

Riders, though only nine in number, qualified as overwhelming, had been met with laughter by Harbarth and Ulfhild alike. *Odin grant that they are right and I wrong*, Bloodsong thought as she wrapped a bandaged hand around the hilt of her sword and slowly drew the blade.

The Death Riders came into view in the distance. The heavy clouds racing ahead of them overhead quickly covered the sun. The purple fires in their eyes became visible.

The Death Riders could simply ride the wind over the shield-wall, Bloodsong knew. *They may not fight the Berserkers at all but come straight for me, unless Odin's magic in the Berserkers forces Hel's slaves to confront them.*

She and the others stood waiting. Suddenly she gasped with pain, the burns around her throat flaring to agony. Her hands flew to her neck, her sword falling to the ground.

"Bloodsong!" Grimnir cried.

"My neck!" she gasped, crumpling to her knees. "It's on . . . fire!"

Grimnir knelt beside her, put an arm around her shoulders as she shuddered with the pain, and tried to comfort her, helpless to do more.

As suddenly as it had come, the pain was gone. She heard a howling arise from the Berserkers that nearly covered the moaning of the Hel-wind. She picked up her sword and got back to her feet.

The Death Riders are indeed going to fight the Berserkers, she suddenly knew, but did not stop to question how she knew it, and she also suddenly knew that she had been right. Only in beastform could they defeat the Death Riders. "Don't fight them as humans!" she shouted. "Harbarth! Ulfhild! Shapeshift! I was right!" But there was no time. The nine Death Riders charged the shield-wall, engaged the Berserkers.

Harbarth's people began to fight and die. Some were slain at once, decaying as they fell. Others seemed unaffected by the death-touch and fought the Death Riders as they would have any foe. But then, some of those not at first affected by the death-touch began to succumb, and the ones who yet fought

on soon found all their battle skills ineffectual against the
preternatural speed of the Death Riders.

"Shape-shift, curse you!" Bloodsong screamed, filled with
a rising fury as she saw more and more Berserkers fall decaying.

All around her the Berserkers continued to fight and fall,
those who still stood fighting on with the ferocity of their kind,
meeting death without flinching, battling to the last.

The fury boiling within Bloodsong erupted in a ragged scream
of rage. She started forward to do battle, shook off Grimnir's
attempt to pull her back, her emotions overflowing, out of
control, sweeping away all rational thought. She ran toward
the collapsing shield-wall, screaming a battle cry that quickly
became more and more like the howling of a maddened beast.

Decaying bodies lay everywhere. Howls and shouts of Odin's
name mixed with the moaning of the Hel-wind as the Berserkers
kept fighting and the Death Riders continued to reap their
harvest of death, corpse-faces glaring down in triumph at those
they were killing from atop their blood-splattered white steeds,
black swords rising and falling like executioners, tirelessly,
relentlessly, eyes of purple fire flaring brighter with each kill,
skeletal mouths grinning the smile of Hel, the grimace of Death.

Then suddenly a howl ripped the air that gave even the
Death Riders pause. Fiery purple eyes looked up from their
grim harvest. Hel-horses shied nervously. Black swords stopped
in mid-stroke.

With another howl, a berserking, raven-black beast leapt
among them and began tearing at dead throats with stiletto
fangs, slashing through sunken, mail-clad chests with razor
claws, howling and slavering with boundless bloodlust and
fury. Thin, keening screams squeezed from the Death Rider's
skeletal throats and emerged from their gaping death grins.

A Hel-horse sped away, riderless, leaving a Death Rider
writhing on the ground, headless, his decaying flesh turning
to maggot-ridden, slime-coated dust.

Another Death Rider fell as the slavering beast tore at him
and then at the others, the beast suffering deep cuts from black

blades without pausing, moving with blinding speed, evading whirring strokes that might have proved fatal, but ignoring less serious wounds as it continued to tear at its enemies. Another Death Rider succumbed to the beast's fury and fell writhing to the ground.

The remaining six Death Riders turned and sped away.

The beast pursued them a short distance, howling for more of their putrifying blood, then it stopped, collapsed onto the ground, jerked spasmodically several times, and lay still, blood pouring from its wounds.

Bloodsong groaned and opened her eyes. Grimnir was kneeling on the ground, cradling her head in his lap, grim lines of concern etched into his face as he soothingly stroked her raven-black hair.

"The battle!" she said, starting to sit up. Pain shot through her.

"Lie still," Grimnir ordered sternly, easing her back down onto his lap. "Your wounds have stopped bleeding and seem to be healing, but if you move too soon, they might open again."

"Wounds? My throat and hands?"

"You don't remember what happened?" he asked. "Three of the Death Riders were slain, the other six driven away."

Bloodsong frowned, memories flitting on the edge of her consciousness. "I'm beginning to remember, I think. A black beast? A Berserker who finally did as I ordered and shape-shifted! One of Harbarth's people. You were right, Grimnir. Odin's magic gave Harbarth's people victory!"

"Odin's magic, yes," Grimnir answered, continuing to stroke her hair, "but it was not one of Harbarth's people who came to our aid."

"Then who—" she began, but stopped as other memories arose.

By the expression which then covered her face, by the look of horror and disgust in her eyes, Grimnir knew he would not have to tell her who had saved them. She knew.

She had herself become the beast.

31
Blackwolf

"We know now how she broke the gallows' noose," Ulfhild said to Harbarth, watching from a distance as Bloodsong lay with her head in Grimnir's lap. At Ulfhild's feet were Bloodsong's sword, the bandages that had covered her throat and hands, and the shredded remnants of her doeskin breeches and tunic.

"Aye," Harbarth agreed. "Odin's magic burned the runes in her neck while yet she hung, and the runes called forth the beast."

"Her flesh expanded as she shape-shifted to beastform," Ulfhild continued, "breaking the rope just as she broke the seams of her clothes when she shifted to beastform during the battle. Do you suppose she'll ask us to repair these clothes again, Harbarth? Their tearing was not our doing this time. Why won't she just let her flesh be free like ours? Then she would only have a breechclout about which to worry when she shape-shifts. Odin curse me if I'm going to be her seamstress every time she takes beastform."

Bloodsong turned her head. Over the distance between them her eyes met Ulfhild's.

"Harbarth," Ulfhild whispered, "I think we'd best watch our words around her from now on. I believe the beast's appearance awakened her senses, and from the look on her face, I don't think she realizes it's a blessing instead of a curse."

Harbarth nodded, Bloodsong's eyes now meeting his. "We became shape-shifters because it was natural to our souls," he said, "but Bloodsong has had it thrust upon her without warning. Odin knows why."

Ulfhild picked up the shredded clothing, then they walked toward Bloodsong and Grimnir.

"I will not ask you to repair my clothing, Ulfhild," Bloodsong said coldly when they'd reached her. "I will mend it myself as we ride."

She sat up, most of her pain gone, most of her wounds healed except for her palms, the rune burns around her neck, and the spear wounds from her testing.

"Only wounds received in beastform heal afterward," Harbarth told her, "as long as they are not fatal *while* in beastform, of course."

Bloodsong got to her feet, and faced the two Berserkers. "How many of your people died?"

"Many now feast in Valhalla with Odin, but more than half remain alive."

Bloodsong looked beyond him to the sprawled, decaying corpses that marked the battleground, looked at the Berserkers still on their feet. "But nearly half died," she finally said, "and *all* would have died had I not become that . . ." Her voice trailed away, face twisting with disgust. She mastered her emotions and looked back at Harbarth and Ulfhild.

"Odin's magic was strong in you both, and in the others who survived the Death Riders' death-touch. Those who fell first were not so deeply imbued with Odin's force. But in time you would all have succumbed. When the Death Riders appear again, shape-shift at once and fight in beastform. Surely you see now that no honor will be lost."

"Aye," Harbarth agreed.

"And you, Blackwolf?" Ulfhild asked. "Will you also shape-shift and do battle by our sides?"

Bloodsong said nothing.

"It's a blessing, Blackwolf, not a curse."

"The beast she became was not exactly a wolf, Ulfhild," Harbarth commented, "nor exactly a bear."

"Then what name would *you* give to honor her victory?" Ulfhild asked, irritated. Her ability to invent appropriate names was well-known among the Berserkers.

Harbarth knew that he should have kept silent and tried to shrug it away. "Blackwolf is a *good* name, Nameweaver," he hastily agreed, winking at Grimnir and nodding vigorously, "though in truth I've never seen the like of the beast she became. It was more like a wolf than anything else, I suppose, but Odin knows what its true name might be."

"Why don't you decipher the runes around her throat," Ulfhild taunted, knowing that it would sting his pride to remind him of his inability to read those runes. "Odin probably wrote the beast's true name there for all to see, don't you agree, Runesmith?"

"I told you I thought Blackwolf a *good* name."

"But you did not mean it. I saw the wink you gave Grimnir. I know what you really—"

"Enough!" Bloodsong cried. She tore her shredded clothing from Ulfhild's hand, pushed roughly past the startled Berserkers, and stalked to her horse. She jerked her rolled cloak from its saddle thongs and slipped it around her bare shoulders, then rolled up her torn clothing and tied the bundle behind her saddle.

"I did not mean to upset her," Ulfhild said to Grimnir.

"Nor I," Harbarth agreed.

"I know that, and so does she," Grimnir assured them, then walked toward Bloodsong.

Magnus approached her, holding a bundle of clothing in his arms. "If you like," he said, standing just out of reach, "you may have these."

"Afraid I will rip your head from your shoulders if you come too near?" she asked. "That's what beasts do, isn't it?"

Magnus looked at Grimnir as the red-bearded warrior came

up to them. "I . . . collected an extra pair of breeches and a tunic from my crew. We are grateful for what she did. We would all have died otherwise."

Grimnir nodded, took the offered bundle, and then motioned for Magnus to leave.

He held the clothes out to Bloodsong. "Put them on," he urged, his voice low and soothing.

"Perhaps Ulfhild is right. Perhaps I should go naked like they do, like a beast—"

"Stop it, Bloodsong. Think, woman. Odin has given you a power that may help you rescue Guthrun and destroy Thokk. And even if you never use that power again, it has saved us this day from certain defeat. Ulfhild is right about its being a blessing and not a curse. And you are *not* a beast. Beasts no doubt dwell in *all* of us. Odin's magic and fury merely give it form, and the Gods help me if I ever should become your enemy. I saw what you did to the Death Riders, the way you fought. I've never seen anything so . . ."

"Horrible?"

"Magnificent. Would that Odin had blessed me in such a manner during my testing on the gallows' tree."

Bloodsong looked away, watched Harbarth and Ulfhild helping to pile their dead in preparation for burning. She cursed softly and looked back at Grimnir. "When I realized what I had become, that I had lost all humanity, I—"

Grimnir's gentle touch on her face stopped her. He bent forward, kissed her lightly on her lips, pulled back, and looked deeply into her eyes. "You did not lose your humanity. You killed only enemies. Do you see any disgust in my eyes for you?" he asked. "Do you?"

She shook her head negatively and looked away.

"Then feel none for yourself. You've nothing for which to be ashamed, and everything for which to be proud."

"I don't want to . . . become that thing, ever again."

"Perhaps it won't be necessary," Grimnir suggested.

"I said I did not *want* to become that beast again, not that I wouldn't."

Grimnir nodded and squeezed her shoulder. "Should I ask Ulfhild to put more salve on your palms and throat and bandage them again?"

"I will ask her myself, but first let me put on these clothes, though Freya knows I'll look foolish. They're bound to be too large, as were the woodcutter's."

"Somehow," Grimnir said, "I doubt that anyone will laugh."

When Bloodsong had dressed and Ulfhild had again cared for her palms and throat, she went to help the Berserkers care for their dead. Soon the only bodies not heaped on the funeral pyre were the remains of the three fallen Death Riders.

Bloodsong looked down at them, forcing herself to remember that it was she who had destroyed them, fighting her revulsion with the knowledge that she had been able to do what she could not have done before the gallows' ride. She had been able to combat Hel's magic and win.

She prodded the black mail shirt of a Death Rider with the toe of a boot, which, like all the clothes she now wore, was too large.

Nothing remained of the Death Riders' flesh but dust. She reached down and picked up a black-bladed sword a Death Rider had but recently wielded. A silver skull gleamed on the pommel.

When she had fought Nidhug in Hel's name, she had worn black mail and wielded a black-bladed sword much like the one she now held. She looked thoughtfully down at the empty mail shirt at her feet, at the black leather breeches, the black steel battle-helm. She caught the mail shirt on the point of her sword, and lifted it into the air. Several maggots fell out of it onto the ground and squirmed madly in the sunlight.

She carried the mail shirt to the fire that was consuming the bodies of the slain Berserkers, held it over the flames a moment on the outstretched sword, pulled it back, and dropped it onto the ground to cool.

Grimnir watched her and guessed her intent.

She walked back to the Death Riders' remains and picked up a Death Rider's shield.

The black circular shield was emblazoned with a silver Bjork rune, the rune that encompassed the mysteries of Hel. Bloodsong remembered holding just such a shield during her battles to reach Nastrond and Nidhug.

She placed the shield on the ground, bundled onto it a pair of black leather breeches, boots, sword belt and scabbard, and a steel battle-helm, then lifted the shield and carried it all back to the fire.

Bloodsong sat the shield on the ground near the fire, checked the mail shirt, and found it now cool to the touch. She felt Grimnir's gaze and looked up into his eyes for a long moment, then began to dress herself in the clothing of the Dead.

32
Allegiance

"You are not stupid, Guthrun," Thokk fumed, "and you're not a fool. Why do you insist upon acting like both?"

Guthrun laughed. "You expect me to give allegiance to you and Hel after what your precious Lokith has caused me to suffer? Nothing you can do to me could be worse than what I experienced with him. How long did you leave me there? Two days alone with him? Three? More?"

"You are not harmed."

"Only because he healed me whenever I slipped too near death! He *wants* me dead. He wants *you* dead. We're threats to his power."

"I am no threat to him. If not for me—"

"And if not for me he would not be alive, or as alive as he can be. You don't have to take my word. Probe his thoughts as you do mine. Learn the truth for yourself."

Thokk was silent.

"You *can* probe his thoughts, can't you?"

There was still no response.

"You can't?" Guthrun suddenly understood. "Freya's teeth.

You can't. You can't control him, either. He's truly as much a threat to you as he is to me. What other powers does he have, Thokk? I know he can see in the dark and heal wounds. What other magic have you given him? Surely not everything you know. If that were true, even you would be helpless against him."

"Enough!" Thokk commanded. She had been sitting in the chair in Guthrun's room. Now she rose to her feet and glared down at Bloodsong's daughter, who sat on the bed. Guthrun got to her feet, too, and glanced around the small room that had once again become her prison.

"I don't know what you had planned for Lokith and me, Thokk," Guthrun continued, "but surely this small room from which you don't dare let me go was not the goal, not for me. You've talked about my becoming a Hel-Witch. I refuse. I will always refuse. You've talked about dark powers waiting to be given freedom within me. I refuse to let that happen, too, though I've come to believe that they are probably indeed there. I've felt them stirring when I was near death in Lokith's chamber.

"And Lokith, Thokk? I assume that he was to have been my partner of sorts. Instead he wants both me and you dead. Surely not as you planned, either. Perhaps we two should begin to make new plans, Hel-Witch—plans to destroy Lokith before he can destroy us."

Thokk stared angrily at Guthrun. Guthrun was right about one thing at least. Things were not at all happening as planned, but they were far from out of her control, she felt certain. She had probed Guthrun's thoughts, learned that Guthrun was not trying to trick her this time, did truly feel great fear of Lokith, really believed him a threat to them both. And Guthrun's thoughts had also revealed the things he had done to the young woman—horrible, brutal things Thokk had not expected. His brutality had pushed Guthrun away from acceptance of Hel instead of toward it, had caused Guthrun to become once again as stubbornly resistant as when she'd first been captured. But in truth she could not lay *all* the blame for Guthrun's renewed resistance upon Lokith. There were also the memories in Guthrun's mind of touching Bloodsong's thoughts and drawing strength from them, a thing that never should have been able to happen within the confines of Thokk's castle, yet had.

Thokk paced a few steps, stopped, and came back to face Guthrun. The Hel-Witch felt her frustration rising, her self-control slipping, her thoughts not as clear as usual, anger with the situation defeating her normal calm. And she was beginning to feel physically exhausted, too, as if some force were draining her strength. Even her sleep had not been sound for the past few days since...

Since Lokith awakened? Thokk suddenly thought. *No, it can't be. I gave him strength while healing him over the years, but he can't still be draining my energy now. Not without my permission. Yet, if he were, and if he might also be projecting mental magic at me, causing my self-control to slip, my anger with Guthrun to rise...*

No, Thokk denied. *I won't believe that of him, not without more proof. Guthrun is my main problem, not Lokith.*

"I have not used Witchcraft on your soul, Guthrun," Thokk finally said, "because that would have inhibited the free flow of the powers I wished to awaken within you. I can probe your thoughts or, as you've learned, strip away your consciousness with a sudden burst of pain, but those do not touch your soul. However, since you continue to resist, obviously something more drastic must be done. If trying to reason with you through mental and physical means has failed to do what must be done, then I must do that which I had hoped to avoid."

"Admit defeat?" Guthrun suggested. "Help me destroy Lokith?"

Thokk forced down an explosively angry reply and took a deep breath in an attempt to calm herself. "No, Guthrun. I speak of a shock to your soul, something that will momentarily stop you from denying and repressing your true self, your true powers. Not a manipulation of your soul, understand, but a shock. A death-shock to be exact, a rune-bladed dagger plunged into your heart and, after a moment, withdrawn, then the wound quickly healed and your flesh returned to life. You have said that you felt your powers stirring when near death in Lokith's chamber. The dagger will enhance that affect, and in that moment of truth, when you die, you will come face-to-face with your inner self, see that what I've been patiently telling you is true. After that, since as I've already said, you're neither stupid nor a fool, you will stop this ridiculous resistance and become that which you were born to become, a leader of Hel's army of Witches and warriors, Lokith and you and I working together to establish a new order on Earth according to Hel's wishes."

Carefully Guthrun had made sure that she looked bored during Thokk's speech, glancing around the room, purposefully yawning while chilled deep within.

"Perhaps you should go talk to Lokith, Thokk. He might enjoy the sound of your voice more than I do. Or maybe he will entertain you by making you scream like he did me."

Thokk's angry gaze pierced Guthrun's eyes. Bloodsong's laughter forced another yawn and stretched out on the bed. Not until Thokk had left the room and locked the door behind her did Guthrun allow her face to show the fear she felt. *Hurry, Mother,* she thought over and over again like a prayer. *Please, hurry.*

Lokith smiled coldly. Alone in his small cell, he had reached out with his mind and detected all that had happened in Guthrun's room, thoughts as well as actions. He had become tense only once: when Thokk began to suspect the truth about his draining her strength and using mental magic to cloud her thoughts. But his will had been stronger than hers, and he had quickly led her suspicions and concerns away from him and back toward Guthrun.

The death-shock will be a shock to both Guthrun and to you, Thokk, he thought, laughing softly, *when I prevent my dear sister from being brought back to life. You will yourself, Thokk, have killed Hel's Deadborn Witch-child. I will then have no choice but to execute you. Such a traitor to Hel's plans*

could not, of course, be allowed to go unpunished. No matter
that the death-shock came into your mind at my bidding and
that it will be my hand that prevents Guthrun from being brought
back from the dead. But I will need support to accomplish this
plan, and I know exactly where to find it.

He went to the door and hissed the spell to open locks. A
blast of purple fire exploded the door outward. He strode through
and turned up the stairs. It was time to seal Guthrun's doom,
and Thokk's. Time to begin his ascent to the throne of the
world.

"A word with you, Thokk!" Kovna demanded as he stepped
into the hallway ahead of her. He glanced at Vafthrudnir, standing behind Thokk, then settled his gaze on the Hel-Witch
herself.

"I've no time to talk with you just now," she said, and tried
to brush past him. He stepped to block her path. Styrki and a
group of warriors with drawn weapons emerged into the hallway to stand behind him, fear in all their eyes.

Curse my preoccupation with Guthrun, Thokk thought. *I*
should have sensed Kovna's presence, detected his thought
and avoided him, just as I should have detected it when Hula
freed herself from the spell-chains in the Chamber of Decay
before getting herself killed. Why can't I think clearly? Why
can't I sense dangers before they occur as I always have been
able to do before? For just a moment her thoughts went to
Lokith, but were just as swiftly pushed back to Guthrun. *Curse*
that girl's stubbornness, Thokk angrily thought.

"I tried to tell you that I smelled humans," Vafthrudnir
rumbled behind her. "Shall I tear their heads from their shoulders, Mistress?"

Thokk shook her head negatively. "I could blast them all
myself with but a word and a thought," she said, holding
Kovna's gaze, "if I so desired. What is worth risking your life
and soul in this manner, Kovna?"

"Is it true that the Death Riders you sent for Bloodsong
have returned?"

"You have spies about my castle, do you?" she asked with
laugh, probing his thoughts and learning that it was true.
Yes, you *do* have spies. But it is not a secret, Kovna. The
Death Riders did indeed return."

"You sent nine. Only six returned."

"You are wasting my time, Kovna. You ask questions for
which you already know the answers."

"Did the six who returned bring evidence that Bloodsong
s dead?"

"She is dead," Thokk assured him, then thought about Guth-
an's mental contact with Bloodsong. *No, she must not be
dead. Why didn't I think of that? What's wrong with me? Why
m I suddenly making these dangerous mistakes?*

"Why did only six return? What happened to the other
aree?"

"I will send the Death Riders out again to make certain. I
ill have them bring back her head. Will that be proof enough?"

"Have your Jotun open the gateway, Thokk. I wish to send
en to scout the mountain trails leading to this castle. I have
warriors' instincts. I can sense that my enemy is still alive,
nd if that is true, she will be plotting to attack your castle."

"Let her!" Thokk laughed. "She will be destroyed."

"You are talking about the woman who nearly single-hand-
dly destroyed Nidhug. You can take nothing for granted when
ealing with Bloodsong. You don't *know* what happened to
ose three Death Riders, do you? I'll *tell* you, then. The Gods
now how, but Bloodsong has found some means of killing
em."

"Kill Death Riders?" Thokk laughed again, feeling uneasy.
t's not possible. Only the power of a God or Goddess could
o that."

"Then Bloodsong has obtained the aid of a God or Goddess."

"Such things are not easily accomplished."

"Difficulties have never stopped Bloodsong before. She led
slave revolt and escaped Nastrond when hardly more than a
irl. Open the gate, Thokk. For both our sakes. Let me send
ut patrols."

"There is no need. I will use magic to discover if she is a threat and to stop whatever she is planning, if she is indeed plotting a foolish attack."

"Open the gate. I wish to send patrols, anyway. I care nothing for your magics. I do not trust them. And there is another matter as well. My men brought two women to your castle, one not much more than a girl. Is it true that you allowed the older one to escape? The Witch who was Bloodsong's friend and helped destroy King Nidhug? She might even now be plotting with Bloodsong."

"She did not *escape*, Kovna. She *died*. I probed with my mind and could not find hers. And if you won't take *my* word, I sent Vafthrudnir to look for her too. He lost the trail. For a Jotun, that can only happen, when the one he seeks no longer exists in the flesh. It angered me for her to escape me by dying, but I content myself that her soul is screaming in Helheim and that her death, at the hands of a Shadow Beast in my Chamber of Decay, was suitably unpleasant."

"Open the gate," Kovna repeated. "Order your Jotun to open the gate."

"Order him yourself."

"He takes orders only from you."

"Then I suppose the gate will stay closed, since I want you to stay here. All of you. Because I don't trust you, either Kovna. Not in the least. I want you and your men here where my powers are the strongest, here where I can spy on you too."

The Hel-Witch brushed by Kovna.

Kovna signaled not to stop her. Vafthrudnir casually back handed Styrki as he passed. Styrki was hurled into a wall cursed with pain, got to his feet, and took a step after the Jotun.

"No," Kovna ordered.

Styrki controlled his anger with difficulty, and saluted his general instead of attacking the Frost Giant.

"We will try to open the gate ourselves," Kovna decided and led the way toward the courtyard.

They will never succeed, Thokk thought as she continued

her way, casting her mind back to detect Kovna's thoughts. *e gate is sealed by magic as much as by the bolt only fthrudnir can draw. But he is right about Bloodsong. I must nd the Death Riders out again. Why didn't I think of that fore? But I will do it now.* . . . Her thoughts trailed away and came unfocused. She tried to remember what it was she had en about to do, could not, continued on her way, the Death ders forgotten.

Lokith breathed a sigh of relief. He had only barely managed divert Thokk's thoughts from the Death Riders. *No, Thokk,* smiled as he continued on his way to the stables. *You will t send my Death Riders out. I am going to need them here * my own purposes. Bloodsong is no threat to me, not with * powers I possess, powers which I am beginning to realize ike yours insignificant by comparison. Hel has given me* *ore powers than you guessed, Thokk, powers beyond even ur imagining. I only need to become fully awake to them, rn to use them to their fullest extent, which I will soon be le to do, once you and Guthrun are no longer a threat to * sovereignty.*

Lokith entered the stable, found a trapdoor, and swung it and back. Below, darkness reigned. Lokith's eyes adjusted d began to flicker with purple fire. He descended a short ght of stairs and stood looking at the six black-clad warriors ng upon the rat-infested dirt floor.

The Death Riders lay upon their backs, hands folded upon *e*ir chests, dressed in full battle gear, ready to rise and obey. *Yes,* Lokith thought, *to obey me and only me.*

He traced runes in the air, faint lines of pulsing purple light iling in his finger's wake. He whispered a word of power. *e* Death Riders stirred, turned decay-ridden faces toward *n*. Within their empty eye sockets purple fires began to cker.

"I am Lokith," he said, "your new master, the one for whom u've waited, the one about whom Hel has whispered in your rkest dreams."

The Death Riders got to their feet, dried flesh creaking li
old leather. They stood silently staring at Lokith. *Thokk is o
mistress,* one of the Death Riders replied, his thoughts touchi
Lokith's mind.

Thokk cares nothing for you, Lokith responded in kin
Three of your number have been slain because of Thokk.
this not true?

We did as ordered. We found our prey, the warrior call
Bloodsong. But she had Odin's aid, became a Corpse Bea
such as those which stalked Hel herself in Time's Dawnin
We tried to kill her but could not. Mother Hel sensed our plig
and commanded us to retreat. Hel's orders overrule Thokk'
We returned here.

A Corpse Beast? Lokith responded. *Then she might inde*
be a danger after all. I will deal with her when Guthrun a
Thokk are dead. You did all you could, he told the Death Ride
then walked forward, placed his hand on the Death Rider
shoulder and gripped it firmly. *You did well, Axel Ironhand*

You . . . know my life-name? And you touch me without fa
ing? How is this possible? Even Thokk cannot do that, and s
has never used my life-name.

I know all your life-names, Lokith answered, *looking at t*
others. You are Einar—he nodded at one—*and you are Tho*
vald, and you Rolfgar, Bjorn, and Karl. I also know the nam
of your friends who died fighting Bloodsong and the name
every other Death Rider and Hel-warrior waiting in Helhe
*for the order to ride forth and conquer the Earth, for I am *
who will lead that conquest!

The Death Riders stood silently waiting, and Lokith kne
for what—the final sign that he was indeed whom he claime

He moved from one to the other, stopping before eac
leaning forward, kissing them on their fleshless mouths.
the touch of his lips upon their skullish faces, the purple fir
in their eyes burned brighter, each feeling more alive than th
had ever imagined it possible to feel again, the pain that po
sessed their every nerve suddenly fading away, ending t
agony they had felt since becoming the living Dead.

From within the glowing eye sockets of the Death Riders, drops of moisture emerged and slid downward over chilled bone and tattered flesh, as each in turn went onto one knee and bowed his head in allegiance and thanks to Lokith.

Arise and stand like the proud warriors you are, Lokith commanded, then waited until they had done so. *You will now obey only me. And through me you shall become masters of the new order that we will soon establish upon the Earth.*

The Death Riders drew their swords and held them in salute to their new leader. *Hail, Lokith!* they said as one with their thoughts, pledging allegiance to their new leader.

And Lokith laughed with joy.

33
Death-shock

Eyes of fire flickered in the dark. Ulfhild saw them f
and hissed a warning.

Though far from Ulfhild, Bloodsong heard the warning v
the enhanced hearing she now possessed. She drew her swo
then passed the word to Grimnir and the others riding near k
Then she saw the eyes herself. But they were not the pur
fire of Hel-magic. They were a golden-yellow, like the e
of a Freya-Witch using a night-vision spell. Like Huld's .

Bloodsong sniffed the air. In the days since the manifesta
of her beastform, she had worked to make using her enhan
physical senses automatic. Her nostrils flared. A death ste
still hovered around the Death Rider's clothing and armor
wore, but there was another death-stench just detectable on
cold night air.

She called a halt and rode forward alone through the ra
of the Berserkers until she reached Harbarth and Ulfhild.
sniffed the air again and frowned thoughtfully at another so
beneath the death-stench.

The eyes of yellow fire suddenly moved in her directio

"Bloodsong!" Huld cried, running toward her down the snow-covered mountain trail.

Several Berserkers raised their weapons.

"Let her pass!" Bloodsong commanded, recognizing her friend's voice, leaping to the ground and running forward. "It's Huld! A friend!"

The two women met, embraced.

"Guthrun?" Bloodsong asked at once.

"Still in the castle," Huld excitedly replied, "along with Valgerth and Thorfinn. I escaped and used my Witchcraft to make them think I had been killed. I wasn't sure it would work, but it did. I have been hiding here in the mountains for days, trying to think of a way to rescue them and destroy Thokk. I thought I would have to do it alone."

"Just as you once thought you could rescue Norda from Nidhug's fortress all by yourself," Bloodsong noted, then hugged the Freya-Witch to her again. "Thank Freya you're alive."

"I was told that you were probably dead, along with everyone in Eirik's Vale."

"Jalna survived too," Bloodsong quietly replied as they walked through the ranks of Berserkers. "She is here, as are Grimnir and others pledged to help rescue Guthrun."

"I saw Norda . . . die," Huld said, her voice catching slightly. "She tried to help me escape. It nearly worked. But there is a Jotun in Thokk's service, Vafthrudnir. He stopped Guthrun and me. I haven't seen Guthrun for some time, but Thokk has special plans for her, so I'm certain she's still alive."

"As am I. I will tell you how later."

"Your hands and throat . . . bandaged. I will heal them so you can better wield your sword. And who are these people?" she asked, eyeing the Berserkers they were passing. "Aren't they cold? They're nearly naked, and there's snow on the ground."

"Do wolves and bears get cold in the snow?" Bloodsong responded.

"What does that have to do with—" Huld began, then stopped. "Berserkers? Shape-shifters? Yes, I can sense Odin's magic pulsing in them, and . . . in you?"

"I'll explain that later too."

They reached Harbarth and Ulfhild. "This is Huld," Bloodsong told them. "She has escaped from the castle."

"We heard all you have said to each other," Harbarth replied. "Welcome, Huld. I am especially anxious to meet Vafthrudnir. His kind and mine are age-old enemies. His death will earn me much honor."

"Welcome, Fire-eyes," Ulfhild said to Huld. Her nose wrinkled at Huld's scent. "You stink of death."

"Thank Freya it's only my clothing," Huld replied, "though had I not escaped, it might well have been otherwise."

"I also wear the clothes of the Dead," Bloodsong noted, glancing down at the black leather and mail.

Ulfhild's nose wrinkled again. "Aye. It's enough to make me want to become your seamstress after all."

"And when we finally met Jalna and Tyrulf near Eirik's Vale," Bloodsong said, finishing her quick explanation to Huld of all that had happened, "we learned that their quest had been successful, too, though *how* successful and in just what way we are not sure. Perhaps you can tell us, Huld. Jalna, show her your rune-engraved sword and the bloodstained cloth."

Jalna drew her sword and handed it to Huld. The runes engraved upon the once-smooth blade began to glow with yellow-gold light the moment the Freya-Witch touched the hilt.

"Freya," Huld whispered reverently, raised the glowing blade to her lips and kissed it. "I have heard of the mound to the west. Norda talked of it often. She had visited it once as a youth, intended to take me there someday . . ." Her voice trailed away, tears glistening.

"We will all miss Norda," Jalna said, touching Huld's hand.

Huld nodded, pushed thoughts of Norda aside, and concentrated on the blade. "I cannot tell you all of Freya's mysteries influencing this blade, not without more time to study the runes and conjure visions. But I am *certain* that you need not fear the death-touch merely from this blade striking the sword of a Death Rider. Freya's magic is too strong in it for whoever wields it to be so easily slain. And it may slay a Death Rider as well, if the cut is well aimed. I would suggest the neck, severing the entire head if possible."

"And the cloth?" Tyrulf asked.

Huld reluctantly returned the sword to Jalna. The runes stopped glowing when it left her hand. She took the tattered cloth Jalna handed her and dropped it with a cry of pain.

"Freya's teeth," she cursed. "There is no subtlety in Thor, that blustering God. I could have had a headache for weeks if I'd not let go at once. I should have prepared myself."

She concentrated a moment, intoned lilting syllables, reached out, and cautiously picked up the cloth. This time there was only a sharp intake of her breath instead of an outcry of pain. She held it in her hands, lips moving soundlessly, eyes half closed, then slowly raised it to her face, carefully reached out with the tip of her tongue, and touched a dark stain. Her brows knit together in a frown, and she grimaced distastefully. She tossed the cloth back to Jalna.

"Thor's blood," she said, "no doubt about it. Does someone have some water or wine to wash the taste from my mouth?"

"Thor is a stalwart God, a friend of humankind," Tyrulf said defensively.

Grimnir handed Huld a wineskin. She gratefully took several long sips then handed it back.

"I meant no insult to Thor," Huld said to Tyrulf, "but he's a bit too ... well ..."

Grimnir laughed and took a drink of wine himself.

"How would you suggest using the Thor-magic in the cloth?" Jalna asked Huld.

"Yes, Huld," Bloodsong joined in. "Because of our enemy's position within the castle, and for Guthrun's sake, we dared not wait for a better opportunity, we had planned merely to try to surprise Thokk and Kovna, overwhelm them with the Berserkers in beast form. Harbarth and Ulfhild assure me that they can easily leap a castle's walls. But now that you are here and we've heard your description of the castle, perhaps there is a better way. I've some proposals to make myself, but what do you suggest?"

Huld was thoughtful for a moment. "Do you have some food?" she finally asked. "I've barely eaten for days. While I eat I'll think and talk, and then, afterward, heal your hands and throat."

"The rune burns on my throat may not respond to your Freya-magic," Bloodsong replied, handing Huld the food-pouch.

"We shall see," Huld said, biting into a hunk of cheese. "We shall see."

"Mistress Thokk," Vafthrudnir said as he brought Guthrun into the candlelit Chapel of Hel. Guthrun kicked and struggled wildly in his arms, cursing and trying to get free. Vafthrudnir all but ignored her efforts.

Thokk looked up from the preparations she was making at a slab of stone which served as an altar. Spell-chains and manacles were anchored along its sides.

"Humans are trying to open the gate," he told her as he reached the altar.

"Will they succeed?"

Vafthrudnir laughed.

"Of course not," Thokk agreed. "Even if their combined muscles were the equal of yours, my magic would keep it shut. Now place Guthrun on the altar, but be gentle, Vafthrudnir. In spite of her stubborn resistance, she is still my honored guest."

The Jotun easily controlled Guthrun's struggles. Within moments she felt the bite of manacles on her wrists and ankles holding her spread-eagled on the slab. Behind the altar rose a dais, and upon it Valgerth and Thorfinn were chained upright in X configurations. Guthrun knew that after her awakening she was to slay them both as proof of her new awareness and loyalty.

The Chapel of Hel soon filled with the castle's inhabitants, the black-hooded and -cloaked Hel-worshipers who served Thokk and, through her, Hel. A low murmur of voices permeated the incense-laden air as they talked of the anxiously awaited ceremony in which Guthrun, the Deadborn Witch-child of Hel, would soon have her Witch-powers awakened.

Thokk hooked her fingers in the neck of Guthrun's sleeping shift. Guthrun fought her chains.

"Soon you will revere Hel, your true mother," Thokk promised. "Soon you will awaken to your true self."

The Hel-Witch tore the shift away, leaving Guthrun naked. "When you awaken to your true self, you will be bathed, groomed, and given new clothing of purple and black. Then will your life truly begin, Guthrun, Hel's Daughter."

A stench of death wafted into the Chapel of Hel. The murmur of the Hel-worshipers suddenly stopped. Thokk looked up. Just inside the doorway stood Lokith and the six Death Riders.

He laughed at her expression. "Why so surprised, Thokk?" he asked. He was dressed in the black mail and leather of a Hel-warrior. At his side hung a scabbarded sword. "Surely you don't object to my watching my dear sister's awakening?"

"I did not intend you to—"

"Yes, I know. You had a grand ceremony planned to introduce me to Hel's followers. But now I'm here and can introduce myself. I am Lokith," he said to the Hel-worshipers. "There, now, Thokk. They know who I am. Continue with my sister's awakening."

"And you have introduced yourself to the Death Riders as well," Thokk noted, glancing at the six corpse-warriors.

Lokith smiled and walked toward the altar. The Death Riders stayed by the door, hands on sword hilts, blocking the way. Thokk glanced at Vafthrudnir, suddenly very glad for his presence.

"Good morning, Sister," Lokith said, reaching out to touch Guthrun's raven-black hair. She stiffened at his touch. He ran his hand lightly down the length of her body. "It *is* morning, you know. The sun will soon rise on a new day. Appropriate, wouldn't you say, Sister? A new day is dawning in your life too."

Guthrun spit toward him but missed his face.

Lokith drew back his hand to strike her.

"You will *not* strike her!" Thokk commanded.

Lokith laughed, lowered his hand, and patted Guthrun's

head instead. Then he looked up and smiled at Thokk. "Continue whenever you wish," he told her.

"He wants us *both* dead!" Guthrun said, twisting in her chains to catch Thokk's gaze. "Don't perform the ceremony with him here! He'll stop your healing my death wound, then probably kill you too!"

"Nonsense, Guthrun," Thokk snapped.

"I spent all those days locked in with him, Thokk. I know how he thinks. Please, Thokk! Listen to me. Don't trust him. Make him leave! If you can..." She shuddered.

"Who will you trust, Thokk?" Lokith grinned. "Will you trust me, who reveres Mother Hel and is anxious to serve her? Or will you trust this fool, who denies her birthright and seeks to stop Hel's plans?"

"Vafthrudnir," Thokk said quietly, eyes locked with Lokith's, "let nothing interfere with my actions during the ceremony. *Nothing*."

"Of course, Mistress Thokk," Vafthrudnir answered.

Lokith stepped back from the altar and motioned for Thokk to proceed.

Thokk struggled to think clearly. Why were her thoughts so confused? Perhaps she should wait to perform the ceremony. Perhaps she should not trust Lokith. Perhaps...

Her eyes touched his. Her confusion cleared. *There is no reason to wait any longer*, she suddenly thought. *Lokith can be trusted*, she was suddenly certain.

Lokith laughed softly to himself as Thokk's doubts were vanquished.

Thokk turned her attention to a black-bladed rune dagger on a richly carved and gilded pedestal near the altar. A silver skull gleamed on the dagger's pommel. She picked up the blade and held it close to Guthrun's face. "Behold the instrument of your awakening," Thokk intoned, then moved the dagger downward, touched the sharp point to the bare flesh over Guthrun's heart, and pushed inward slightly, just enough to draw a single drop of blood.

The Hel-Witch touched the blood-consecrated tip of the

dagger to her tongue, then she began to chant runes as she cut the air with the dagger, tracing runes of power, runes of Death.

Guthrun jerked wildly at her chains. Overhead, the ceiling of the Chapel of Hel was decorated with scenes of death and decay. Countless carved skulls grinned mercilessly down at her as she struggled futilely to get free. Behind the altar, Valgerth and Thorfinn also struggled without success to get free.

The low murmur of the crowd arose again and grew steadily louder and more impatient until suddenly Thokk raised the dagger, point downward, over Guthrun's straining, sweat-slicked nudity.

The crowd fell silent. Thokk's eyes began to blaze with purple fire as she concentrated every fiber of her will upon the dagger. The runes carved into the dagger's black blade began pulsing with purple fire. Guthrun screamed her denial of what was about to happen over and over and over as she writhed madly in her chains. Valgerth and Thorfinn hurled themselves against their bonds. Vafthrudnir watched Lokith and the Death Riders. Lokith ignored the Jotun and pretended to be absorbed in the ceremony, smiling coldly as he prepared to signal his Death Riders into action. Then suddenly Thokk screamed Hel-runes and plunged the dagger deep into Guthrun's racing heart.

34
Invaders

Bloodsong cried out in sudden pain, clutched at her heart, and reeled in her saddle.

"Bloodsong!" Grimnir cried as he urged his stallion closer.

The pain vanished as quickly as it had come. "I am . . . all right," she said, dazed, her breath coming in irregular gasps. "There was a pain in my chest, and . . ." Her voice trailed away.

"Guthrun," she said, moaning. "Something has happened to her. I know it. She—" Her voice broke, tears glistening. "Freya help me and her. I think we are too late. I think . . . she is dead."

No one spoke. The sun had risen, but the sky was heavily overcast. In the gray light Bloodsong looked at her companions.

They had decided that while the Berserkers attacked the castle in beastform from the outside, the rest would enter through the escape tunnel to invade and attack from within, Huld using the magic in the Freya-empowered swords and the bloodstained cloth to open locks and shield them from Thokk's detection.

Bloodsong pulled herself straight in her saddle. "We will proceed as planned," she said, her voice tight with rage and hurt, hoping that it might be possible to take Thokk alive, a need for vengeance burning molten in her heart.

Thokk jerked the dagger from Guthrun's heart and immediately began to intone the runes of resurrection and healing, her hands outstretched over the bleeding wound in Guthrun's chest, her eyes tightly closed in concentration.

Vafthrudnir saw Lokith motion to the Death Riders and reach for his sword. The Jotun started forward toward Lokith, saw a whir of movement out of the corner of his eye, jerked back, felt pain burn in his left shoulder as an ax hurled by a Death Rider buried itself to the bone in his flesh. Had he not moved in time, the blade would have found his skull instead.

The Jotun jerked the ax free, threw it at the Death Rider, saw it strike the corpse-warrior in the chest, hurling him backward with the force of the impact. Again there was movement out of the corner of his eye as Lokith rushed at Thokk with his sword.

Vafthrudnir dove forward, reaching for Lokith. Lokith threw himself back just in time, evading the Jotun's hands.

The Hel-worshipers in the chapel felt confusion for a few moments, then panic. They began trying to flee the Chapel of Hel, but found their way blocked by the Death Riders. Their panic grew. They started to curse and scream and fight among themselves as they tried to escape.

The distractions around her threatened to break Thokk's concentration, but she fought to keep her will focused, kept intoning the runes of healing and rebirth. Her hands began to glow with purple fire. A purple healing ray suddenly shot downward and bathed the bleeding wound in Guthrun's chest.

Lokith backed away from the Jotun, cursing, motioning his Death Riders forward.

Vafthrudnir picked up the heavy pedestal where the rune dagger had rested and hurled it at the approaching Death Riders. They avoided it, kept moving forward.

As the doorway cleared of Death Riders, the Hel-worshipers fought even harder to get through the portal.

Lokith noticed that only five Death Riders were advancing, saw the sixth lying unmoving near the door, an ax buried in his chest. Hel-worshipers were avoiding the skeletal body as they fought to escape through the door.

"Kill them all!" Lokith ordered his Death Riders, pointing at the altar, then hurried to the fallen Death Rider and pushed fleeing Hel-worshipers aside. He wrenched the ax out of the Death Rider's chest, traced runes in the air, spoke words of power. "Arise, Axel Ironhand," he ordered. The Death Rider jerked spasmodically, then struggled back to his feet.

Guthrun's body jerked once, twice, three times on the altar. Breath hissed into and out of her lungs once more, the wound in her chest healed. She opened her eyes, saw Thokk staring down at her.

The Hel-Witch laughed at the haunted look in Guthrun's eyes. *It succeeded*! Thokk knew, then turned her attention to her surroundings and saw the Death Riders nearing the altar, Vafthrudnir blocking their way.

Bloodsong reined Freehoof to a halt at the base of a cliff. "You are certain?" she asked Huld, looking upward at the seemingly solid, jagged rock wall.

"You can't see the escape tunnel's entrance from the ground," Huld replied, dismounting. "I assume that it was designed that way to keep it a secret."

Bloodsong dismounted and flexed her hands out of habit, then stopped. There was no longer any stiffness or pain. Before dawn, Huld's magic had healed her hands, but as she'd expected, not the burns on her throat, which remained bandaged.

"You're staring at me again," Huld growled, looking Ulfhild in the eye. "I don't like it."

"Why do you wear no hair on your head?" Ulfhild innocently asked.

"So *that's* why you've been staring. It's Thokk doing. But since I escaped her power, it's started to grow back. Be careful during the fight or she might do the same to you."

For a brief instant apprehension widened Ulfhild's eyes. Huld turned quickly away to conceal a grin, then her smile faded as she contemplated the cliff and the ordeal to come within the Castle of Thokk.

Bloodsong started to speak to the Berserkers, but suddenly she was shaken from within by a deep throbbing of emotion. She steadied herself against the cliff, momentarily dizzy.

"Bloodsong?" Grimnir asked with concern, moving closer.

"I . . . I'm all right. It's just that for a moment I felt as I did once long ago, when I first set eyes upon Guthrun after her birth. I think . . . yes! I know it. She lives once more!"

For a heartbeat no one spoke, then Huld said, suspiciously, "Thokk's magic?"

"Or maybe Guthrun was not truly dead?" Jalna suggested.

"A trick of some kind?" Grimnir asked.

"Aye," Tyrulf agreed. "The Hel-Witch seeks to trick us."

Bloodsong straightened. "All that matters is that Guthrun is alive, and by the Gods, she is going to stay that way! Speed is now essential. Caution be damned. Hurry, Huld, lead the way up the cliff!"

Thokk screamed words of power, raised her arms above her head, and flung them out to the sides. Thunder exploded within the Chapel of Hel. A blazing curtain of purple fire formed between the altar and the Death Riders, cutting them and Lokith off from their prey.

The corpse-warriors tried to pass through the fire, but could not.

"Why, Lokith?" Thokk cried, locking gazes with him through the curtain of purple fire.

His answer was to concentrate his will and intone words of power. The curtain of fire began to fade.

Thokk renewed the spell of protection. The curtain flared brighter again.

"I am stronger than you!" Lokith shouted. "Surrender, Thokk. I will let you live!"

"You are endangering Hel's plans!" she cried back.

"Am I? Perhaps Hel and I have plans about which you do not know."

"Don't do this, Lokith! Stop it now! I did not labor for thirteen years to heal you and help you to become what you now are only for you to—"

"Kill my sister and I will let you live," Lokith said, cutting her off.

"She, too, is part of Hel's plan!"

"Hel and I have made new plans, Thokk. Kill her. Now."

"You must kill me or set me free," Guthrun said, catching Thokk's gaze. "I can feel power within me, Thokk, and the knowledge to wield it, just as you promised. I ache to use that power. Let me. Together we can beat him. Alone you cannot. Take these spell-chains from me so that I may use my magic to aid you."

"Kill her, Thokk," Lokith urged. "You taught me well. I know all you know and more, and being who I am, who you and Hel have made me, I am more powerful too. Plunge that cursed dagger back into her heart."

"Choose, Thokk," Guthrun said. "You can't have both, and I am your only chance to live."

"You are both important!" Thokk cried.

"The fire curtain is fading again," Vafthrudnir noted, his deep voice tight with pain, blood pouring from his wounded shoulder. "And if you could spare some energy to heal this wound, I may live long enough to help you fight."

"Release me!" Guthrun demanded. "I will heal his wound while you keep the fire spell strong!"

Thokk hesitated a moment longer, glancing from one to the other, all her plans and dreams collapsing around her. Then, with a curse, she intoned the spell to open locks, and Guthrun's chains fell away.

On her last passage through the tunnel, Huld had replaced the rocks at the cave-in as best she could, to make it seem like she had never left the Chamber of Decay. Now she helped hastily remove the rocks once more. Then, when there was an opening large enough for even Grimnir to crawl through, Huld led the way, Bloodsong following behind. Once on the other side, Bloodsong unstrapped her shield from her back and unsheathed her black-bladed sword while Huld invoked her night-vision spell, her eyes immediately beginning to glow with yellow-gold fire.

As soon as Grimnir, Jalna, Tyrulf, and Magnus and his men were also through the opening, Jalna and Tyrulf handed their Freya-empowered swords to the Witch. When her hands touched the hilts, the runes upon the blades began glowing with yellow-gold light, dimly illuminating the walls of the narrow tunnel for Bloodsong and the others.

"I don't suppose I need tell you," the Witch said, "but keep all your senses sharp. My concentration will be on using my powers, enhanced by these swords, to shield our presence from Thokk's sorcerous senses, so I'll not be able to use my magic to sense danger if it awaits us or approaches. To do so would probably alert Thokk, anyway. I'm not even certain I can keep her from detecting us as it is. Without the power in these swords I know I could not."

Bloodsong nodded and motioned impatiently up the tunnel with her drawn sword for Huld to lead the way.

The air became steadily more tainted by a death stench as they hurried onward. Soon the tunnel widened and they entered the region of corpses and rats, the floor gradually becoming covered with more and more crawling things until they walked through then ankle-deep.

Huld watched closely for moving shadows, remembering the thing that had attacked her there, but no more of the shadowy beast-things appeared, and soon they reached the locked door.

"If we could force it open by physical means, we wouldn't risk Thokk detecting my use of magic," Huld told them.

Grimnir examined the lock, then removed the ax on his belt, drew the weapon back, and struck. An instant before the ax reached the lock a bolt of purple fire shot forth and struck the ax, turning it aside to thunk into the wood of the door. The warrior cursed and released the handle, his hands hot with pain. But learning that his skin had not actually been burned by the blast, he angrily wrenched the ax free and aimed another blow at the lock.

"No, Grimnir," Bloodsong said, stopping him before he could try a second time. "The same will only happen again, perhaps actually harming you this time. We must use Huld's magic. Whether Thokk detects us or not, we have no choice."

Huld held the glowing swords with their points aimed at the lock. "Take the cloth and cover the lock," Huld tensely ordered.

Bloodsong took the bloodstained cloth from a pouch on Huld's belt and held it over the lock, feeling a tingling sensation where her fingers touched the Thor-empowered cloth.

Huld again pointed the swords at the lock, then concentrated her will and intoned lilting syllables of power.

Beneath the bloodstained cloth the lock began pulsing with purple light, resisting Huld's magic, trying to burn through the shielding Thor-magic in the cloth to strike at the Witch.

Huld's face streamed sweat as she repeated the spell over and over. A small circle of purple light blazed as a small hole, its edges charred, appeared in the cloth, then another and another.

A spear of purple fire jabbed through one hole toward Huld. A tongue of yellow-gold fire from the Freya-swords intercepted it. The magical forces canceled each other with a crackling of power and an explosion of purple-and-yellow sparks.

The Freya-Witch kept at it, refusing to be beaten by the magic of her enemy. Another purple ray and then another was countered by yellow rays from the swords as Huld continued to intone the spell, her body now trembling with the strain.

Suddenly there came a loud hissing amidst a shower of purple sparks fountaining from beneath the cloth, then the metal of the lock, reduced to a molten, red-hot ooze, began seeping toward the floor, cutting flaming channels in the aged surface of the nail-studded wooden door.

Bloodsong jerked back the cloth and used her gloved hands

to slap out one flaming corner, then she quickly stuffed the cloth back into Huld's belt pouch, kicked open the burning door, and motioned Huld ahead. When Huld did not immediately move, she looked more closely at the Witch and saw Huld sway unsteadily on her feet, a frown of pain creasing her brow.

"Huld?" Bloodsong asked.

"I'm all right," the Witch panted.

"Then hurry!"

The Witch hastily garnered her strength and pushed past Bloodsong into the spiderweb-draped corridor, the glowing swords in her hands.

Up stairway after stairway they ran, meeting no attackers. The door to the cell in which Huld had been tortured stood open. The Witch quickly checked inside and saw that it was empty.

"Valgerth and Thorfinn were chained there when last I was here," she explained as she hurried to lead the way up the next stairway.

"This is too easy," Grimnir growled as they hastened up the stairs. "We must be walking straight into a trap."

"Perhaps it's just that Huld's magic is shielding us as we'd hoped," Jalna suggested.

"I agree with Grimnir," Tyrulf said.

"Turn back, then," Bloodsong angrily suggested, "but trap or not, nothing is going to stop me from reaching my daughter."

No one turned back

When the black walls of Thokk's castle came into view around a bend in the mountain trail, the Berserkers quickly discarded their weapons and breechclouts.

"Wolfraven and Odin," Harbarth said softly, for stealth's sake resisting the urge to shout the battle cry as he raised his right fist skyward and faced his people.

"Wolfraven and Odin," they repeated, also softly, fists raised.

"And may those who fall this day feast in Valhalla this night," Ulfhild added. Suddenly she glanced at Harbarth. He caught her gaze and frowned at the look in her eyes, then thought he understood. A chill slipped through him. He took her in his arms.

"And are we then to part this day?" he gently asked.

Ulfhild said nothing, tears suddenly springing to her eyes as she returned his embrace.

"If I today meet Odin," he said, "know that I have loved you long and well, my mate." Then he quickly kissed her, stepped away, closed his eyes in concentration, and began to transform himself, his human features rapidly altering, hair thickening, teeth elongating, flesh rippling and reforming into the likeness of a towering, massively muscled, gray-furred bear.

Ulfhild cursed her momentary lapse and hastened to join the others in beast form. Soon a giant, red-furred wolf stood in the tracks left in the snow by her human feet. Then, together with Harbarth and the rest of her people, she loped smoothly and swiftly toward Thokk's castle, glorying in the feel of Odin's power coursing like molten metal through her veins, anxious for the battle to begin.

35
Death

A red-furred form leapt high over the towering walls of the Castle of Thokk, landed in the courtyard on all fours, fangs bared, eyes blazing with a white-hot lust for blood.

Kovna, Styrki, and the men who had been trying to open the gate cursed with surprise, drew their swords, and pressed back against the spiked wall as more and more beasts appeared in the courtyard.

"Shape-shifters," Kovna said, terror in his eyes and voice. "I saw one once before, prayed that I would never see another. We can't fight them alone. We need the rest of the men. Cover me! I'm going to make a run for the side entrance!"

He began running along the wall, then angled away across the courtyard toward his goal. The beasts saw him at once and gave pursuit. Styrki formed the men with him into a shield-wall between Kovna and the beasts.

Kovna heard Styrki and the others curse and scream in pain as they tried to stop the berserking beasts. Then there were no more death cries, and glancing back, he saw a monstrous red wolf nearly upon him.

He threw himself through the side entrance just in time, barred the thick wooden door behind him, and heard howls of rage and claws digging at the wood on the other side.

Kovna turned and ran, cursing, somehow knowing that Bloodsong was behind the attack. She had somehow gained the allegiance of shape-shifters.

If we could leave the castle, I would gather the men and ride away, leave Thokk to the shape-shifters and Bloodsong, he thought. *But we can't get out, can't open the gate. Our only hope is to make a stand, hope that a chance to survive will present itself, and be ready to take it if it does.*

Cursing again and again as he ran, heart pounding with terror, Kovna raced on to muster his men.

Ulfhild loped back to the main entrance, frustrated that her prey had escaped, and saw Harbarth waiting there, towering over her in his gray-furred bearlike beastform. Blood from the men they had killed dripped from both their fangs and claws. Others of their people had already entered the castle at Harbarth's direction. Their eyes met, communication passing between them. Ulfhild growled with anticipation and entered the castle, Harbarth at her side.

At first there was no resistance; the castle was seemingly deserted. But then a group of warriors burst into view, weapons raised, their eyes widening in fear as they beheld those they faced.

With a savage howl Ulfhild leapt forward, twisted with lightning speed to avoid a sword thrust, lurched upward, and tore out a warrior's throat, hot blood spurting into her face from the severed jugular. She jerked sideways to avoid another blade, leapt back, then forward and to one side. Her jaws clamped down upon another soft throat, and she violently jerked her head sideways, ripping and tearing. Beside her, Harbarth broke the back of one man, ignored a deep cut on his left leg, swept out with his claws and left a screaming warrior's face a fountain of crimson gore, one ruined eye hanging by a string of flesh upon a blood-drenched, raw-skinned cheek.

*   *   *

Within the Chapel of Hel, Lokith cursed at the sounds of fighting. He reached out with his Hel-senses, cursed again, ordered two Death Riders to his side, and sent one to aid Kovna's men, the other to stop the invaders approaching from below. Then he returned his attention to his own struggle in the chapel and once more strove to concentrate on Thokk's defeat.

Still concentrating her energies on trying to shield their presence from Thokk, Huld could not risk reaching out with her Witch-senses to seek Bloodsong's daughter, so when they reached the torchlit level where Guthrun's room had been, she quickly led them to the room but found it empty.

Huld still leading the way, they hurriedly retraced their path from Guthrun's room. When they reached the main torchlit corridor, the Witch revoked her night-vision spell but kept hold of the Freya-swords, hoping that their power might help her continue attempting to shield their presence from Thokk. Then she led them to the next stairway, noticing that the sounds from the shadowed ceiling and rooms were now gone.

"Be wary of a sudden drop in the temperature," Huld urged as they mounted the stairs. "If the Jotun approaches, the cold might give us a moment's warning. And," she added, remembering the things he had done to her, "if by chance he survives the battle to become our captive, I claim the right to execute him however I choose. I owe him much pain."

Bloodsong nodded her agreement as they came to the top of the stairs and headed down another corridor, not caring what happened to the Jotun, thinking only of reaching Guthrun and slaying Thokk.

At the top of the next stairway Bloodsong suddenly called a halt, her enhanced beast-senses straining. "There are sounds of battle on the level above and a scent of death growing stronger. Huld, return the swords to Jalna and Tyrulf. The death-stench may mean the approach of Death Riders."

Huld gave back the swords and stopped trying to shield

them from Thokk's detection, no longer seeing any point since the battle had started. She quickly reached out with her Witch-senses. "Guthrun is on the next level, too," she told Bloodsong a moment later, "and Thokk's presence is near your daughter's. I'll lead us to her."

Bloodsong followed Huld at a run up the next stairway, nostrils flaring as the death-stench grew rapidly stronger. Then at the top of the stairs appeared a skeletal figure in black armor, black-bladed sword held ready. It started down toward them.

Jalna and Tyrulf pushed past Bloodsong and Huld to confront the corpse warrior with the Freya swords. Using a maneuver they'd worked out before dawn, Jalna feinted to the left as Tyrulf held back, waiting to strike from the right. The Death Rider's preternatural speed nearly got past Jalna's guard, but she parried in time and was relieved that, as Huld had predicted, the Freya-empowered sword protected her from the death-touch.

Tyrulf struck from the right, but the Death Rider's speed allowed him to easily parry the stoke and strike back. Tyrulf blocked the cut and jerked sideways to avoid the corpse-warrior's return stroke as Jalna sliced at the flesh-tattered remains of the Death Rider's skeletal neck.

Once more the Death Rider's speed protected him, but as he thrust his black blade toward Jalna in retaliation, Tyrulf risked a two-handed blow at the corpse-warrior's neck, knowing that if the reckless cut did not succeed, he might not be able to block the Death Rider's lightning return stroke.

A black steel helmet containing little more than a skull clattered down the stairs as the corpse-warrior's skeletal body collapsed.

Without a word, Huld ran on up the stairs, Bloodsong and the others in her wake, to emerge on the next level. As they raced down a wide corridor the sounds of battle ahead became audible to everyone: men's screams and the frenzied howling of beasts.

Three terrified warriors running away from the battle suddenly came toward them down the corridor. Bloodsong and

Grimnir met them, his battle-ax and her black-bladed sword quickly slipping through their faltering guard.

They hurried past the fallen three, boots splashing in the spreading pool of blood gushing from the warriors' death wounds.

Down two more corridors the battle came into view. Though the Berserkers were outnumbered, they were having little trouble slaying the enemy except for one, a Death Rider. At the black-clad corpse-warrior's feet lay the bodies of several dead Berserkers.

Jalna and Tyrulf rushed forward and attacked the Death Rider as Bloodsong and the others followed Huld to find Guthrun. "She's not far now," Huld promised, her Witch-senses guiding her, urging her toward an arched doorway carved with scenes of death and decay, the entrance to the Chapel of Hel.

Vafthrudnir looked down into Guthrun's eyes. She had done as promised. His shoulder was healed. "Thank you, little human," he said, then turned his attention back to the curtain of fire.

The four remaining Death Riders still stood poised on the other side, waiting to attack if Lokith's magic succeeded in breaching the barrier. Behind them, Lokith's face was a mask of rage as he stood watching Guthrun free of the chains. He glanced around, momentarily distracted by the increasing sounds of battle outside the Chapel of Hel. Again he reached out with his Hel-senses, discovered that the Death Rider he had sent below had been slain and that enemies were nearing the Chapel of Hel. With a curse and a glance at Thokk and Guthrun, he ordered two Death Riders to his side to await the more immediate threat of the invaders. And then, in the entrance to the Chapel of Hel, they appeared.

"Welcome, Mother," Lokith hissed. "Slay her," he ordered the Death Riders.

Bloodsong stood, momentarily stunned by Lokith's appearance, so like that of her dead husband, Eirik. It could have been Eirik himself come back from the grave.

The two Death Riders attacked. Bloodsong stepped forward to meet them.

"No, Bloodsong!" Grimnir cried. "The death-touch! Shapeshift! Don't fight them in human form!"

But Bloodsong ignored his warning, thinking only of reaching Guthrun. Her black-bladed sword met the black blade of a Death Rider. Purple sparks flew. She did not fall.

"The Odin-magic in her protects her!" Huld cried, then whipped the bloodstained cloth from her belt pouch and quickly wadded it into a ball.

Bloodsong blocked a cut with her shield, ducked to avoid the lightning thrust of the other warrior's blade, sliced with her sword and cut through one of the Death Rider's legs at the knee. The corpse-warrior fell, crippled but still filled with unnatural Helish life. But even as his companion fell, the other Death Rider was attacking. Bloodsong parried the cut but not in time to avoid being staggered. She slipped to one knee and brought her blade up to parry again.

Something fluttered through the air into the Death Rider's face. Blue-white light flashed and thunder exploded as the object touched the warrior's skullish face. He dropped his sword and clawed at his eyes as if in great pain.

Bloodsong leapt to her feet and cut his head from his shoulders. His remains writhed momentarily on the floor, then became a maggot-riddled ooze within the black armor. Bloodsong's sword sliced downward and decapitated the crippled corpse-warrior. Soon he, too, was no more than a putrifying death-ooze.

Huld grabbed up the bloodstained cloth she had thrown in the Death Rider's face and held it clenched ready in her right hand.

Lokith, seeing his Death Riders defeated, backed up toward the altar, cursing. "A truce, Thokk!" he called. "Unless we destroy the invaders, neither of us will live to spread Hel's conquests! Death Riders!" he shouted. "Do not harm those behind the fire curtain. Slay those who approach!"

The Death Riders turned away from the altar and faced Bloodsong and her companions.

"Guthrun!" Bloodsong shouted, her eyes touching her daughter's through the curtain of fire. For a heartbeat a stranger seemed to look out at her from behind Guthrun's eyes, then recognition came.

"Mother!" Guthrun cried.

A bolt of purple fire blazed from Lokith's upraised fist toward Bloodsong. Huld leapt in front of her friend and held the bloodstained cloth like a shield. With a clap of thunder and a shower of purple and blue-white sparks, Lokith's ray of death dissipated.

Thokk grasped Guthrun from behind and pressed the rune dagger to her throat. "Throw down your weapons or she dies!" the Hel-Witch warned.

Guthrun kicked back and brought her heel down hard on Thokk's instep. The Witch cried out with pain and rage, her grip loosening slightly. Guthrun rammed an elbow into Thokk's solar plexus, wrenched herself free, then turned and grabbed Thokk's wrist and began struggling to get possession of the dagger.

Bloodsong rushed forward toward Lokith and the two remaining Death Riders, Huld by her side. Behind Bloodsong, Grimnir growled with frustration, wanting to join the fight, knowing that he was not immune to the death touch but prepared to throw himself into the fight, anyway, should it be Bloodsong's only hope.

The red-bearded warrior glanced around at Magnus and his men, then beyond them to the battle between the Berserkers and Kovna's men. He now saw others in the fight as well, black-robed servants of Hel, some of whom were trying to wield magic against the shape-shifters. He looked for Jalna and Tyrulf, caught sight of them just in time to see Jalna's Freya-sword shear through the neck of the Death Rider they had been fighting.

He stepped outside the Chapel of Hel. "Jalna! Tyrulf! Your help is needed here!" he shouted, and saw them begin to race toward him. Behind them came the towering bulk of a gray-furred bear. "Magnus," Grimnir continued, "take your men and help the Berserkers."

Bloodsong blocked with her shield the stroke of the Death Rider to her left and parried with her sword the thrust of the one to her right. Behind her, Huld stood ready with the blood-stained cloth should Lokith again attack with magic, her eyes flicking back and forth between Lokith and the curtain of fire.

The fiery barrier was rapidly fading, Thokk's concentration now being split between it and the struggle with Guthrun. Then suddenly the purple fire was gone and the way to the altar clear.

Vafthrudnir grabbed Guthrun and held her arms pinned to her sides. Thokk's face was twisted with anger. "You betray not only me but your true self!" she cried. "I saw it in your eyes when you awakened. You now *know* that all I have told you about yourself was true! Help me fight the invaders! They're your enemies too!"

"You were going to slay me a moment ago!" Guthrun yelled back, struggling helplessly in the Jotun's icy grip.

"A trick to disarm them!" Thokk protested. "I would not have harmed you!"

"You've already harmed me countless times!"

"Only to lead you to the truth!"

Jalna and Tyrulf rushed into the chapel, followed by a hulking, gray-furred bear rearing on his hind legs. As the two warriors began to fight the Death Riders Bloodsong had been facing, the bear saw the Jotun and roared a challenge.

Vafthrudnir jerked his head around toward the sound. His eyes locked with those of the shape-shifter.

The Frost Giant released Guthrun, roared a Jotun battle cry, and rushed to grapple with the Berserker.

In the battle outside the Chapel of Hel, Grimnir suddenly caught sight of a face that brought hate boiling into his heart, the face of the man who long years before had killed his wife and children.

"Kovna!" he shouted, gave a final glance at the battle in the Chapel of Hel, and decided that with Jalna and Tyrulf helping Bloodsong he could afford to go in search of prey of his own. Remembering what Kovna had done to his wife and children and what had been done to Bloodsong at Eirik's Vale, Grimnir lifted his battle-ax in a two-handed grip and ran toward his hated enemy.

Guthrun saw Thokk raising her arms to wield magic. She threw herself forward, head down, tackled the Hel-Witch, and grabbed for the rune dagger once more. Cursing beneath Guthrun on the floor, Thokk tried to cast a spell of unconsciousness on the young woman, but the awakened Hel-powers in Guthrun automatically deflected the spell.

"Be true to yourself!" Thokk cried. "Stop fighting me and the truth!"

"Bloodsong and freedom!" Guthrun shouted, and kept fighting for the dagger.

Jalna was now battling one Hel-warrior, Tyrulf the other, while Bloodsong faced Lokith.

Lokith raised his sword.

"Don't fight me, my son," she pleaded, torn by his haunting resemblance to her dead husband.

Lokith lowered his sword. "Of course, Mother." He smiled. "I'm so glad you have come to free me and my sister. At last I am free of Thokk's evil!"

Bloodsong kept her sword at the ready, wanting to believe him but unable to do so. "Throw down your sword," she ordered, and glanced to where she'd last seen her daughter. Her gaze lingered when she could not immediately see Guthrun, who was still battling with Thokk on the floor behind the altar.

Lokith aimed a lightning stroke at Bloodsong's neck while her attention was diverted.

She caught the movement out of the corner of her eye and parried the stroke. "I don't want to slay you!" she shouted as she blocked a slicing blow with her shield and parried another cut and then another, fighting defensively, unwilling to attack her own son.

Behind the altar, Valgerth and Thorfinn wrenched at their chains, desperate to get free and join the fight.

Thokk finally managed to throw Guthrun from atop her.

The Hel-Witch rolled away and came to her feet, still clutching the dagger. Guthrun threw herself at her again. Thokk hissed words of power. A ray of purple light shot out from her left hand and struck Guthrun, hurling her back, even Guthrun's awakened Hel-powers being no match for a ray of pure Hel-force.

Guthrun struck the wall hard, the force of the blow stunning her. She struggled to stay on her feet, vision swimming, saw Thokk raising her arms to hurl deadly magic at Bloodsong and forced herself to stagger forward toward the Hel-Witch, knowing that she was not going to be in time.

Huld saw Thokk raising her arms. "Freya and Folkvang!" the Freya-Witch screamed, raised the bloodstained cloth like a shield, and intercepted a bolt of purple fire from the Hel-Witch's hands. The Thor-imbued cloth steamed with the Hel-force it had deflected. Huld raced forward, concentrating on a spell as she ran. A thin beam of yellow-gold fire shot from her left hand. With a gesture of contempt Thokk easily turned it aside.

Having seen Guthrun strike the wall out of the corner of her eye, Bloodsong gave a cry of frustration and rage and began battling Lokith in earnest. If a choice between her son or daughter had to be made, it would be made in Guthrun's favor.

Her black-bladed sword caught Lokith's, purple sparks flying. She feinted to the left and cut through his guard. Speed nearly that of a Death Rider saved him as he jerked back just in time. But he was now momentarily off-balance and Bloodsong pressed her advantage, battering at him with stroke after stroke to keep him that way.

Guthrun, her vision rapidly clearing and strength returning, reached Thokk and began grappling for the dagger once more. Moments later Huld reached the Hel-Witch and whipped the Thor-empowered cloth around Thokk's neck.

Thokk screamed in agony as her throat blistered where touched by the cloth. Huld tightened the choking cloth. Thokk dropped the dagger and clawed at the Thor-empowered cloth around her neck. Guthrun quickly grabbed up the dagger and sank it to the hilt in Thokk's heart.

The Hel-Witch screamed again and again, weakened but not slain, black ooze seeping from the wound while her neck continued to burn from the bloodstained cloth, blisters rapidly spreading upward to cover her once beautiful face.

Guthrun wrenched out the dagger and turned to aid her mother while Huld kept the Thor-cloth around Thokk's throat, muscles trembling with the strain of pulling it steadily tighter and tighter.

Bloodsong cut through Lokith's guard again, but this time he was not quick enough to avoid the stroke. He cried out with pain, the sound tearing at Bloodsong's heart as putrefying black blood oozed from a deep cut on his left arm.

"Throw down your sword!" she shouted at him.

Eyes filled with pain, he shook his head negatively and raised his blade once more.

Guthrun hurled the rune dagger, aiming for Lokith's exposed neck above his black mail. The dagger missed and went slightly wide to the right of his head. He flinched, momentarily distracted as the blade whirred close to his ear. Bloodsong's blade sheared down through his neck, nearly severing his head. A look of hatred frozen on his face, his eyes glazed and he fell unmoving to the floor, black ooze pouring from the gaping wound in his neck.

A sob of horror at what she had been forced to do bubbled from Bloodsong's throat, but then she turned and saw Guthrun racing toward her. She opened her arms and embraced her naked daughter while nearby Harbarth and Vafthrudnir howled and cursed in a battle frenzy and Jalna and Tyrulf fought the two Death Riders.

Guthrun pulled away from her mother's embrace and hurried to the doorway. She grabbed up a black-bladed sword from one of the fallen Death Riders there and ran back to Bloodsong's side. "Together we can slay a Death Rider," she said to her mother. "Jalna and Tyrulf need our help."

Bloodsong nodded and advanced with her daughter against

the Death Rider Tyrulf was fighting. Tyrulf shouted his thank
and hurried to aid Jalna in her fight with the other corpse
warrior.

"Back toward the altar!" Bloodsong ordered. Guthru
understood and backed away beside her mother as they bot
parried the strokes of the Death Rider, leading him toward th
altar.

When they reached the raised structure, Guthrun quickl
turned, leapt onto it, and began aiming strokes at the Deat
Rider from above. A moment later Bloodsong joined her o
the altar, the two women using the advantage of higher groun
to force the Death Rider to fight defensively.

Jalna and Tyrulf suddenly found the Death Rider they fougl
unwilling to continue the fight. The skeletal warrior backe
away, twisting his head from side to side as if listening t
something only he could hear. Then he turned and ran to Lok
ith's corpse, lifted his fallen leader, and placed him over hi
left shoulder. Holding him there, he advanced upon Jalna an
Tyrulf once more.

Again he began to fight them, but suddenly purple fir
bathed his skeletal body, and his lightning movements becam
even faster, his sword arm blurring nearly too fast to follow
making Jalna and Tyrulf fall back until soon they were presse
against a wall, desperately trying to parry every blow, knowin
that a single cut on their flesh would bypass the protection c
the Freya-blades and deliver them to the death-touch.

"I can't keep this up much longer!" Tyrulf panted, muscle
trembling with the strain.

Suddenly the Death Rider backed away again and raced lik
a wind-driven shadow from the Chapel of Hel.

Atop the altar Bloodsong finally got through the Death Ric
er's guard and sheared his head from his shoulders, sendin
his skeletal body to the floor to become a pile of crawling
ooze-drenched dust.

Bloodsong gripped Guthrun's shoulder. "You fight well
daughter," she proudly said. "I thought you had been killed,
she added, embracing her as she glanced around to make certai
no other danger was approaching.

Another ragged scream tore the air where Huld still held the Thor-cloth around Thokk's throat.

Huld now knelt on the floor where the Hel-Witch's body writhed in relentless agony. Thokk's entire body was now blistered and burned, smoke starting to rise from beneath her clothing, her scalp a blackened mass of charred hair and flesh. But still she thrashed and struggled, refusing to give in to the death she had avoided for over a century.

Huld began shouting Freya-runes, eyes blazing with triumph and hate. Thokk's pain grew even worse. Her body arched into a rigid bow, supported only by head and heels, every muscle straining and trembling, charred, skeletal hands clawing at the cloth Huld held around her neck.

"She's prolonging it!" Guthrun exclaimed, her awakened Hel-Witch powers giving her an understanding of what Huld was doing. "End it, Huld!" she cried, and jumped down from the altar and ran to the Freya-Witch's side. "She's suffered enough!"

Huld glanced up, her face a mask of hate. Her eyes and Guthrun's met. Reason slowly returned. The Freya-Witch nodded and quietly spoke one final word of power.

The cloth flared white-hot. Thokk's neck and head burst into flames.

Huld jumped back and watched as Thokk writhed screaming upon the floor a few moments more. Then slowly the Hel-Witch's cries dwindled to wheezing sobs and stopped.

36
Hel-Witch

All was suddenly silent in the Chapel of Hel. Thokk's corps
lay at Huld's feet, the fires consuming her skull slowly dwin
dling, the remains of her charred body withered and dried. Th
bloodstained cloth had itself been consumed by the final flames.

Jalna and Tyrulf stood panting near the door, trying to rega
their strength after the frenzied fight with the Death Rider. B
the bearlike beast form of Harbarth lay unmoving within Va
thrudnir's spine-crushing embrace. Vafthrudnir, however, wa
also dead, his neck a gaping blood-red ruin where Harbarth
teeth had torn out his throat.

A red-furred, blood-splattered wolf entered the chape
Ulfhild saw her fallen mate, slowly padded to Harbarth's sid
sniffed at his unmoving body, nuzzled him with her nose, the
sat back on her haunches and whimpered low in her throat.

Bloodsong slipped a hand around Guthrun's bare shoulde
and pulled her daughter close, then looked for the body of h
son.

"The Death Rider we fought carried him away," Jalna sai
approaching the altar. "We tried to stop him but couldn't."

256

With a cry of rage Bloodsong ran from Chapel of Hel to
y to recover her son's corpse, Ulfhild, Huld, Jalna, and Tyrulf
ose behind.

"You won't find him!" Guthrun shouted, but Bloodsong and
e others were already gone.

Guthrun looked down at Thokk's corpse for a moment, then
at Valgerth and Thorfinn. She stepped onto the dais and
oved toward them, the black-bladed sword still in her hand.

"Thank Skadi *you* remembered us." Valgerth laughed, jerk-
g impatiently on her chains.

Guthrun stopped in front of the bound warriors, sword in
nd. "I was supposed to slay you both," she quietly said, then
anced around at Thokk's corpse. "There's no need to do that
w."

"Of course not!" Thorfinn exclaimed. "Get us free of these
rsed chains so that we may find our children! Hurry, Guthrun!
rry!"

Guthrun hesitated a moment more, eyes haunted, then, with
urse, she hurled the sword away and hissed words of power.
e locks upon their manacles clicked open. Valgerth and
orfinn rushed from the Chapel of Hel to seek their children,
ving Guthrun alone.

Guthrun went to Thokk's corpse, stood looking down for a
g moment, started to walk away, stopped, went back, lifted
okk's remains onto the Altar of Hel, stood silently for a
oment more, then turned and left the chapel.

Bloodsong raced through the Castle of Thokk, Ulfhild lop-
along at her side, both following the scent of decayed flesh
t in the Death Riders' wake. Behind them came Huld, Jalna,
d Tyrulf. All around lay the sprawled bodies of Kovna's
in warriors and the black-robed corpses of Hel-worshipers,
ile beasts patiently searched for any who might have es-
ed. Of Grimnir there was no sign.

Bloodsong and Ulfhild followed the death-scent into the
bles and to a trapdoor. Bloodsong wrenched it open. Dark-
ss waited below. An overpowering stench of death wafted

up from the dark hole. Bloodsong heard no movement with
"Huld," Bloodsong said.

The Freya-Witch understood, intoned her night-vision sp
and cautiously peered into the dark opening with her eyes
yellow-gold fire. She bent nearer, carefully examining the sm
room below. "Empty," she finally announced.

"Axel Ironhand, the Death Rider, has taken Lokith to H
heim," Guthrun said from behind them. She stood in the sta
doorway dressed in the bloodstained black robe of a slain H
worshiper. "I heard Hel call to him during the battle. Then
empowered him with extra life-energy and commanded him
return to Helheim with Lokith's corpse."

"You *heard*?" Bloodsong asked. "How . . ."

Guthrun did not reply.

"Guthrun, the one you call Lokith was your brother, Th
bjorn. Didn't you know?"

"Of course. But his name *is* Lokith. Someday I will dest
him, have revenge for all the pain he caused me. You th
you killed him during the battle, Mother, but he was not al
in the way you think of life, and death will not mean for h
what it means for most."

Guthrun's gaze shifted to Tyrulf. She walked to face h
hatred in her eyes. "What is an enemy doing among us? T
is the man who led those that captured me." She looked
Huld. "He helped kill Norda and capture us for Thokk."

Huld moved to stand beside Guthrun, eyes boring i
Tyrulf's.

"I did not kill the old woman," Tyrulf told them.

"That is true," Huld agreed, her voice tight with hate, "
she only faked her death with Witchcraft in the hut and
not truly die until later. But she would still be alive if not
Thokk and Kovna and those who served them—men like y
You should be fed to the beasts like the others."

"Yes," Guthrun agreed. "He is no better than—"

"No," Jalna cut in, standing close beside Tyrulf. "He
proven himself our ally. He helped obtain the magic that
feated Thokk."

Bloodsong caught Tyrulf's gaze. "I did not know you led the men who captured Guthrun." Her eyes touched Jalna's. "Did you know, Jalna?"

Jalna nodded slowly. "I did, and I meant to tell you several times, but it never seemed the right moment."

Bloodsong searched Jalna's eyes. "You were afraid that I would not let him come with us if I knew, afraid I might even kill him."

"No," Jalna quickly denied, "that is, not at first. I . . . *should* have told you."

"Yes, you should have."

"I would have told you myself," Tyrulf responded, "but for the very reasons you named. After finding Jalna again I was determined to let nothing separate me from her. I still am. And knowing her loyalty to you . . ." He ended with a shrug.

Bloodsong looked from one to the other. "You have aided us, Tyrulf. For that you have my thanks. But for helping Thokk to harm my daughter I will not forgive you. Jalna, if I decide that he may not remain with us, will you stay with us or go with him?"

Jalna started to reply that she would stay, then hesitated, glanced at Tyrulf, back at Bloodsong, but could not answer, torn between loyalty to Bloodsong and feelings for Tyrulf she could not yet name. "I don't know," she finally said.

Bloodsong nodded her understanding. "I won't decide now," she told them. "When I do, you will be told at once."

"I will have much to say about that decision," Guthrun promised, hate still burning in her eyes.

"And I," Huld agreed. "Norda's vengeance will not be complete until he is slain like those he once served."

"Perhaps," Tyrulf replied, "I will not *choose* to remain among you." He glanced at Jalna and held her eyes a moment until she looked away.

Bloodsong turned and led the way from the stable and across the courtyard, all following except Ulfhild, who held back to reappear in human form a moment later. She hurried forward to walk beside Bloodsong.

"Where will you go now, Ropebreaker?" she asked. "You will always be welcome on Wolfraven."

"My thanks, Ulfhild, but you heard what my daughter said about my son being taken to Helheim. If Hel chooses to restore life to his dead flesh once more, in time he will surely return, leading other Death Riders. I must stop him if he does and ... destroy him for all time. I must therefore go to the northern frontier in the direction of Hel-gate to prepare and wait."

"Your battles are mine and my people's, Blackwolf," Ulfhild replied. "You shall not go north alone."

Bloodsong shook her head negatively and started to speak, but Ulfhild laughed and quickly said, "Protest all you like, Swordsister. We're going with you."

A moment later Bloodsong smiled, deeply touched, and nodded. "Again, my thanks, Ulfhild, for that and for all you and your people have done. My sympathies are with you for Harbarth's passing. I know what it is to lose a mate," she said, thinking of Eirik, then she found her thoughts turning to Grimnir. Why had he not re-joined them after the battle?

"Harbarth feasts with Odin," Ulfhild said proudly, tears glistening. "His death was magnificent. He killed the Jotun. He will be remembered as Ulfhild's Mate, Jotun Killer, Vafthrudnir's Bane."

The heavy clouds were breaking up overhead. Brilliant sunlight glistened dazzlingly off the snow-covered ground.

Valgerth and Thorfinn were standing near the closed gate, Thora and Yngvar in their arms. "We found them riding atop the back of a ... bear?" Valgerth ventured, glancing around at the hulking beast that had followed them into the courtyard.

"The Berserkers were told to watch for two small children," Bloodsong told her, went closer, embraced her friend, and clasped Thorfinn's shoulder.

Grimnir emerged from the castle, wiping blood and sweat from his face. He carried something dangling from one hand.

Bloodsong hurried toward him, hesitated, then embraced him. "You are alive," she whispered, holding him close.

"Aye," Grimnir replied, "as, praise Odin, are you. But Kovna's not." He dropped the object he'd been carrying onto the ground at Bloodsong's feet. Kovna's head stared up at her, glazed eyes filled with horror.

"Kovna's warriors were no match for the Berserkers," Grimnir said, "nor was Kovna for me."

Like Ulfhild, some of the Berserkers had begun to resume human form. Others still hunted for any warriors or Hel-worshipers in hiding. Occasional screams indicated that another had been found. Five males still in beast form were working to open the gate, standing on their powerful hind legs, pushing up on the ponderous bar with all their strength, but without the slightest success.

"Thokk's magic was strong," Huld noted. "It still keeps the gate closed tight. But Freya's magic is stronger. I will have it open in moments. Tell them to stand back."

"No," Guthrun said, placing a hand on Huld's shoulder. "If you try to open it with Freya's magic, you will die. It's not just a spell of closure that holds the bar. The spell that keeps the gate closed has survived Thokk because unseen demons still hold the bar in place. They must be ordered to return to Helheim, then the gate will easily open, but they will not obey a Freya-Witch."

Huld stared at Guthrun. *The dark power within her has been awakened,* Huld realized, suppressing a shudder. *It will require all my skill and power to undo what Thokk has done, but by Freya, by Norda's soul, and by my own, I am going to try.*

The Freya-Witch concentrated her will and spoke lilting words of power to allow her to see if what Guthrun had said were true.

She saw, then turned away from the gate, sickened.

"What did Thokk do to you?" Bloodsong asked Guthrun.

Guthrun did not reply, turned her attention on the gate instead, closed her eyes, and concentrated her will.

"Before you arrived, Freyadis," Valgerth said, touching Bloodsong's arm, "Thokk performed a ceremony."

"Guthrun has Witch-powers now," Thorfinn quietly added. "She opened our manacles with magic."

"And heard Hel call to the Death Rider during the battle," Bloodsong remembered, chilled, carefully watching her daughter.

Guthrun ordered the beasts at the gate to one side, traced runes in the air, then shouted ragged, guttural words of power.

"Try it now," she told the Berserkers. They reared up on hind legs once more. The bar easily gave way, and the gate creaked open.

Bloodsong walked forward and looked into Guthrun's eyes. "You wield Hel-magic now, Daughter," she said, trying without success to keep the distaste from her voice.

Guthrun slowly nodded. "And you have changed, too, Mother. I can sense the beast in you, hungry to be free."

The two women stood unmoving for several long moments, then Bloodsong reached out and pulled Guthrun close. "We've both been changed by all that has happened," she said at last, "but we're both still alive and together once again."

Guthrun hugged Bloodsong back.

Soon they had piled their dead in the castle courtyard and set the funeral pyre aflame. Magnus and most of the men who had followed him had been slain, as had Harbarth and several other of the Berserkers.

The survivors stood around the blazing funeral fire, honoring their dead, Huld singing prayers to Freya, Ulfhild to Odin, and when at last the flames died away, they left the Castle of Thokk, Bloodsong and her daughter leading the way.

When they came to the horses near the tunnel entrance, Grimnir formally presented Frosthoof to Guthrun. She patted the stallion's neck and stroked his mane, delighted, then surprised Grimnir by hugging the red-bearded warrior and giving him a quick kiss.

Bloodsong grinned at his momentary embarrassment.

Grimnir looked at her and, after a moment, grinned back. "Your mother has a beautiful smile, Guthrun," he said. "We must see that she uses it more often from now on."

"Aye," Guthrun agreed, mounting Frosthoof, "that we must."

Bloodsong gave them each a frown, but a moment later her

expression softened and she smiled again as she mounted Free-hoof. She took a deep breath of clean mountain air and looked up at the sun blazing in the clear blue sky. Beside her she saw Guthrun do the same and was unexpectedly comforted by the sight. Then, when everyone was ready, they began riding down the mountain trail, away from the deserted Castle of Thokk, Bloodsong and Guthrun leading the way, mother and daughter together once more, Grimnir riding closely by their side.

By the year 2000, 2 out of 3 Americans could be illiterate.

It's true.

Today, 75 million adults… about one American in three, can't read adequately. And by the year 2000, U.S. News & World Report envisions an America with a literacy rate of only 30%.

Before that America comes to be, you can stop it… by joining the fight against illiteracy today.

Call the Coalition for Literacy at toll-free **1-800-228-8813** and volunteer.

Volunteer Against Illiteracy. The only degree you need is a degree of caring.

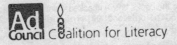

Ad Council • Coalition for Literacy

Warner Books is proud to be an active supporter of the Coalition for Literacy.